BLINDED BY PASSION

BLINDED BY PASSION

Shelley LeBlanc

iUniverse, Inc.
New York Lincoln Shanghai

Blinded By Passion

Copyright © 2006 by Shelley P. LeBlanc

All rights reserved. No part of this book may be used or reproduced by any means, graphic, electronic, or mechanical, including photocopying, recording, taping or by any information storage retrieval system without the written permission of the publisher except in the case of brief quotations embodied in critical articles and reviews.

iUniverse books may be ordered through booksellers or by contacting:

iUniverse
2021 Pine Lake Road, Suite 100
Lincoln, NE 68512
www.iuniverse.com
1-800-Authors (1-800-288-4677)

ISBN-13: 978-0-595-39208-7 (pbk)
ISBN-13: 978-0-595-83599-7 (ebk)
ISBN-10: 0-595-39208-3 (pbk)
ISBN-10: 0-595-83599-6 (ebk)

Printed in the United States of America

Acknowledgments

For my mother-in-law, Helen, an avid romance reader, and to my mother, Portia. Thanks to both of you for your encouragement and support. And to my husband, Wendell, and my daughter, Haley, for listening to me speak about my characters as though they were my best friends. I love you.

CHAPTER 1

❀

Darkness fell over downtown Los Angeles as Catherine Sheldon stood beside the window in her office, staring out at the fading horizon. Thoughts of the past few months churned through her mind, a sudden death, the loss of a friend.

A tear streamed down her cheek and she wiped it away with her fingertips. Crossing her arms over her chest, she turned around. She walked to her desk and sat down. Her gaze shifted to the stack of contracts sitting in front of her. With a light touch, she pressed the palm of her hand down on the top page, then slowly traced her fingertips across the print, down to the bottom of the page, to the signature line. Below the line, she focused on her name which had been typed in capital letters, above it, her signature.

"I hope I did the right thing," she mumbled to herself.

Overwhelmed by the days events, she buried her face in her hands. "I'm exhausted," she sighed. She closed her eyes and took two deep breaths, then slowly opened them. Her focus shifted to a note written in bold red ink beside the date on the calendar. Squinting her tired eyes, she read the words "Engagement Party 7pm." Her heart began to race. "Oh, no! I'm late. Antoinette's going to kill me!" she said aloud.

Leaping to her feet, she paced across the spacious office, grabbed her purse and briefcase then quickly rushed out the door. "I have to go," she informed her secretary, running past her in the hall. "Can you call Jackson and tell him that I'm coming down? I need him to take me to Antoinette's…Thanks…I'll see you on Monday," she called racing toward the elevator.

Once inside, the elevator doors closed. "I can't go like this," she uttered, seeing her reflection in the shiny brass doors. She looked up. The elevator had already made its way down to the eleventh floor, now ten, now nine. She had to think fast.

Dropping her belongings on the floor beside her feet, she pulled off her black silk business jacket, revealing a sleeveless sheath dress.

The elevator dropped to five. She stooped down and pulled a hairpin out of her purse. Rising to her feet, she pinned up her curly golden brown locks.

Two, one. The elevator doors opened, and she gracefully stepped out. Since the lobby was empty she picked up the pace. Dashing toward the exit, her high heels pattered against the slick marble floor with every step she took.

Outside, her chauffeur waited patiently beside the long, shiny black limousine. As she moved closer, he pulled the back door open. "Good evening, Miss Sheldon," he said with a smile.

Catherine slid onto the smooth tan seat.

"Good evening, Jackson. How are you this evening?"

"I'm mighty fine. Thanks for asking," Jackson replied with a warm smile.

Catherine had hired Jackson ten years earlier. His given name was Herman L. Jackson, but he preferred to be called Jackson. During their first meeting, she discovered that he had just moved to Los Angeles from down south in Mississippi, and because she had grown up in Louisiana, they hit it off immediately.

Jackson closed the door and walked around to the driver's side. Sliding behind the steering wheel, he glanced into the rear view mirror. "It's going to be a beautiful evening," he said, attempting to start a conversation.

Cupping her cheek in the palm of her hand, Catherine propped her elbow against the wooden door frame, and glared up at the sky. "Yes. The sky's clear tonight," she mumbled.

Jackson peered into the mirror again. "And the moon's full," he said. "Strange things happen when the moon's full."

Nodding in agreement, Catherine relaxed her shoulders, pressing them back against the cool leather seat, and closed her eyes. Ordinarily, she would have jumped into a conversation with him, but she wasn't in the mood for small talk. Her day had been a long, grueling one and fatigue had set in.

Sensing the distance in her demeanor, Jackson turned his attention to the road ahead and drove quietly.

As the limousine raced through the city streets, Catherine's thoughts wandered back in time. Back to when she had talked the owner of a small gift shop in New York into letting her rent a corner of his boutique to peddle her clothing designs to anyone who showed any interest.

A lot had changed since then.

At thirty-five, she was now one of the most successful fashion designers in the world. But fame had come at a high price. Over the years, the fun of designing had been replaced by long days and nights at the office, contracts and negotiations. Her life had become her work.

Looking down at her diamond watch, her eyes fixated on the time. It was already nine o'clock. "Damn, I'm two hours late," she muttered. "Antoinette's going to be furious."

She couldn't understand how she could have forgotten about the party. Antoinette had made a point of reminding her every day since she'd sent the invitation. She'd even left a message with Catherine's secretary earlier in the day. It should have been embedded in her brain, but it wasn't.

Jackson made a turn off the highway through the iron gates of the estate down a long, winding lane leading to the main house. The lane glistened with white lights highlighting the shrubbery, and the evening sky looked incredible as the light of the moon illuminated down on the magnificent mansion.

As the car veered closer, Catherine lowered the tinted window, taking pleasure in feeling the cool breeze against her skin. Drawing a deep breath, she listened to the sound of music echoing from the ballroom. Normally, the rhythm would have invigorated her, but it didn't. Weary from the long day, she wasn't feeling up to a party. But she'd made a promise to attend…and Catherine never breaks her promises.

The car's motion came to a halt.

Before stepping out, Catherine pulled the lighted mirror down from the headliner. Her flawless olive skin and big brown eyes radiated in the dim light while she applied her favorite red lipstick and a couple of dabs of powder, giving her face a matte finish. Noticing that her eyes were swollen from all the crying she'd done earlier, she patted some extra powder around them. "That's the best I can do," she whispered to herself.

When she finished, Jackson opened the door.

Without hesitating, she emerged, stopping momentarily to stare up at the palatial white mansion. Taking a deep breath, she turned to her faithful driver. "Well, here I go," she commented. "Wish me luck."

Smiling softly, she turned back toward the mansion and started to walk up the well-lit entryway. "Have a nice time," she heard Jackson call from behind.

"Yes. A nice time," she repeated beneath her breath. "A nice time would be relaxing in a hot bath tub."

As Catherine walked up the steps, the front door opened and Antoinette came into view. "Where have you been?" Antoinette scolded. "I was worried about you."

Stepping over the threshold, Catherine hurried to explain. "I'm sorry. The party slipped my mind," she admitted bravely, in a quick tone.

Antoinette frowned. "It slipped your mind. How did it slip your mind? I just left a message for you this morning."

"I know…but I had a lot on my mind today."

Sensing that Catherine was upset, the pained expression on Antoinette's face began to diminish, and she pulled her close for a hug. "Are you okay? Is there anything you want to talk about?" she asked in a soft tone.

Catherine's eyes filled with tears and she pulled away from her dear friend. "Yes. But not now," she replied hesitantly. "We can talk about it later."

Although Catherine wanted to confide in Antoinette, she realized it was neither the time nor the place so she wiped away her tears, put on her best smile and changed the subject. "By the way, you look wonderful," Catherine complimented. "That color is exquisite on you. The blue matches your eyes perfectly. Your designer did an excellent job," she joked, referring to the elegant gown that she had designed.

"She certainly did!" Antoinette giggled.

A former beauty queen, Antoinette was always stylishly dressed, her shoulder length blonde hair well groomed, and her makeup carefully applied. Tonight was no exception.

During their long friendship, Catherine and Antoinette had spent a lot of time together, sharing many happy moments. Over the years, Catherine had grown to become the daughter Antoinette never had. And like mother and daughter, they shared with one another many intimate details about their lives.

As they walked down the long, elegant foyer, Antoinette began to ramble about a big surprise she had for Catherine.

"What kind of surprise?" Catherine asked suspiciously while waving to the Senator and his wife.

"Actually, I have a few surprises."

Catherine's mind drifted.

"Are you listening?" Antoinette questioned impatiently.

"Yes. I'm listening."

Gazing into the ballroom, Catherine turned back to Antoinette with a suspicious look on her face. "Politicians, doctors, bankers—Isn't this an odd group for your son's engagement party?"

Antoinette's expression soured. "Yes. It is. Daniel put most of them on the guest list. If it would have been solely up to me, I would have only invited our family and close friends. But you know how he is?"

"I sure do," Catherine uttered sarcastically.

Just as she started to say something more about Antoinette's ex-husband, her eyes focused on another strange site. Across the room, a group of men were huddled in front of the bar, all gazing in her direction. "Who are they?" Catherine asked without pointing.

She didn't give Antoinette a chance to respond. "My goodness. They're all pretty boys," she poked. "And why are they all smiling at me?"

"Well, that's what I've been trying to tell you, dear. I've invited them for you."

Antoinette had finally managed to get her attention.

Eager for an explanation, Catherine turned back to Antoinette. Her brown eyes widened. "For me, what do you mean, for me?" she asked abruptly.

"They're here to meet you," Antoinette disclosed. "It's not like you have to marry any of them. I just want you to have a little fun for a change."

Catherine frowned. "Please tell me you didn't do this. Not tonight?"

Antoinette didn't respond.

Catherine's day was getting worse by the minute. This hadn't been the first time that Antoinette had taken on the role of matchmaker. Over the last couple of years, Antoinette had tried on numerous occasions to set her up on blind dates, but Catherine had always flatly refused the offers. It had been over six months since Antoinette's last attempt and Catherine assumed she'd given up.

But now it was clear, she'd only moved on to more elaborate schemes.

Despite the fact that Catherine was upset by Antoinette's plan, in fear of hurting her feelings, she decided to go along. What would it hurt? All she had to do was smile graciously and meet a few of them. Then, at the end of the evening, she would break the news to Antoinette that none of the men were of interest to her. Better than that, she would eliminate all of Antoinette's eligible bachelors in one night. It might be years before Antoinette could try again.

Catherine thought about it for a moment, then turned toward the ballroom. "Well, what are we waiting for?" she announced. "Why don't you introduce me to some of the men you invited?"

Surprised, Antoinette smiled brightly. "You mean it?"

Catherine smiled despite herself. "Yes. I mean it."

As Antoinette led Catherine through the crowded room, Catherine saw Antoinette's ex-husband headed their way. "Speaking of a pretty boy," she whispered.

Daniel Drew stepped in front of them. His eyes red and glazed over, he looked at Catherine first. "I was wondering what had happened to my lovely ex-wife," he blurted. "It's time to make a toast to our son and his fiancée."

"All right," Antoinette replied forcefully. "I'll meet you on stage in few minutes."

The odor of whiskey rolled off his breath as he turned back to Catherine. "I thought this party was to celebrate our son's engagement, but I think Antoinette would like for it to be your engagement party, too. What do you think about that?"

The scent of the liquor made Catherine's stomach churn. She could tell that he was trying to pick a fight, and she wasn't in the mood for his games. With a look of distaste, she replied, "I don't think I'm quite ready for marriage, but I don't think it would hurt to do a little testing."

Arrogantly waving his glass in the air, Daniel nodded. "Well, good luck with your testing," he snickered, and then walked away.

Embarrassed by his bad manners, Antoinette apologized. "I'm sorry about that. I don't know why he has to be so rude."

Catherine laughed. "You don't have to apologize for him. We both know how much of an ass he is."

Trading laughs with her best friend, Catherine's eyes softened. "Now, why don't you go to make the toast," she suggested. "We can talk later."

Agreeing, Antoinette turned and headed toward the stage.

While Antoinette graced the crowd with a speech, Catherine began to think about how much she disliked Daniel. From the first time they'd met, she couldn't stand him. He was always sneering at her, driving her crazy with rude comments. She figured that he had married Antoinette for her money, and it turned out she was right. After only two months of dating, Antoinette fell madly in love with him. He proposed soon after, and she accepted. Back then, he was an attorney with a bright future, but shortly after they wed, he decided to stop practicing law, and lived solely off her wealth. He spent most of his days on the tennis court with his pals, and his nights drinking and playing around with other women!

Antoinette put up with his indiscretions for eighteen long years, and finally divorced him right after their son graduated from high school.

Catherine never understood how Antoinette could have spent so many years with a man that she couldn't trust. In today's society, most women wouldn't have been so tolerant, but then again, Antoinette had grown up in the fifties when people's ideals about marriage were different, and staying together for the sake of the children was a common occurrence.

Undeserving, Daniel walked away from the marriage with a very substantial settlement. But Antoinette was just happy to get rid of him.

Catherine walked farther into the ballroom, stopping momentarily to accept a glass of champagne from one of the servers.

Thanking him, she took a glass, and then walked to the right side of the room. The lights lowered and the orchestra began to play a Benny Goodman classic.

Everyone seemed to be having a ball.

During the evening, Catherine was approached by most of the men Antoinette had invited but none of them appealed to her. They were all self-proclaimed studs, all acting like God's gift to women, and that was a big turnoff for her.

Managing to escape the last of her suitors, Catherine grabbed another glass of champagne and quickly headed toward the door leading outside. On the way out, Antoinette grabbed Catherine's arm. "Not so fast," she said. "There's still one more man you have to meet."

Not wanting Antoinette to see the look of dread on her face, Catherine turned around slowly. "One more, huh?"

Antoinette smiled. "Yes. Follow me," she directed. "He's right over here."

Catherine followed Antoinette through the crowded ballroom. "Here we go again," Catherine mumbled.

"What dear?"

Catherine hadn't realized she'd spoken loud enough for Antoinette to hear. "Oh, nothing," she replied. "I just said that I'm having a great time."

Antoinette peered around. "I don't know where he went. He was right here a minute ago," she pointed.

"Maybe he left," Catherine mentioned, hoping that he had.

Antoinette spotted him in the other direction. "Ah, there he is," she said, relieved that she'd found him.

"Oh, great," Catherine sighed.

Turning around, she found herself face to face with one of the most handsome men she'd ever seen. Flustered by his appearance, she tried to listen while Antoinette introduced him, but the only words she heard were, "Justin Scott—an architect."

Catherine took an involuntary step backward. "Hi, It's nice to meet you," she said reaching out to shake his hand. The palm of his hand was smooth with a few calluses lingering around the base of his fingers, a sign that he was certainly not a business executive.

Smiling proudly, Antoinette discreetly walked away, leaving the two alone.

Catherine gulped her last sip of champagne and asked the first question that came to her mind. "So, how do you know Antoinette?"

Justin's eyes brightened. "I've known Antoinette all of my life. She and my parents were friends for many years." He stopped talking and pointed to her glass. "Would you like another glass of champagne?"

She smiled. "Yes. I'd love one."

She watched carefully while he signaled one of the servers. A young man walked over with a tray filled with champagne glasses and Justin took two. "Thanks, chief," Justin said with a smile.

Catherine giggled beneath her breath. *Chief*, she thought, *where's this guy from?*

After the young man walked away, Justin turned his attention back to Catherine. Smiling softly, he gave her one of the glasses.

Catherine smiled nervously. It had been a year since she had been attracted to anyone, and the normally confident Catherine suddenly became bashful. She glanced around the room in search of Antoinette, but she didn't see her. Shifting her eyes back to Justin, she gulped another sip of champagne. "So. You're an architect?" she asked in a half question, half statement sort of way.

"Yes. I've been an architect for about ten years," he said, then paused. She hoped he wouldn't stop there, and her wish came true as Justin began to tell her about his work, speaking about it with great pride, and enthusiasm.

While he spoke, she found herself studying every inch of his body; his lean tall figure, strong shoulders, beautiful smile and perfectly shaped lips. And his eyes. He had the most striking blue eyes, set against short sandy blonde hair.

Unlike the other men she had met, there was something rugged about him.

She liked that.

The band began to play a slow song and Justin invited her to dance. Accepting the offer, they set their champagne glasses on a nearby table, and Catherine followed him to the center of the dance floor. An awkward silence filled the air, and they smiled nervously at one another. Gently gripping her hands, Justin pulled her close. Catherine placed her hand firmly against the back of his black tuxedo jacket. It was soft.

While they danced, Catherine took a deep breath and closed her eyes. Instinctively, her hand glided to the tanned skin on the back of his neck, cupping it softly in her palm. His skin was warm. His cheek brushed lightly against hers, it was smooth. She smiled.

Enticed by the scent of her perfume, Justin pulled her closer and glided her around the room. Her hand felt soft, her fingers long. Shifting his gaze downward, he wanted to see if her hand matched the way that it felt. It did. It was the most beautiful hand he'd ever seen, her fingernails well manicured with clear polish, her ring finger adorned by a pretty sapphire and diamond ring. He shifted his gaze back up, over her shoulder. She moved her head slightly, and his nose touched one of her golden brown curls, it was soft. Her hair smelled good. Being close to her stirred emotions that he never knew existed. Holding her in his arms felt perfectly natural.

Out of the corner of her eye, Antoinette spotted the couple from across the room. "My plan worked perfectly," she muttered. "I knew she would choose him." Happy with her selection, she smiled, and then went back to what she was doing.

What Catherine didn't know or would never find out, was that Antoinette had orchestrated the entire evening, knowing that out of all the men in attendance, Catherine would be drawn to Justin.

Near the end of the song, Justin shifted his head to look at Catherine. "I'm going to have to leave soon," he said. I'm going fishing with one of my buddies tomorrow morning and we have to get an early start."

It wasn't what she wanted to hear, but she understood. "I think I'm going to head out in a little while myself," she replied softly.

The song ended and the band broke into a pulsating Latino rhythm. The crowd around them went insane, each performing their own version of the mambo. Gazing around, Justin laughed. "I think that's my cue to leave," he said, "before I'm inclined to make a fool of myself."

Without warning, arms and legs of the dancers began to swing near their bodies. The dance floor was becoming dangerous. Protecting Catherine from being hit, Justin grabbed her hand and led her off the dance floor. "It's like a war zone out there," he shouted.

Sharing a laugh, Justin's expression turned serious. Catherine could tell that he wanted to say something but the music was so loud he couldn't. Leaning forward, he spoke softly against her ear. "Would you like to have dinner with me sometime?"

The warmth of his breath caused her ear to tingle. She smiled. "That would be great. I'd love to." She couldn't believe she'd said yes. So much had happened in her life lately, she didn't feel ready to date anyone.

Reaching for her handbag, Catherine pulled out a business card and an ink pen. Holding the card firmly against her handbag, she wrote her home telephone number on the back and handed the card to Justin.

Grinning, he accepted it happily.

Although he was apprehensive about leaving, he knew that he had to go. He looked down at his watch. It was close to midnight and he planned to leave for his fishing trip at four in the morning. He wouldn't get much sleep. He smiled and pointed to the door. "Well, I'd better get going."

Catherine smiled again and nodded.

Out of the blue, Justin leaned forward, kissing her softly on the cheek. "I had a really nice time tonight," he whispered. "I wasn't going to come, but I'm glad I did."

She smiled, and then watched as he walked away.

After Justin left, Catherine decided to take a walk through the beautiful gardens of the estate. Stepping onto the large flagstone balcony, she asked the bartender for a bottle of wine and a glass. Of course, he obliged.

Although it was the middle of August, there was a cool breeze. It was the perfect night for a stroll.

While walking, she looked up at the darkened sky. The full moon was gleaming, and the sky was filled with thousands of stars shining down from the heavens. For a moment, she thought about lying in the grass to relish the view but decided she'd better not. She giggled at the thought of falling asleep, only to be awakened by a group of gardeners looking down upon her, wondering what she might be doing lying all alone in the grass with a glass and an empty bottle of wine nestled beside her. That wouldn't have been a pretty sight, so instead, she decided take a walk down to the swimming pool.

As she approached the pool, she found herself alone with only echoes of laughter in the distance. She turned around to see if any guests were on the balcony of the mansion, but it was too far to see clearly. She removed her shoes and stockings, and then sat on the edge of the pool, putting her tired feet in the water. The water felt so warm, so soothing and so inviting.

It's the perfect night for a swim, she thought.

Looking around one last time, she made a quick decision to take a dip. Not wasting any time, she slipped out of her dress, then out of her panties and bra, and hurried down the steps into the water.

She swam with a gliding motion, being careful not to wet her hair. As she moved around the pool, the warmth from the water began to loosen the tension that had built up in her neck and shoulders from her grueling day. Closing her eyes, she moved her shoulders in circular motions, relaxing the tight muscles.

She opened her eyes and looked up at the sky. Taking a deep breath, she shifted her gaze. Her eyes focused on a man standing beside the pool.

Neither said a word.

He stood motionless, sipping a drink, glaring down at her.

Quickly, she crossed her arms to hide her breasts. He didn't speak.

"Excuse me. Would you please turn around while I step out?" she asked kindly.

She thought he would do as she asked, but he didn't.

"Oh, don't mind me," he remarked sarcastically. "I'm enjoying the view. In fact, I was thinking about joining you," he replied slyly, with an untrustworthy grin.

Catherine didn't share his amusement. With tension in her voice, she lifted her brows. "How long have you been leering at me?" she inquired sternly.

"Leering at you?" he repeated arrogantly.

"Yes, you heard me. Leering at me."

He thought for a second, and then rubbed his chin. "I guess I would have to say I began leering just about the same time you decided to go for your little romp." He laughed and snickered, "I was getting ready to introduce myself, but you slipped out of your clothes before I had the chance. I didn't come forward because I didn't want to startle you."

"If you didn't want to startle me, then why didn't you just leave the pool area like any gentleman would have done, without letting me know you were here in the first place?"

"I guess I could have done that. But I'm not feeling too much like a gentleman right now," he said boisterously, waving his glass in the air.

"You're right. And you're not acting like one either!"

She waited a moment, but he didn't leave.

Ignoring her request completely, he continued to stare.

She thought for a moment, and then had an idea. With a look of defiance she stared into his eyes and released her arms. Like a cat eyeing its prey, she rose up the steps. Water dripped down her body as she walked past him, lightly brushing her arm against his tuxedo jacket. "Do you like what you see?" she asked in a sexy voice.

His eyes followed her motion, but he didn't respond.

She walked over to her clothes. "You better look now, because you'll never have the opportunity to see it again!" she said loudly.

He watched intently as she used her fingertips to remove the water from her body, then she began to dress. She could tell her movements had caught him off guard and she was pleased with what she had done.

Grinning, he shook his head in disbelief. "I guess I deserved that." He started to walk away, then turned back. "But if you didn't want an audience, then why would you even think about going for a skinny dip in the first place?" He pointed to the house. "There's a party going on less than 500 feet from here. Anyone could have seen you. It just happened to be me."

He walked closer. "And for your information, I wasn't leering at you." He pointed to the table at the other end of the pool. "I was just sitting over there minding my own business. Then, there you were taking your clothes off."

For the first time, she was speechless.

He waited a moment for a response, and then strolled away.

As she dressed, she thought about what he'd said. She hated to admit it, but he was right. Anyone could have seen her. Where was her head?

For the first time in her life, she had done something without thinking about the consequences of her action. For the life of her, she couldn't understand what had gotten into her. Maybe it was the full moon, or maybe somewhere deep inside, she was tired of doing what was always expected of her. For the first time, she'd acted on a whim. It was exciting.

After dressing, Catherine walked back to the main house. The party had ended and the ballroom was empty, except for the cleaning staff.

Catherine approached an older gentleman who was sweeping the floor. "Excuse me. Do you know where I can find Mrs. Drew?" she asked graciously.

"Yes, ma'am," he replied. "She's in the kitchen."

Thanking him, Catherine walked toward the kitchen. Just as she entered, Antoinette bolted around the corner. "Catherine, where have you been?" she questioned, flinging her arms in the air. "I've been looking for you everywhere!"

"I'm sorry. I took a walk down to the pool, and I went for a swim."

"Were you able to find my extra swimsuits in the pool house?"

"Actually, I swam in my birthday suit…and got caught by one of your guests."

"How embarrassing," Antoinette remarked, covering her mouth with her hand.

"Yes, quite embarrassing. And to make matters worse, he refused to turn around to let me dress."

"Well, what did you do?"

Catherine giggled. "What do you think? I gave him a close look of what he was trying so hard to see."

Antoinette was shocked. "Oh no. You didn't?" Do you know who he was?"

Catherine smiled sarcastically. "I don't think asking his name was high on my list of priorities at the time." Then Catherine yawned. "Well, I think I've had enough surprises for one evening. I'm going to go home."

Antoinette escorted Catherine outside. "By the way. What about Justin?"

"Ah, yes—Justin," she replied. "I had a nice time with him."

"Well? Are you going to see him again?"

"I think so. He asked me to have dinner with him."

"I hope you accepted?"

"Yes, and I gave him my telephone number."

"That's terrific. "I think the two of you would make a delightful couple."

Catherine laughed. "We'll see about that," she said, then turned to leave.

When Catherine arrived home, she locked the door, then walked around the house, turning off lights that had been left on. Walking around the lower level, she thought about the time she'd spent with Justin. She smiled thinking about how pleasurable it had been to dance with him. He was such a wonderful dancer.

Smiling softly, she took off her earrings. His scent began to come back to her. His cologne wasn't musky, like most. It had a smooth, fresh, clean scent. She thought about it for a minute, then realized that it probably wasn't cologne at all. It was probably an after-shave lotion that he'd smoothed over his closely shaven beard. And his eyes. He had the most incredible eyes, a mixture of turquoise and sky blue. She could get lost in those eyes.

Shaking her head, she removed her watch. "What am I doing?" she whispered to herself, feeling silly. "It's been much too long since you've been with a man," she mumbled.

And it had been a long time. Over the years, her hectic schedule had allowed little time for dating. Most of her time had been spent building her multi-million dollar corporation. She did manage to date a few men, but the relationships never lasted for more than a couple of months.

Clinching her jewelry in her hand, she slowly made her way up the winding staircase to the bedroom. Worn out from the events of the day, she couldn't wait to climb into the solitude of her warm, cozy bed.

CHAPTER 2

On Monday morning, Catherine held a meeting with her top executives. During that time, she made an alarming announcement, telling everyone that she'd made the decision to step down as chief executive officer of her company. Doing so would allow her more time to focus on her true love, design, and less time on product innovation and paperwork. And more importantly, she wouldn't be chained to the office anymore. She'd finally have more free time to spend with her friends and family—away from work.

Eyes lit up around the room, all hoping for a chance at the job.

"I've already made my decision," she added, "and he's already accepted."

In the corner of the room stood a tall, gray-haired, neatly dressed man. Standing with his hands in his pockets, unaffected by what she was saying.

Theodore Nelson had been with her since the beginning, serving as her first financial advisor when she opened her first boutique. He was trustworthy, loyal and shrewd with crunching numbers. He was also a man who was well liked and highly respected in the business world, and her only choice for the job.

"Without further delay, I'd like to introduce the new chief executive officer of Sheldon Enterprises, Mr. Theodore Nelson," she revealed, graciously walking over to shake his hand.

The sound of clapping erupted around the room, everyone agreeing favorably with her choice. "Thank you," Theodore said, smiling delightedly. Clearing his throat, he walked to the head of the table. Tears filled Catherine's eyes as he focused on her. "It has been an absolute privilege to have worked side by side with one of the most talented and savvy business minds in the industry, a woman of pure courage and sheer determination. I am truly honored to become your successor." He turned to the executives. "As you all know, over the last year Catherine has worked relentlessly putting together our latest venture, a cosmetic and fragrance line which will be launched in just a few short weeks. I look forward to continuing the work that she has begun, and I will strive to make this corporation the best that it can be." He paused. "I would also like to take a moment to thank all of you for your many years of loyal service to our company. Speaking not only for myself, but for Catherine also, your commitment has not gone unnoticed."

Nodding in agreement, Catherine dried her tears. Everyone applauded.

Even though she would remain in charge of fashion design, and chairman of the board of directors, she still felt an enormous amount of sorrow for giving up something that meant so much.

At the close of the meeting, Catherine headed back to her office. She sat at her desk but couldn't work. Her head was filled with mixed emotions. *Did I do the right thing*? she thought, second-guessing herself.

She began to think about her friend who had died, and the wife and kids he'd left behind. Johnny Siegel was only thirty-six years old when he died suddenly of a brain aneurysm. His future was a bright one, in charge of his own public relations firm; and his most important job, fathering three children all under the age of seven.

Catherine had met Johnny while in college. It was then they became friends, each inspiring the other to never give up on their dreams. Over the years, she had kept in close contact with him, both professionally and personally. And it had been Johnny's company who'd handled her most successful advertising campaigns.

By his death, Johnny had impelled Catherine to change her life. She had finally realized that life isn't about working fourteen hours a day, and then going home to an empty house. Life is about family and friends, finding true happiness.

A knock on the door interrupted her thoughts. "Come in," she called out, shifting her gaze to the doorway.

Slowly, the door opened, and Theodore stepped inside. "I just wanted to check on you," he said softly. "Are you all right?"

Standing up, she walked toward him extending her hands out. "Yes, I'm fine," she replied. But she wasn't fine. Gripping his hands, tears welled in her big brown eyes. "I know that I made the right decision, but it's just going to take a little while for me to adjust."

Overwhelmed by her sadness, Theodore pulled her close for a hug, then reached in his pocket and pulled out a handkerchief. "Here you go," he said, handing it to her.

Backing away, Catherine accepted the handkerchief. "Thanks," she said quietly, wiping the tears from her cheeks.

Just then, the sound of loud chatter erupted in the hallway. Turning their attention to the door, they watched as Catherine's design team strolled across the threshold, laughing and joking with one another.

Catherine looked down at her watch. "Oh, my…Please excuse me. I lost track of time," she admitted to the group.

Standing tall, she turned to Theodore. "Well, I guess it's time for me to get back to work. I have a show to plan."

Smiling, Theodore nodded his head, and then exited the office, giving her an encouraging wink on the way out.

When he was gone, she turned to her staff. "Good Morning. I'm sure you've already heard the news."

A young redheaded lady stepped forward. "Yes, we heard, and speaking for everyone here, we're pleased to finally have you all to ourselves," she divulged.

"Thank you," Catherine replied softly. "Now, why don't we get to work."

While the group took their seats around a large round conference table, Catherine pulled the sketches of her evening gowns out of her black leather portfolio. "Well, here they are," she said, laying them out on the table for them to view.

Anxiously awaiting their reaction, she backed away from the table, nervously rubbing her hands together.

The group gathered around the sketches.

"Oh, wow," someone said, "These gowns are exquisite."

"These are your best ever," said another.

"They're fabulous," said one of the gentlemen. "I can't wait to see them when they're finished."

Relieved by their reaction, Catherine took a deep breath, and walked toward her desk. "I'm so happy you like them." Shifting her gaze downward, she pushed the button on the intercom. "Kay, can you please have someone bring the fabric in," she instructed.

Soon after, the group's attention turned to the doorway, where an office assistant wheeled a large cart into the office.

"As you can see, we have a lot of work ahead of us," Catherine announced, looking at the cart, filled with bolts of fabric. "So far, we've accomplished most of our goals for the Milan show. Our business and casual lines are complete. Now, all we have to do is finish the evening gown collection."

By the end of the day, Catherine and her staff had finished what they'd set out to do. The fabric for each design had been chosen. All that was left was to work with the cutters and seamstresses to put it all together.

On the way home, Catherine stopped for a bite to eat at her favorite Italian restaurant. When she arrived, the owner, Lucio, greeted her. "Hello, Miss Catherine," he said in his heavy Italian accent. "It's been a while since you've been in. We've missed you," he said loudly, flinging his arms in the air. "Your beautiful face always brightens my dreary restaurant."

"Thank you Lucio. That's very kind of you to say," she replied, following him to an open table.

Once seated, the waiter came over to take her order. Having skipped lunch, she was quite hungry. She ordered a salad and plate of cannelloni, along with a glass of Chianti.

The restaurant wasn't crowded, so it didn't take long to be served. While eating, she browsed around the dining room, noticing three men talking and laughing over drinks at a table near the bar. She saw two of their faces clearly, but the other man's back was facing her. Somehow, he seemed familiar and she was anxious to get a closer look.

Less than a minute later, all three men stood. Two left, but the other man stayed behind. She watched intently while he walked to the bar to order a drink. *I wish he would turn around*, she thought.

At last, he did.

That's when she realized…she did know him. It was the rude man from Antoinette's party. Not wanting him to see her, she used the wine list to hide her face. It was too late. He was strolling toward her table. Her heart began to race and her face reddened with every step that he took. She hoped that he would walk past. As he got closer, she quickly turned away. At one point, she even thought about racing to the bathroom. But she was stuck. He was standing in front of her.

"So, we meet again," he said in an upbeat voice. "I almost didn't recognize you with your clothes on!"

Disgusted by his comment, she looked up. "Oh, it's you again," she said abruptly, then hurried to look down again. She didn't want to look at him and she hoped that he would leave.

"Would you like to join me for a drink?"

Her gaze shifted upwards, and her eyes widened. "A drink. I don't think so," she replied harshly.

He pressed. "Come on. I hate to drink alone. Please say you'll join me."

Her face reddened even more. "No thank you," she said. She deliberately paused for a moment. "And to be honest with you, I'm not even interested in having this conversation, so I hope that you'll be considerate enough to allow me to finish my meal in peace," she remarked bluntly.

Shocked by her attitude, he slammed his glass down on the table. "I'm sorry for intruding," he sneered, then walked away.

Stunned by what he'd done, she looked at the glass to see if it had cracked. It hadn't. Shifting her gaze up, she looked around the room. Their argument had gotten the attention of some of the other restaurant patrons.

Catherine watched as whispers broke out around the room, while nameless faces focused on her, as if she'd done something wrong. Ignoring the stares, Catherine turned her attention back to the man, watching as he marched toward the front door.

He started to push the door open, then stopped, shook his head, and turned around. *What's he doing now?* she thought. Taking a sip of wine, she lifted the dessert menu with her other hand, and peeked from behind. He perched his bottom side on one of the barstools at the bar, his back facing her. "I'll have another drink," she heard him say to the bartender.

"Dammit. Why isn't he leaving?" she mumbled.

She gazed down. Half a plate of cannelloni was left in front of her, and the other half felt balled up inside her stomach. Her appetite lost, she pushed the plate away.

Lifting the glass to her lips, she took a sip of wine, and thought about what had happened. Maybe she'd been too hard on him. She'd always been taught to treat others kindly, even if they acted like asses. But with him, she couldn't help herself.

The waiter noticed that she had finished eating, and brought the check over, laying it face down beside her hand. She looked up and their eyes met. He smiled politely, but didn't say a word. He didn't have to, because his eyes spoke for him. In his opinion, she had been too rough on the man.

Catherine paid the bill, and then walked across the restaurant to leave. Her mind was telling her to get out of there as quickly as possible, but her heart was telling her differently. It was saying to swallow her pride, and apologize for her bad behavior.

Moving closer, she made a bold move. She stood beside him at the bar. At first, he didn't see her. She even thought about walking away. But it was too late. With a blind stare, he looked at her, waiting for her to speak.

She had to say something. "Excuse me," she said politely.

He gazed into her dark expressive eyes. "Are you talking to me?" he asked.

Her toes curled inside her shoes. She should have known he would make the apology difficult.

Curling her mouth to the side, she stared at him, and then looked around. She wanted desperately to run away.

"I thought you never wanted to see me again?" he snickered.

Catherine sighed, and rolled her eyes. "That's beside the point," she said. "It's just that I owe you an apology. What I did to you was wrong, and I'm sorry for being so rude."

Perplexed, he shook his head. Had he heard correctly? Did she just apologize?

She'd caught him off guard, left him speechless.

"Well, that's all that I wanted to say," she said, then she turned and walked out of the restaurant.

Once outside, she took a couple of deep breaths of the night air to clear her head. Then she thought about what her mom had always told her, "No matter how badly people treat you, kill them with kindness." And her mom was right. It had taken a lot of courage for her to apologize to him, but after the deed was done, she felt good.

She just hoped she'd never have to see him again.

CHAPTER 3

❧

The moment she'd been waiting for finally arrived. Three days before the fashion show, Catherine flew to Milan to join her design staff, who had arrived earlier in the week to set up for the big event.

Over the next three days, she worked incessantly with the production crew on set decorations and seating arrangements. On the afternoon of the show, she had all the models attend a final fitting and rehearsal. With the exception of a few minor details, things went well.

Catherine rushed home to eat dinner, shower and change, and then rushed back two hours before the show to work with the stylists to get everyone ready. Along with her staff and the models, the backstage area was filled with reporters from major magazines around the globe. A sense of organized chaos existed as she made her way from model to model, checking every detail. From head to toe, everything had to be perfect.

The show was set to begin. The backstage crowd dispersed, making their way to the seating area. The time had finally arrived. The lights lowered. Upbeat music filled the air. The crowd began to sizzle.

One by one, Catherine made a final check of each model, and then, one at a time, sent them down the runway. Each time, she held her breath, listening for the crowd's response.

After sending her final model down the runway, her hands began to tremble. Anxious to get a glimpse of their faces, Catherine peeked from behind the curtain, but was blinded by the flashing white lights of the camera bulbs.

At last, it was time for her to greet the audience.

Everyone applauded in delight as she calmly led the group of models down the runway. The audience stood, honoring her with a standing ovation.

Humbled by their attention, her eyes began to tear. Gracefully, she bowed, and then backed away giving credit to the models. In the background, she stood tall, feeling proud of what she'd accomplished. The show had been a huge success.

Slowly, she made her way backstage to congratulate her team. As the caterers handed out the glasses, she got the party underway by popping the cork off the first bottle of champagne, then made a toast to everyone who'd helped make the show a success. At the end of her speech, she found herself surrounded by a group of reporters who wanted to interview her.

Despite the fact that she was exhausted, she took time to answer each and every question, while posing for hundreds of photographs and signing numerous autographs.

The following morning, Catherine woke up early to find out what the critics were saying. Stumbling out of bed, she hurried to the computer, and then sat quietly, reading the fashion reviews from around the world. The reviews were remarkable!

She was ecstatic.

She placed a call to her office, and found out that orders were pouring in from buyers around the world. Suddenly it hit her. It was all over. All of the planning, all of the work was finally complete.

Later in the morning, Catherine received a telephone call from Bernardo Marcello, a dear friend and local newspaper reporter, whom she'd met on her first visit to Milan. Over the years, Bernardo had not only become a friend to Catherine, but also a confidant, having proven himself an invaluable asset with dealing with the media for her fashion shows.

Sinking her body into an oversized ivory chair near the window, Catherine sat sideways, propping her feet on the arm of the chair. She spoke with Bernardo for nearly an hour, talking about their times together, and their families.

Three years earlier, Bernardo had married for the second time. His new wife was now eight months pregnant with their first child. With good reason, Bernardo was elated. Plagued by fertility problems, it had taken the couple two and a half years to conceive. During that time, they'd tried everything, from taking his wife's temperature every morning, to taking fertility drugs, to keeping her hips lifted on top of pillows after intercourse. They'd been through it all. They'd been through all of the pain, and now all of the joy accompanying the upcoming birth.

Bernardo had been blessed with only one other child, a son from his first marriage. He and the boy's mother had separated when his son turned two, but shared joint custody of the child. Bernardo was a devoted father, always there whenever he was needed by either his son or his former wife. And through the trauma of the divorce, for the sake of their young son, they'd remained friends.

Near the end of the conversation, Bernardo invited Catherine to his parents' home, located south of Florence in the Tuscany region, to celebrate his son's seventh birthday. And she graciously agreed.

It would be the perfect way to end her stay in Italy.

They spoke for a few minutes more, finalizing the details, then hung up. It was all set. Catherine would leave the following day, traveling by airplane from Milan to Florence, there a car would be waiting to take her to the Marcello home, where she would spend the next two nights with his family.

Catherine peered out the window of the small twin engine airplane as they flew away from the industrialized city of Milan and entered the lush landscapes of the Italian countryside; flying low over the ancient latticed hills and woods of the region.

Once the airplane landed, Catherine was whisked away by car, first driving down a two lane paved highway, then a dusty white gravel road leading through the rolling hillsides; passing solitary farm houses, and medieval villages along the way.

The driver turned onto another gravel road, and Catherine's eyes focused off in the distance on a group of houses sitting atop the hillside. She pointed in that direction. "Is that it?" she asked the driver, anxiously awaiting his reply.

"Si, signorina," he replied in his heavy Italian accent. He pointed out over the vast olive gardens and vineyards in the valley below. "That's the Marcello's land," he added.

Looking out the window, Catherine wondered if the people who had lived centuries before had seen it the same way…The endless, timeless beauty of the valley.

Driving through the narrow gates of the complex, Catherine turned her attention to the two story terra-cotta roofed farmhouse nestled among thick cypress and olive trees of the hillside.

As the car veered closer, she reached down to pick up her purse, then looked up again. The car slowed to stop, and Catherine smiled when she saw a group of people running to meet her. Leading them was Bernardo, dressed in a pair of blue jeans with a white shirt, wearing a huge grin. And by his side, his wife, Giovanna, dressed in a floral maternity dress, her huge belly protruding in front.

Catherine chuckled when she saw her. "Yep. She's definitely pregnant," she mumbled to herself.

Bernardo pulled the door open, and smiled. "My dear sweet Catherine," he said, reaching for her hand. "It's so nice to see you again."

Stepping out, Catherine gripped his hands and they shared a hug. Over his shoulder, Giovanna's friendly round face came into view, glowing with happiness. Tears welled in Catherine's eyes as she reached around to hug her. "I'm so happy for you!" she said.

Giovanna smiled and stepped back while Bernardo introduced Catherine to the others. His mother and father, Vincenzio and Lucianna Marcello, stepped up first. "It's so nice to finally meet you," his father said, reaching his hand out to shake hers. "Bernardo has spoken about you for many years," he said, his accent thick.

Looking directly into his big brown eyes, Catherine gripped his hand firmly. Against hers, his hand felt rough and dry. She could tell that he'd worked in the fields often. Beyond the weathered skin of his face stood a handsome man with a dark black mustache, and a head full of thick black hair. From his looks, Catherine couldn't tell how old he was, but she figured he was in his late fifties.

Bernardo's mother moved closer, a beautiful woman with her vibrant red hair swept back away from her face. Catherine thought that she was going to shake her hand, but instead she gave her a warm hug, and in a soft tone said, "We were so happy when we heard you were coming. Welcome to our home."

Bernardo's mother gripped Catherine's hand while Bernardo introduced his grandparents, Ernesto and Carlotta Marcello. His grandmother, the stereotypical motherly-type Italian woman; a short, plump woman dressed in a black dress with her graying black hair pulled back in a roll. And his grandfather, a short, thin man, his dark complexion weathered from the sun, with gray hair sticking out from beneath the straw of his wide-brimmed hat.

Catherine shook their hands, then watched as a little boy stepped up from behind Bernardo. "And you remember my son," Bernardo said, setting his hands atop the young boy's shoulders.

Catherine stepped back to take a closer look at Donatello Marcello. Although his hair and skin had gotten darker, she recognized his sweet face immediately. Donatello was four years old the last time she'd seen him. Now he was getting ready to turn seven, nearly half her size, and shooting up like a sprout.

While everyone looked on, Catherine stooped down to say hello. "I hear that you have a birthday coming soon," she said with a smile.

Donatello smiled sweetly, and nodded his head.

Reaching inside her purse, Catherine pulled out a small box, and handed it to him. "Well, I have a special present for you," she said.

Donatello's eyes lit up, as he accepted the gift from her.

"But you can't open it until tomorrow," his father said sternly from behind.

Donatello turned around, acknowledging his father's request, then he turned back to Catherine, and thanked her for the gift. Touched by his impeccable manners, Catherine leaned forward and kissed him on the cheek. Donatello blushed, then broke out in a smile. He looked so sweet, so young.

Bernardo put his hands on his son's shoulders again. "That was his first kiss from a beautiful woman," he said. "Now, you've made his day."

Smiling, Catherine stood and took hold of Donatello's hand. Led by Bernardo's mother, they started to walk toward the house, leaving Bernardo behind to struggle with the luggage. Bernardo laughed. "What do you have in here?" he yelled. "Did you bring some rocks with you?"

In response to his comment, Catherine jokingly cast a set of evil eyes in Bernardo's direction. "Yes," she said. "I thought you might like some rocks from the states. I pulled them out of the Pacific Ocean right before I left home."

Humored by what she'd said, Bernardo laughed, then picked up his pace to catch up with the group.

Bernardo's mother led Catherine into their home. Inside the worn bricked farmhouse loomed a stucco interior with arched door frames and a cypress timbered ceiling. Beneath Catherine's feet, warm, inviting terra-cotta tiles.

Although the furniture in the house was plain, the interior didn't lack Tuscan charm. Through the corner of her eye, Catherine caught a glimpse of two large windows. Walking closer, she cast her eyes on a heavenly sight, a magnificent view of the olive gardens and vineyards surrounding the home. It felt as though she'd been taken back in time.

Bernardo dropped Catherine's luggage on the floor, making a loud noise that startled her back to reality. Catherine hurried to turn around, watching while Bernardo sat down to catch his breath.

Shaking her head in disbelief, Catherine turned back to his family and they traded smiles. Bernardo's mother took hold of Catherine's arm. "Come right this way, and I'll show you to your room," she said, leading her up the cypress staircase.

At the top of the stairs, his mother led her into a small densely furnished bedroom. Catherine looked down at the bed, noticing the olive green crocheted bedspread. She figured it had been there for many years, along with a painting of the Virgin Mary gracing the wall above the headboard.

From across the double bed, Catherine watched as Mrs. Marcello went over to the windows to pull the curtains back, letting in a stream of light. Then she flung the windows open to air out the room.

As Catherine walked to the window to look out, her long golden brown hair blew backwards from the warm breeze. It felt wonderful. Peering out, she cast her eyes on a magnificent view of the vineyards.

Catherine stared out for a moment, then turned around to look at the room again. The change was incredible. By opening the curtains, the plain bedroom had been transformed into something rather amazing. Someplace like no other in the world. A shaded oasis in the middle of what she thought to be God's country.

Standing beside the window, Mrs. Marcello pointed out the boundaries of their property. Then she pointed to the other buildings in the complex, explaining what each was for.

While she was speaking, Bernardo walked into the room. Once again, he dropped the suitcases on the floor. Huffing and puffing, he tried to catch his breath.

Catherine turned around and laughed. "You're unbelievable," she said. "We're going to have to get you started on an exercise program," she joked.

He pointed to the suitcases. "I don't know what you have in there, but they're heavy!" he complained.

And he was right. Not knowing how she would spend her free time while in Italy, Catherine had packed clothes for every occasion. And she was happy that she had, otherwise, she wouldn't have had any casual clothes to wear while in Tuscany.

Mrs. Marcello excused herself, and Bernardo followed close behind, leaving Catherine to rest for a while before dinner.

Exhausted from the trip, Catherine slipped out of her clothes and into a soft, flowing yellow dress and a pair of comfortable brown leather sandals. Then she laid down on the bed to rest. She looked up at the sky through the window. It was clear blue, with only a few clouds that she could see. She studied the sky for a few minutes, then closed her eyes to rest them for a moment. Soon after, she fell into a deep slumber.

Catherine awoke to the sound of laughter coming from outside the window. Rolling over, she looked down at her watch. It was already six o'clock. Shifting her gaze to the window, she noticed that the sun was beginning to set over the countryside.

She couldn't believe she'd fallen asleep.

Standing up, she walked over to the window to look out. Down below, the family was gathering, and she wondered what they were doing.

Bernardo saw her and called out. "Hello," he said. "Would you like to join us for a *la passeggiata*?"

"What's that?" she yelled back.

Remembering that she spoke little Italian, Bernardo laughed. "We're going for an evening stroll through the vineyards. Would you like to come with us?"

"I'd love to. I'll be right down," she shouted.

Hurrying away from the window, Catherine ran downstairs to meet the family where they'd now gathered near the edge of the vineyard. Running up, she saw his mother first. "Did you sleep well?" Mrs. Marcello asked.

The others started to walk, while they stayed behind.

Catherine blushed. "Yes. I slept very well. Thank you," she said. "And I'd like to apologize. I closed my eyes for a moment, and I fell asleep."

Mrs. Marcello shook her head, and spoke in her sweet Italian accent. "Don't worry about that," she said. "You were tired from your trip."

"What are the two of you waiting for?" Bernardo shouted from the vineyards.

Catherine and his mother smiled but didn't answer him. They walked side-by-side through the wide passage separating two of the rows of vines. His mother loved to talk, and Catherine loved listening to her speak. While strolling, they talked about everything from the Marcello family heritage to Catherine's work as a designer. Catherine could tell that Mrs. Marcello had strong, family oriented values, and loved being a wife and mother. In a way, Catherine envied her.

When the group returned home, Bernardo's grandparents retired for the evening, and Giovanna excused herself to get Donatello ready for bed. Because Catherine had missed dinner, Bernardo and his parents took Catherine to the kitchen to fix a plate of food for her.

While she ate, they talked about how much the vineyards meant to the Marcello family, having existed since the seventeenth century, handed down from generation to generation.

What an amazing gift their ancestors had given them.

The following morning, the family began to set up for Donatello's birthday celebration. Soon after they finished, family, friends and neighbors started to arrive, filling the land around the farmhouse with high spirits and good cheer.

Catherine took off her shoes to walk around. The grass felt like soft carpet. Dressed in a pretty pastel pink dress, she found a spot beneath one of the large cypress trees and sat down to watch how the guests interacted with one another, while all the children ran around the hillside kicking a ball around.

Everyone looked so happy.

Scanning the hillside with her eyes, Catherine spotted a beautiful little girl with long, flowing brown hair standing still in a white dress adorned by a pretty pink sash, waiting for the ball to come her way. A little boy kicked the ball, and it flew past her, landing on the ground beside Catherine's feet. As the girl ran toward her, Catherine picked up the ball and clinched it in her hands. When she got closer, Catherine looked into her beautiful brown eyes, and smiled. "Here you go," Catherine said, handing the ball to her. The girl smiled back, and Catherine's heart melted. She hoped one day to have a child just as beautiful.

Catherine turned and caught a glimpse of Bernardo putting his ear to Giovanna's stomach, playing the role of the proud parent, while Giovanna looked down upon him with an exuberant smile. They looked so happy, so much in love.

Thinking about how it would feel to be pregnant, Catherine smiled. Just the thought of carrying another life inside her body began to stir emotions that she never knew existed. She remembered when she was a teenager, and how she dreamed of one day marrying and having children. But that was before college, before other challenges came along.

Sitting on the ground overlooking the tranquil countryside, she took a deep breath of the fresh air, and looked out over the unspoiled land of the Tuscany hills.

Although she'd been to Italy many times before, each visit seemed like the first. Each time, she discovered something new. On this trip, she'd discovered a wonderful, loving family, full of rich family heritage.

Looking out over the hillside, she wondered if she'd have the opportunity to see this place again. She hoped that she would. She'd found a special place, filled with special people. She wanted to visit again and again. And hopefully one day, she would have the chance to return with children of her own, to show them this special place. A place without pollution, without the sound of airplanes flying overhead, without traffic jams, without overcrowded neighborhoods. A simple place, where life is simple.

A voice called out, interrupting her thoughts. Bernardo was announcing that it was time to eat.

Catherine stood up, and walked over to one of the long tables, and sat down beside Bernardo. The local priest led everyone in a prayer to bless the meal, and when he was finished, everyone dug in.

One thing was certain. There wasn't a shortage of food. Looking across the table, Catherine spotted many appetizing dishes being passed around, and she couldn't wait to eat. Some of her favorites were lasagna, spaghetti bolognese, tortellini, an array of cheeses, and homemade Italian bread.

Best of all, the olive-oil and wine had been created from the land surrounding them. It couldn't have been any better.

After eating, the kids played a while longer, then one of the ladies brought a cake out for Donatello's birthday. On top, seven candles burned brightly.

When Donatello saw it, his face lit up, and he ran over to make a wish and blow the candles out. The delight in his eyes filled Catherine's heart with joy.

After the birthday celebration, Catherine watched while the guests either went inside, or laid on blankets below the trees for their daily siesta. Looking on, Catherine smiled brightly. Every afternoon the people of Tuscany stop to rest. And today, for the first time, she understood why. With such a wide array of food, they had all eaten too much and would probably explode if they didn't lie down. The siesta gave everyone the time needed to digest their food, and get ready for the evening. For these people, it was a daily ritual, one that would probably never change.

While everyone else rested, Catherine went back to the spot on the hillside where she'd been sitting earlier, and sat below the same cypress tree. She began to reflect back on the day, remembering the expression on Bernardo's face when he cradled his wife's belly. He had such a loving look on his face, filled with excitement, dreams and aspirations for his baby's future. He was a proud father indeed.

She thought that maybe one day she would find that kind of happiness. That kind of peacefulness. But first, she had to find a special man to share it all with.

CHAPTER 4

❧

When Catherine returned to Los Angeles, she had lunch with Antoinette. While dining, Antoinette questioned her about the trip to Milan. "So, did you have any sexy Italian lovers while you were away?" Antoinette joked.

Catherine laughed. "No. I didn't run across any on this trip."

"Oh, well. Maybe next time," Antoinette giggled.

Catherine's expression turned serious, and she began to confide her innermost thoughts. "I didn't find a lover, but I do have some good news for you," she divulged.

Antoinette's eyes widened as she listened intently. "After the show, I had time to think about my life, and what I want for my future…" Antoinette put her forearms on the table and leaned closer. "I realized that I've been alone much too long."

Antoinette laughed. "My darling, that's what I've been trying to tell you for years. So, what do you plan to do with your new found knowledge?"

"I've decided to find someone to share my life with," Catherine announced.

Delighted with the decision, Antoinette smiled in approval. "That's wonderful news!" she exclaimed reaching for Catherine's hands. Antoinette thought about it for a moment, then joked, "You know, you're not getting any younger. How old are you now? Thirty-Seven?"

Catherine rolled her eyes. "No. I'm thirty-five."

"Ah, yes, that's right. Well, if you want to have children, you need to start soon!"

Catherine giggled. "I think I have a few more good years in me." Her expression turned serious. "I'm laughing about it, but to be honest, I have been thinking about starting a family lately. And you're right, I'm not getting any younger. But don't you think I should wait until I'm married to consider getting pregnant?"

Antoinette chuckled in agreement. "And speaking of your new found freedom," she mentioned. "Why didn't you tell me that you were planning to step down as CEO of Sheldon Enterprises? While you were out of town, I picked up the financial section of the newspaper, and there it was…the top story of the day. I couldn't believe my eyes."

Catherine knew she was in trouble. "I'm sorry," she apologized solemnly. "I've just been so busy—."

Antoinette stopped her. "It's all right. I understand," Antoinette said sweetly. "It's just that it took me by surprise. I had no idea that you were thinking of giving it up."

Catherine's face turned sad, and Antoinette could tell she'd touched on a sore spot.

"It's okay," Antoinette said, stroking the top of Catherine's hand in reassurance. "In fact, if I were you, I would have done it years ago." She laughed.

"I spent many sleepless nights trying to make that decision," Catherine explained. The tears welled in her eyes. "But it was Johnny's death…"

Antoinette's eyes softened and she clasped Catherine's hand. "I know, Dear."

Catherine took a deep breath, then finished. "After he passed away, I realized that I wanted more…I just had to do it. I had to take my life back!"

"I know. And you did the right thing," Antoinette agreed with a smile. She had to change the subject. "So, how about those Italian lovers," she blurted. "How many did you say you had?"

After lunch, Catherine stopped at the grocery store for a loaf of wheat bread, a pound of freshly ground coffee and a cantaloupe. While waiting to check out, she glanced around the small store. Standing beside the apples in the produce section, she saw the man from the restaurant, and Antoinette's party. Once again their eyes met. But this time it was different. This time she didn't turn away. It was as if she'd been placed in a hypnotic trance.

Her heart began to race and her stomach felt like it was tied in knots. And if that wasn't bad enough, her hands trembled with the fear that he might speak with her.

She stood silently, gazing in his direction. "Excuse me, Miss. I'm ready for you," the cashier announced.

Catherine didn't hear. "Miss…I'm ready for you."

In a blind stare, she turned to the young girl. "I'm sorry. Did you say something?"

"Yeah…I'm ready to ring up your groceries," she snarled.

Placing the items on the conveyer belt, Catherine apologized, then peeked over the rows of candy displays to see if he was still there. *That was close*, she thought, relieved to see that he wasn't. The last thing she wanted was to have another encounter with him. She just wanted to get out of there as soon as possible.

After paying, she grabbed the bag, and rushed out of the store. Walking briskly towards her car, she heard a man's voice calling from behind. "Wait. Please stop!" he shouted. She recognized the voice immediately. It was him.

"Hold up. I'd like to speak with you," he said.

Her hands began to sweat. Slowly, she stopped to turn around.

Walking up, he laughed. "Don't you think it's time we introduce ourselves. That is, especially if we're going to keep meeting this way."

He stuck his hand out. "My name is William Moorehouse. What's yours?"

She swept the hair out of her eyes, then extended her hand. "My name is Catherine Sheldon."

"Are you the designer, Catherine Sheldon?"

"Yes. That's me," she stuttered, clutching the bag of groceries.

Her mind went blank. She was frightened, but at the same time drawn to him. They looked at one another for a moment, then out of the blue, he invited her to join him for a cup of coffee. Against her better judgment, she agreed to have one cup at the cafe across the street.

"Here let me take that for you," he suggested, reaching for the brown paper bag. "Before we go, would you like to put the bag in your car?"

"Yes. I parked right over there," she pointed.

Catherine led him to her car. *What are you doing? Are you crazy?* she thought to herself.

After putting the bag inside, they headed across the street. The walk was pleasant, and much to her surprise, he acted like a complete gentleman.

Once they were seated, he started the conversation. Unlike her, he didn't seem to be nervous at all. He told her that he was a Real Estate Developer and his current project was to convert an old office building to luxury condominiums. They spoke about the project for a while, then briefly spoke about her work.

The conversation was going well, until he mentioned the swimming pool incident. She thought he was going to say something offensive, but instead he apologized for his behavior, both at the pool and the restaurant. She accepted the apology, then she too, apologized for being such a bitch. She explained that it had been an embarrassing moment for her, and one she'd rather forget.

"You didn't seem too embarrassed when you got out of the pool." He laughed.

Her face turned flush. "I didn't think that I would ever see you again…Now, can you please forget it ever happened?" she commanded.

He realized that she didn't want to talk about it, or even joke about it, so he decided to drop the subject. They continued to drink their coffee. She was still nervous, but at least they weren't fighting. While sipping her cup of decaf, she sensed that he was staring at her. She looked up. Their eyes met again. Soothingly, he smiled, and she wasn't frightened anymore.

While talking, he got up to retrieve the sugar from another table. And for the first time, she noticed how handsome he was, dressed in a crisp light blue, button-down oxford shirt and a pair of tan pants, with a nice pair of brown saddle oxfords. His tanned face looked great against his blue shirt and his eyes were a divine shade of dark brown. He had short wavy dark brown hair, cut neatly away from his face, enhancing his strong jaw line.

Returning to the table, he sat down. As he held his cup to his lips, she caught a glimpse of his well-manicured fingernails, and on his finger a gold signet ring with the letter M engraved on top.

The waiter walked over and placed the bill on the table. She tried to reach for it, but found herself touching the top of his hand. She hurried to pull away. "The coffee's my treat," he smiled. "It's just another way of saying how sorry I am for the way that I acted."

"I'm sorry too," she admitted once again. Then, she stood, motioning to the door. "Well, I really should get home." She smiled softly. "Thanks for the coffee."

As she began to turn away, he lightly touched her shoulder. She turned back.

"Would it be all right if I walk you to your car?" he asked kindly.

"Sure," she replied, graciously accepting.

Stepping outside, she pulled her sunglasses out of her purse and put them on. Walking side by side, she observed his physique through the darkness of the lenses. He stood a couple of inches taller than her and his body was quite masculine. When they arrived at her car, they both said, "I—," at the same time.

They laughed. "You go first," she instructed.

"I had a really nice time," he said.

"I had a great time, too," she replied, and turned to put her key in the lock.

She thought for a moment, then slipped her hand down into her purse and pulled out a business card. Handing it to him, she urged, "Why don't you give me a call sometime?"

He pulled the door to her silver Mercedes open. "I'll do that," he replied.

While he watched, she slid onto the leather seat. They shared another smile, then he closed the door. She started the engine and drove away.

Driving home, she couldn't get the thought of him out of her head. With every thought, her body temperature rose. She began to wonder what it would feel like to kiss him. "What's wrong with you?" she blurted. "Why did you give him your telephone number? What if you go out with him and he acts ghastly again? Then you'll feel like a real fool!"

She thought about it, then had an idea. "I just won't accept his call. That'll give him the message that I'm not interested. He'll forget about me and I'll forget about him. That's what I'll do!"

When she arrived home, she noticed the red light blinking on the answering machine, indicating that someone had called. Once again, the hot rush came over her body. She began to get excited. "Would he call so soon?" she asked herself out loud. "I hope so…What am I saying? I don't want to go out with him!"

She walked to the machine and reluctantly pushed the play button. The voice on the other end was a man's. "Hello, this is Justin Scott. We met a few weeks ago at Antoinette's party. I was calling to see if you'd like to have dinner with me? Please give me a call if you're interested."

She couldn't believe it. All that time, she hoped the caller was William, instead it had been Justin. She wanted to return his call, but decided to wait a few days to see if William would call first. After all, she hadn't thought about Justin since the night of Antoinette's party.

That night, she dreamt about William. In her dream, he came to her bedroom and stood over her, watching while she slept. He stood beside her bed for hours watching, but never touching.

In the morning, when she awoke, he was gone.

The hours passed slowly during the next couple of days, with no telephone call from William. Catherine felt like a schoolgirl. *I can't go on like this*, she thought. *I'm a grown woman.*

It was then that she made a decision. If William did call to ask her out, she would definitely decline the invitation.

By week's end, she began to get lonely. On Friday, she paced around the house for most of the day, then decided to call Justin.

Sitting beside the telephone, she took a deep breath, put the receiver beside her ear, and dialed his number. The phone rang three times, and she started to get nervous, she even thought about hanging up. It was too late. He answered.

Uncertain of what to say, she paused, then somehow managed to get the words out. "Hello. May I speak with Justin?"

"This is Justin," he answered in a masculine voice.

"Justin. Hi, this is Catherine Sheldon. I'm sorry that it took so long for me to return your call."

"That's okay. I'm glad that you called."

She didn't respond, and Justin figured she was feeling a bit apprehensive about calling a man. He decided to help her along. "If you're not busy tomorrow night. How would like to go out with me?" he asked sweetly.

Her voice shuttered, "Yes. I'd love to. What did you have in mind?"

"How about dinner?" he suggested eagerly.

"Dinner sounds great. Why don't you pick me up around seven?"

"That would be wonderful," he replied anxiously, then he listened while she gave directions to her house. "Okay," he said, "Then, I guess I'll see you tomorrow night."

"Yes. Tomorrow night." Holding the phone beside her ear for a moment, Catherine breathed a sigh of relief, then slowly lowered the receiver.

Though she was enthusiastic about having dinner with Justin, she still couldn't get William out of her mind. She spent the remainder of the night fantasizing about kissing him. Just the thought sent shivers up and down her spine. She wanted to stop thinking about him, but she just couldn't do it. All night, she found herself dreaming about him. That dream…How wonderful it felt.

The following morning, she opened her eyes. Invigorated, she rose from her iron bed and walked to the French doors leading to the balcony. As she pulled the doors open, the sheer drapes were swept aloft by a fresh morning breeze. Catherine stepped onto the patio. It was a lovely day. The sun was shimmering like gold, and the sky was a beautiful shade of blue, with only a few clouds lingering in the air.

Casting her eyes downward, she looked out over the luscious gardens of her backyard. Her eyes focused on the tranquil blue water of the swimming pool, glimmering in the sunshine, and she decided to go for a swim.

She walked back inside to change into a swimsuit and grab a towel, then went downstairs. On most days, the house would have been filled with the sound of rustling pots and pans, or the vacuum cleaner fast at work, but her housekeeper was on vacation, and the house was quiet.

The hardwood floor creaked as she walked across the room and went outside. The warmth of the sun felt good against her skin.

Placing the towel down on one of the gunmetal chairs near the pool, she looked around, smiling when she saw that the flowers in the beds were beginning to open, while large bumblebees made their way from one flower to another. She descended down the steps, then gracefully plunged into the calm water, swimming below to the other side. She swam laps, stopping after the thirteenth, then swam toward the steps and emerged.

After toweling off, she went inside to take a shower. Refreshed and alert, she dressed in a pair of blue jeans with an old tee shirt, then walked downstairs to the kitchen. After brewing a pot of coffee and toasting two English muffins, she set it all on a serving tray and went back outside to enjoy the weather.

While she was eating, the telephone rang. Her heart began to pound. *What if it's William?* she thought. *What if he wants to go out tonight? What will I say?*

She didn't want to face that problem, so she decided to let the machine pick up. A moment later, she heard Antoinette's voice over the loudspeaker, wondering if she wanted to have lunch and go shopping.

She jumped up, and ran to the phone, answering before Antoinette hung up. She spoke without taking a breath. "Hi. I'd love to go. I have a lot to talk to you about. Can you meet me at the coffee house?"

Antoinette agreed, and they decided to meet an hour later.

Dining on a light lunch, Catherine explained everything that had been happening. She told her about William, then went on to talk about the call from Justin.

Antoinette was quite pleased that Justin had called, and that she'd agreed to go out with him. She said that she really liked Justin, and suggested that Catherine keep an open mind while with him. Catherine listened as she explained, "He's reserved and he likes to keep to himself. His parents were killed in an automobile accident when he was a young boy."

Catherine shivered. She had no idea.

Antoinette continued. "After that, he went to live with his grandparents. His parents had left a substantial inheritance to him, but his grandparents never told him about it. They wanted him to appreciate the value of money, so they kept the inheritance a secret until he turned twenty-one. They raised him to become a good, decent man, deserving of everything he has now."

She paused for a minute, then continued. "Now, William on the other hand, has been spoon fed by his mother since he was a baby. His parents are the owners of a shipping company in Boston, and are quite wealthy. His father had dreams of William joining the company and someday taking over the reigns, but William didn't want any part of the family business. He calls himself a real estate developer, but he's only worked on a couple of projects that I know of in Los Angeles. He lived in New York for a while, but I've never heard of any of his accomplishments there."

Concerned for Catherine's well-being, she divulged, "Listen, I don't think that William's the right man for you, but you have to make that decision for yourself."

With an earful to think about, Catherine graciously thanked Antoinette for the advice, then requested that she not worry about her.

After finishing their lunch, and several cups of coffee, they decided to cancel their shopping excursion. It seemed they'd spent two and a half hours at the restaurant discussing Catherine's issues with the men in her life. They settled the bill and left the restaurant together, saying good-bye at Antoinette's car. Before driving off, Antoinette wished Catherine luck on her date and asked her to call the next morning with the details. Waving, Catherine nodded in agreement.

By the time Catherine arrived home, she only had two hours to get ready, so she quickly headed for the shower. She washed and dried her hair, then put on her makeup and began to search through the closet for something to wear. She thought about it for a moment, then decided to dress conservatively. She pulled out a long black crepe skirt, a stylish ivory silk blouse with French cuffs, and a pair of black suede heels. She pinned her beautiful brown hair up in a barrette, allowing her wavy curls to softly touch her shoulders. She finished by putting on her diamond earrings, bracelet and cufflinks.

She looked stunningly elegant.

Just as she finished, the doorbell rang.

Grabbing her black suede handbag, she left the bedroom, and ran down the winding staircase to answer the door. She was relaxed, but at the same time, anxious. When she opened the door, she was pleased with what she saw. Justin was standing there with a boyish grin, holding a bouquet of colorful tropical flowers. He looked terrific, dressed in a tan polo shirt with a nice pair of black slacks.

Enjoying the aroma of the flowers, she thanked him, then invited him in. He followed her through the elegant marble foyer, and down the stone steps leading to a large living area. Gazing around, he noticed the vaulted ceiling and two sets of glass doors overlooking the sparkling water of the rectangular swimming pool. She mentioned that she'd opened a bottle of wine earlier, and asked if he wanted a glass. Agreeing, he followed her to the bar, located near the back of the room.

While she poured the wine, he continued to look around. "Catherine, your home is beautiful," he commented.

Smiling, she replied, "Thank you. I designed the house with the help of one of my friends. She's also an architect but she lives in New York. Maybe you know her? Her name is Zelda Mitchell."

He recognized the name right away. "Ah, yes. She's a wonderful architect. I had the opportunity to meet her a few years ago at one of our conventions. If I can remember correctly, she's famous for designing Mediterranean style houses like yours."

Catherine laughed. "Yes. But mine was the first."

"And who did your interior design work? For such a large and open floor plan they really made the house have a warm and cozy feeling."

Catherine blushed. "Well…I did," she admitted hesitantly. "I chose all of the fabrics throughout the house, then sewed everything with the help of two of my seamstresses. And I did most of my furniture shopping at antique stores."

Catherine stopped talking for a second to see if Justin was still interested, then she continued. "I wanted the swimming pool to be the main focal point of the house. I think that's what we've accomplished." She turned, pointing to the back of the house. "I wanted to bring the serene feeling of the pool inside, so we installed those large windows."

"You did an amazing job. You're very talented."

Catherine blushed again, and took a sip of wine.

Justin looked down at his watch. "We better get going. Our reservations are for eight-thirty."

Agreeing, Catherine picked up her purse from the end table and led Justin to the front entrance. While locking the door, she glanced over her shoulder to get a peek of the car that Justin was driving. It was a white Land Cruiser, which didn't surprise her a bit.

He led her to the passenger side, and opened the door. After she climbed in, he gently shut the door behind her. Catherine giggled under her breath, thinking how happy she was that she hadn't worn one of the short skirts she was so accustomed to wearing.

Justin got in, and smiled warmly, telling her once again how pleased he was that she'd accepted his invitation.

On the way to the restaurant, they spoke about their interests. He began by asking what she liked to do in her spare time.

She laughed. "Well, on those rare occasions when I'm not at the office, I enjoy gardening and swimming. And I love to travel. But I usually wind up mixing my business trips with my personal time."

"What about you? What do you like to do?" she asked.

Justin's face lit up, and Catherine could tell that whatever he liked to do in his spare time made him extremely happy.

With one hand on the steering wheel, Justin kept his eyes on the road while he explained. "A few years ago, I built a cabin in the Sierra Foothills, and that's where I love to spend my time."

He went on to say that he'd built a rustic cabin beside a beautiful lake where he loved to take walks through the woods to a grassy meadow, and down the canyons to the waters of a rushing stream.

Catherine leaned back against the leather seat. "It sounds relaxing."

Justin pulled into the parking lot of a small seaside restaurant. Before shutting the engine off, he told her that the restaurant was owned by two of his friends, a married couple by the name of Bridgett and Gary Moseley. He explained how they'd purchased the once dilapidated cottage ten years earlier, and had done major remodeling work. "Now it's one of the finest restaurants around," he commented with a smile.

Justin got out, and ran around to the passenger side to open Catherine's door. Grinning, he offered his hand to help her out. Smiling, she accepted.

The small gray restaurant sat on the edge of the secluded beach, with large windows on all sides of the quaint little cottage. As they walked up, the ambiance radiated from the building. On the outside wall, Catherine noticed two beautiful gas lanterns hanging on each side of the doorway, lighting the entrance. It was like no other restaurant in the area. As they drew closer, she could see candles adorning the top of each table, glowing in the darkened dining room.

Upon entering, they were immediately greeted by the Moseley's. Gary and Bridgett were a lovely couple, and did not look anything like Catherine had expected. Bridgett was short and petite with brown hair, and Gary, tall, husky and balding. Complete opposites.

Gary shook Catherine's hand. "It's a real pleasure to meet you," he said, then he began to laugh, his cheeks chubby and glowing. "Do you know that you've been on this guy's mind for weeks?" he divulged.

Catherine reached for Justin's strong arm. "No, I didn't know that," she replied, looking over to see Justin's reaction.

Acknowledging the truth of the statement, Justin grinned at his old friend, then nervously shoved his hands in his pockets. It seemed his friend had told a secret.

Looking at Catherine, Gary patted Justin on the shoulder. "Well, in any event, I'm glad that you were able to come tonight. I promise you won't be sorry. Justin's a great guy."

Bridgett stepped closer. "It's wonderful to finally meet you," she said shaking Catherine's hand.

Unlike her husband, Bridgett was a woman of very few words. Quietly, she led them to a secluded table overlooking the ocean. "Oh, what an incredible view," Catherine remarked casting her wide eyes on the golden sienna sunset. Justin pulled her chair out, and she sat down. "I can't believe the view," she commented, watching as the sun gradually began to disappear below the horizon.

"Yes, and this is a special table for us," Gary said, waving for the waiter to come over. "Right after we purchased the restaurant, I proposed to Bridgett in this same spot, on a night similar to this one."

Bridgett softly interrupted her husband's memory. "Now, Gary, Don't go getting all mushy on us. I'm sure Justin and Catherine would like to be alone now."

Agreeing with his wife, Gary handed out the menus. When the waiter walked over, Gary instructed him to bring their finest bottle of wine over, then he scooted out of the way.

It was a joyful day for Gary. Over the years, he had set Justin up on many blind dates, but they never worked. Justin had been talking about Catherine for weeks, but Gary wasn't sure if she was real or if Justin had made her up for his benefit. But she was real, and Gary liked her immediately.

The waiter returned with a bottle of Cabernet Sauvignon, opened it, and then asked to take their order. They'd been talking so much, that Catherine hadn't even looked at the menu.

"I can come back," the young man acknowledged.

"That would be great. I just need a few minutes."

After the waiter left, Catherine turned to Justin. "What are you going to have?"

He pointed to the menu. "I thought that I'd have filet mignon with the lobster."

"Ooh," Catherine admitted, "That sounds good, but that's a lot for me. I think I'll just have the filet, cooked medium."

"What about your side dishes?" he asked. "Salad comes with the meal, along with a baked potato or garlic mashed potatoes."

Catherine laughed. "I think that I'll stay away from the garlic tonight. I'll have the baked potato, with Italian dressing on the salad."

While they ate, they discussed everything from their high school days to their dreams for the future. Justin was a wonderful conversationalist and he kept the discussion alive and vibrant. As he spoke, Catherine couldn't stop looking at him. She thought that he was not only handsome, but witty.

By the time they finished, they'd gone through two bottles of wine. Passing on dessert, they went to say good-bye to the Moseley's. Gary and Bridgett took turns giving hugs while Catherine commented about how much she enjoyed their restaurant. "Your restaurant reminds me of a European Inn that I once visited. I'll definitely recommend it to my friends," she remarked kindly.

Gary shook Justin's hand. Pulling him close, they shared a masculine hug. "You lucky devil! You have a beauty on your hands," he whispered in Justin's ear.

Catherine didn't let it show, but she'd heard everything that Gary had said, and she was trying hard not to giggle.

Once again, they said good-bye. Catherine and Justin walked out the front door and headed to the truck. Justin started to unlock the door, then stopped. "Wait here, I have a great idea. I'll be right back," he said, then ran back into the restaurant.

Catherine could see Gary and Justin through the window. They talked for a moment, then Gary walked away. A few seconds later, he appeared again, and handed something to Justin. They shook hands, then Justin headed back to the front door. As he got closer, she saw that he was holding two glasses and a bottle of wine. Pacing toward her he asked, "How'd you like to go for a moonlight walk?"

Catherine smiled brightly. "That's a great idea."

Walking across the narrow wooden bridge leading from the restaurant to the beach, Catherine led the way. When they reached the end, where the bridge met the sand, she stopped. "Wait a minute," she said. "I'm going to take off my shoes."

Sitting on the end of the bridge, she removed her shoes, then discreetly began to remove her pantyhose.

Embarrassed, Justin nobly looked away. "Let me know when you're ready."

Catherine stood up, and ran toward the water. "I'm ready," she shouted. "I love the feeling of sand between my toes," she yelled. "And did you know it's a great exfoliater, too?"

Justin laughed. "No, I didn't know that."

Reaching down, he removed his shoes. He took his socks off, rolled his pants legs up, and then put his feet in the sand. "You're right. It feels great!" he acknowledged.

Side by side, they headed down the deserted beach. When they could no longer see the restaurant, they stopped to sit on a large group of rocks. Justin opened the wine and poured two glasses. He gave her a glass, then he casually laid back against the rocks. Catherine sat snugly beside him while they watched the waves crash gently into the shoreline. Once again, he commented about how much he loved being outdoors, and how the sound of water calmed him, taking him back to another place in time. "The world doesn't feel so hurried when you're out here," he said. "Looking out over the water makes you understand how big the world is, and how small a part of it you are," he stated eloquently.

Looking off in the distance, Catherine nodded. "I know what you mean. I feel exactly the same way. It's kind of spooky," she added, taking a sip of wine.

"Why is it spooky for you?" he asked curiously.

She squinted her eyes, and looked at him. "It's weird how we both have the same thoughts about things. I've never had this much in common with anyone before. I know it sounds like a cliché, but I feel like I've known you forever."

Justin sat up straight. Leaning forward, he softly kissed her lips. She surrendered to him, sliding her body close to his. Gently, she wrapped her arms around his shoulders. He pulled her body even closer, stirring instant feelings of desire. She exhaled a shaky breath as they shared a soft kiss. Once again, she surrendered. The warmth of his body pressed against her skin. She had second thoughts. "Maybe we should go now," she whispered against his lips.

Justin nodded his head. He stood, reaching his hand out to help her up. And he didn't let go, holding her hand all the way back to the restaurant.

When they approached the parking lot, Justin turned to Catherine. "I'll be right back. I'm just going to run in to give our empty bottle and wine glasses to Gary."

Once again, Catherine watched through the window as Justin handed the empty wine bottle and glasses to Gary. He shook Gary's hand, then walked out of the restaurant to meet her.

When he approached, he opened the door and turned to her. "I'm sorry it got so heated back there. I promise, I didn't plan for that to happen," he uttered in the darkness.

Catherine leaned against the side of the seat and glared deeply into his blue eyes. "I know that you didn't plan it," she said. "I liked it, but it was just a little too fast for me."

Worried that he'd ruined his chances with her, Justin nodded his head as he closed the door. He walked around and got into the truck. Once inside, he hesitated for a moment, then started the engine. Before putting the truck in gear, he turned to her, took a long breath and smiled softly. He was trying to hide his true feelings, but she could see the look of anxiety in his eyes. Looking straight ahead, she thought for a moment, then quickly leaned over, kissing him softly on the cheek. Relieved, he smiled at her, put the truck in gear and drove away.

The ride back to her house was much quieter than the ride to the restaurant. To break the silence, Justin played classical music on the stereo. During the ride, Catherine kept running what had happened over and over again through her mind. And she could tell that Justin was doing the same.

She looked up, noticing that they had arrived back at her house. Justin got out and slowly walked around to open the door. Pulling the door open, he extended his hand. "Come on. I'll walk you to the door."

Accepting without speaking, Catherine got out of the truck.

Slowly and silently, they made their way along the curved brick sidewalk up the steps to the entryway. While he watched, she unlocked the door. Then she turned to him. "Thank you for everything, Justin. I had a really nice time tonight."

Without speaking, he moved closer, gently placing his hands on her shoulders, then kissed her sweetly on the cheek. "I had a good time too," he whispered. "I hope we can do it again sometime."

"I'd like that," she replied in a soft voice.

He began to walk away, then turned around for a second look. "Well, goodnight. I'll call you soon."

It had been a long time since anyone had affected him the way that she had that evening. And for the first time, he looked forward to the possibility of love.

Catherine went inside, locked the door and turned the alarm on. Her emotions were raging and she was angry with herself. It seemed that while she was kissing Justin, she began to think about William Moorehouse. Why couldn't she get him out of her head?

She turned off the lamp in the foyer, then headed upstairs to take a shower before retiring for the night.

Inside the large marble bathroom, Catherine sat at her dressing table to remove her jewelry. When she finished, she stood up, undressed and stepped into the shower.

As the warm water rolled down her body, she began to think about everything that had happened. Although she felt a connection with Justin, she didn't like the way she'd thought about William while kissing him. It felt wrong. Somehow she had to get William out of her mind once and for all.

After toweling off, she dried her hair, put on a blue silk nightgown and climbed into her large cozy iron bed. Once again, she began to analyze what had happened.

She thought about it for a while, then somehow managed to fall fast asleep.

CHAPTER 5

❈

It was early in the morning when Catherine's telephone rang. Barely able to open her eyes, she rolled to the other side of the bed to answer. Lifting the receiver, she lazily answered, "Hello."

"Good Morning, Catherine. This is Antoinette. Did I wake you?"

"Yes," Catherine admitted. "What time is it?" she groaned.

"It's seven-thirty," Antoinette announced in a perky voice.

"Seven-thirty? Are you crazy, calling me at seven-thirty on a Sunday morning?"

"Sorry, I left a message for you last night, but you didn't return my call. I have some place to take you today and we have to get an early start."

"Where do you want to take me?" she mumbled.

"I'm invited to a barbecue in Malibu, and I thought that you might like to go."

"In Malibu. Where in Malibu?" Catherine interrogated.

"It's at the home of the movie producer, Hugh Davenport, and it starts at noon. My helicopter pilot is going to take us. Will you come with me, please….? I promise, you'll have a great time."

"I guess so—What if I meet you at eleven-thirty?"

"Eleven-thirty is perfect. This is one party that I've been looking forward to attending. A few celebrities are supposed to be there," she added.

"Okay, Okay! You don't have to sell me on the idea anymore. I'll see you at eleven-thirty."

Catherine got out of bed and went directly to the shower to wake herself up. Normally, she liked to sleep until at least ten o'clock after a late night, so she was extremely tired. The shower was refreshing and she felt much better when she got out. She combed through her hair, slipped into her terry cloth robe, and then proceeded to go downstairs to have breakfast.

The sun pierced through the window, blinding her, when she entered the kitchen. She realized immediately that she had a hangover from all of the wine she'd consumed with Justin. Her head ached, and her eyelids were swollen. She made a pot of strong coffee, toasted a bagel, and took two pain relievers. Just as she sat down to eat, the telephone rang. *Now who can that be?* she thought.

Massaging her throbbing temples, she picked up the receiver.

She recognized the voice. "Hi, It's Justin. I hope I didn't call too early?"

"No. I've been up for a while now," she mumbled.

"I'm going to the cabin, and I was hoping that you'd join me," he said eagerly.

"Oh, Justin. I'd really like to, but I can't. I promised Antoinette that I'd go to Malibu with her for a barbecue. I must tell you though, I'd much prefer to go with you. I have a horrendous headache from all of the wine we drank last night and I'm not feeling up to being around a crowd. I'd much rather lay on the grass beside the lake or better yet, float on a raft and just relax." She paused for a moment, then asked, "By the way, how are you feeling today?"

"I feel great, but I'm sorry to hear you're not," Justin said sadly. In a sweet voice, he continued, "Well, I guess I should let you go. Have fun today and take care of yourself. I'll be thinking about you," he added.

"I'll be thinking of you, too."

Catherine set the receiver down, and started to think about her date with Justin. And that kiss. How she wished it had been William. But then again, it was a very passionate kiss and it was from Justin's lips. There was still hope something could ignite between she and Justin.

She looked up at the clock. It was already nine-thirty. After eating fast, she leaped to her feet and hurried upstairs to get ready.

Rummaging through her closet, she decided to dress comfortably in a sleeveless white tank style dress, which looked great against her tanned skin, and a pair of gold strappy sandals. She packed a beach bag with a few necessities; a one piece bathing suit, a pair of extra panties, a pair of blue jeans, a shirt, another pair of shoes and a bottle of sunscreen. She put on her makeup, pinned her hair up, put on some perfume and was ready to go.

Because traffic was light, she made it to Antoinette's in record time. Driving up, she could see Antoinette pacing nervously beneath a large elm tree near the driveway. She watched as Antoinette checked the time, then hurried over to the car, flinging the door open. She could tell Antoinette was in a hurry.

"Come on—My helicopter pilot is waiting for us."

Catherine didn't move. Smiling slightly, she removed her dark sunglasses. "Hello to you too," she remarked lazily.

Antoinette stepped closer as Catherine got out of the car. "You don't look too well," she commented. "You look like you have a hangover. Please don't tell me that you do."

"I do, but I'll be okay."

Antoinette made a face. "I hope so because I don't want to leave the party early. A lot of high profile people are going to be there and I want to meet all of them!"

"I can go home if you like," Catherine moaned, pointing back to the car.

Antoinette gripped Catherine's hand. "Oh, no. I want you to come with me," she announced.

As they walked down the path leading to the back of the house, Catherine put her arm around Antoinette's shoulder to console her. "It's okay. If I start to feel bad, I'll go down to the beach and find a spot to relax while you're at the party. I just have to eat some lunch and take a couple more pain relievers, and I'll be fine."

In the distance, Catherine could see the helicopter sitting on the freshly mowed lawn behind the mansion. The pilot saw them and immediately started the engine. Just as Catherine and Antoinette climbed into the small cabin, the blades began to turn. They buckled their seat belts, and the helicopter lifted from the ground.

The flight to Malibu was short, and before they knew it, the pilot announced that they would land shortly. And for that Catherine was grateful, because she was beginning to feel queasy from the ride.

As the helicopter approached the landing pad, Catherine got a birds eye view of the Davenport Estate, which was located on one of the lower cliffs beside the beach. She peered out of the window, getting a glimpse of the contemporary style house centered in the middle of the beautifully landscaped property. Two men were running across the lawn to greet them.

When they got closer, Antoinette mentioned that the distinguished, older gentleman was Hugh and the other man was Hugh's butler. Hugh opened the door, offering Antoinette and Catherine his hand to help them, while the butler took their bags.

He introduced himself to Catherine, then kissed Antoinette on the cheek. Catherine watched as Hugh grabbed Antoinette's hand and headed toward the side entryway while Catherine and the butler followed close behind.

When they entered, Antoinette told Hugh that she and Catherine were going to freshen up and would meet him on the patio. Antoinette led Catherine down a long hallway into a room which seemed to be the master bedroom of the house. As they walked in, Catherine commented, "So, Antoinette. You really do seem to know your way around this house. Is there anything you have to tell me?"

Antoinette laughed. "Oh, Catherine, you know me so well. I can't hide anything from you." She took a deep breath. "I can't lie to you. Hugh and I have been seeing each other for some time now.

He makes me feel young and vibrant again. I feel like I have a life again, I feel—"

Catherine interrupted. "There's no reason for you to explain any further. I understand completely." She reached for Antoinette's hands and pulled her close to share a hug. "If you're happy, then I'm happy, too," Catherine whispered.

Catherine sat on the edge of the bed while Antoinette looked at herself in a large wall mirror. Straightening her skirt, Antoinette looked at Catherine through the mirror. "What about you? How was your date with Justin?" Antoinette inquired quizzically.

Catherine closed her eyes and began to massage her temples. "It was fine," she replied quite simply.

"Just fine," Antoinette said, turning to walk toward her. Realizing that Catherine was in pain, she reached for her head. "Here let me do that," she said, taking over the task. Standing beside her, she waited for Catherine to tell her about the date, but she didn't. "So—what about the date," she inquired again. "Did you have a good time?"

Catherine slowly raised her head to look at Antoinette. "Yes. I had a great time. Justin's a nice man." She didn't seem very enthusiastic.

"Well, are you going to see him again?" Antoinette pressed.

"If he calls, I will," Catherine replied, then she changed the subject. "Can you rub right here?" she asked, pointing to the middle of her forehead.

Antoinette massaged the spot for a minute, then stopped. "We better get outside," she remarked. Catherine didn't move from where she was sitting.

"Are you going to come with me or would you like to rest a while?" Antoinette stated, putting her hand on her hip.

"I'm coming with you," Catherine grumbled as she stood.

A few minutes later they stepped onto the large stone patio. Once again, they were greeted by Hugh and his butler. The butler took drink orders. Antoinette ordered a glass of wine and Catherine told him that a glass of mineral water would be great. Catherine watched as the butler walked across the patio toward the bar to get their drinks. And that's when saw William Moorehouse standing beside the bar conversing with another gentleman.

She couldn't believe her eyes. What was he doing there?

She moved close to Antoinette and tugged on her arm. "You'll never guess who's here?" she whispered.

Excited, Antoinette looked around. "Is it a movie star?" she asked.

"No. He's no movie star. It's William Moorehouse. And don't look now, but he's standing directly across from us."

"What's he doing here?" Antoinette questioned angrily.

Catherine turned to the side, hoping that he wouldn't see her. But not a second later, Antoinette informed her that he was walking toward them.

Catherine put her hand over her face.

Seeing what Catherine was trying to do, Antoinette laughed. "When are you going to learn that you're too beautiful to hide? Didn't you notice that every man on this patio turned to get a glimpse of you as soon as we stepped outside?"

Before Catherine had a chance to respond, William was standing in front of her. He smiled, "Catherine, it's great to see you again. I had no idea you were going to be here today."

She began to feel flush. Her voice shuttered, "Yes, Antoinette invited me." For a moment, she didn't know what to say. "So, how have you been?" she asked.

He moved closer. "I've been great," he said. "By the way, I'm sorry that I haven't called. I've been really busy lately. You probably won't believe it, but I planned to call you later in the week to invite you out for dinner and dancing."

She didn't want to let him know she'd been waiting for him to call, so she pretended his not calling didn't bother her at all. "Oh, I understand. I've been pretty busy myself." Then she smiled. "I didn't expect to see you here either. How did you get invited to this party?"

William laughed. "I'm one of Hugh's neighbors. I guess he had to invite me." He pointed down the beach. "I live about a mile down on the flat portion of the beach."

Looking in that direction, Catherine could see about a dozen houses, closely spaced, near the edge of the beach. She took a sip of mineral water to wet her lips. "Oh, really," she remarked. "I didn't know that you lived in Malibu, but I guess the subject never came up."

"Yeah, I have the beach house but I also have a loft in LA where I spend most of my time," he disclosed.

She thought he was trying to impress her. "Well, I'm glad you're here. It's really nice to see you again," she admitted.

Catherine was nervous. Not knowing what to say next, she turned around to look for Antoinette for support, but she and Hugh had disappeared.

"Are you looking for someone?" William asked suspiciously.

"No—I was just trying to see who else is here that I might recognize."

He shifted his face close to her ear. "To be honest, most of the people here today are really snooty Hollywood types and I don't think you'd enjoy their company," he whispered. "How would you like to hang out with me instead?" he asked, sounding sure of himself.

"So—You think I enjoy your company?" she chuckled.

He grinned. "Well, to be honest, I think if you had to choose between the lesser of two evils, you'd have to choose me."

Catherine broke out in laughter. "Since you put it that way, I guess I'll hang out with you. At least for a little while."

"You have a beautiful smile," he sweetly complimented.

Once again, her face turned flush. "Thank you. That's a nice thing for you to say," she graciously replied.

Catherine started to walk toward the swimming pool, and William followed close behind. Continuing to talk, they stopped beneath a blanket of palm trees surrounding the tranquil water of the swimming pool. They stayed there for a while, then resumed walking around the well-tended lawn, talking and laughing, unaware of how quickly the time was passing.

Later, they took their place at a table with a breathtaking view of the ocean. Deciding to eat lunch, William went over to the large buffet tables, and served two plates of food while she waited at the table. She watched as he lifted each and every silver lid, choosing their meal carefully.

Before long, the sun began to set, and the air started to get chilly. Shivering, Catherine clinched her bare arms. "Are you cold?" William asked softly.

"Yes. I forgot to bring my sweater," she admitted.

William took his jacket off and draped it over her shoulders. "Here, this should warm you," he uttered in a soothing voice.

Smiling, Catherine tugged the lapels, gently pulling the jacket snugly around her body. William moved his chair close to hers, then placed his arm around her shoulders. She looked up, and found herself face to face with him. His big brown eyes glared softly into hers. Slowly, he moved his chin closer, inviting her for a kiss. Uncontrollably, her lips turned into magnets, drawn to his. Her body had taken over and there wasn't anything she could do to stop it. Their lips touched, and gently merged.

After the kiss, Catherine reached for her glass of water, clumsily spilling it on the table. The mood was broken and she quickly stood. "Oh, I'm so sorry," she said wiping the spill with a white linen napkin.

Remaining seated, William watched her closely. He could tell she was nervous. "It's all right," he said stroking the top of her hand.

She looked up at him, and a tear fell from one of her luscious lashes. "What's happening here?" she questioned. "I don't even know you."

"I don't know," he said in a soft tone. "I guess we're just two people who are attracted to one another."

Trying to ignore what he'd said, Catherine continued to wipe up the spill without looking at him.

William looked around the patio. Everyone had gone inside. He realized that she was nervous, and he wanted to relieve some of the pressure that she was feeling. "Listen, why don't we continue our conversation inside?" he suggested.

Willingly, she agreed.

As they made their way inside the spacious living room, she thanked him for the jacket, then handed it back to him. They found a cozy corner near the fireplace to sit. Walking up to the seating area, Catherine chose to sit in a burgundy wing-backed chair, instead of the love seat that was next to it. She sat down, and crossed her legs.

Realizing what she was doing, William grinned and sat in the chair across from her. Once again, they began to talk, but this time they made small talk about the party.

One of the servers came by offering them brandy and they both accepted a glass. To calm her nerves, Catherine took a big gulp, almost choking as she swallowed it.

Eyeing her up and down, William pressed his body back against the chair, then watched her every move. She couldn't bear to look him in the eyes. Instead, she stared downward at her glass, gently swirling the brandy. She took another sip, and their eyes met. He crossed his legs and smiled gently. She could tell by the look in his eyes that he wanted to move closer.

Saying good-bye to the last group of guests, Antoinette and Hugh finally made their way back to speak with them. Walking up,

Antoinette immediately noticed the tension between the two of them. She sat on the arm of Catherine's chair, as if to protect Catherine from William, giving him a set of evil eyes that pierced through him. Antoinette began to speak, but was summoned to the kitchen. "What do they want?" she commented, not wanting to leave Catherine's side.

"Are you going to be all right?" she whispered in Catherine's ear.

Catherine smiled politely and nodded.

Excusing herself, Antoinette stood and walked toward the kitchen. She thought that Hugh would remain behind, but he didn't.

William smiled, stood up, and walked closer. "Well, we're all alone," he said. "How would you like to take a walk down to my place?" he asked smoothly as he reached his hand out.

Looking around the empty room, Catherine took a deep breath.

"It's all right," he said, "I promise to be a perfect gentleman."

Catherine shrugged. "I don't know if that's such a good idea. It's been a long day, and I'm pretty tired."

He coaxed her. "Oh, come on. Just for a little while, then I'll drive you home."

Catherine thought about it for a moment. "Well, I left my car at Antoinette's house, but I guess I can pick it up tomorrow," she reasoned aloud. He smiled, easing the tension. His smile softened her heart, and she agreed. "Okay, but just for a little while, then I really have to get home."

Hugh and Antoinette returned just as Catherine stood. William shook Hugh's hand thanking him for the hospitality, while Catherine walked over to Antoinette. "I'm taking a walk to William's house, then he's going to take me home," she whispered.

Antoinette didn't say a word. She just gave her the look a mother would have given a daughter when she thought her suitor was less than acceptable for her precious little girl. There wasn't anything she could do to stop her.

William draped his jacket over Catherine's shoulders and they walked down a set of steep steps leading to the beach. When they got to the sand, Catherine looked up at the sky. The moon was hidden by silvery clouds quickly rolling across the darkened sky. They began their journey down the beach and halfway there, the waves became violent, crashing against the shoreline. The mild weather was changing rapidly. *Is this a sign of what is to come*, she thought, looking up at the ferocious sky.

A little voice inside her mind told her that she shouldn't have accepted the invitation, but a stronger voice inside her heart had won the battle. What was it about him that made her say yes? She just didn't get it. There she was a strong, intelligent woman drawn to such a smooth talker. Was it because he was so handsome, or was it his persistence. *Just take a chance*, her heart kept saying over and over again. *You'll never know unless you take a chance.* And now, there she was—walking down the beach with him. Ready to take a chance…

Arriving at the door of his beach house, he turned to her. "Now, I just want to warn you. My house is not as glamorous or as large as Hugh's, and you'll be able to tell immediately that a bachelor lives here."

Catherine laughed. "Thanks for the warning."

It began to drizzle. She watched the rain from beneath the patio while William unlocked the door. He turned back, shifting his body close, drawing her soft body nearer to protect her from the rain. He stared into her eyes, caressing her cheeks with his hands. "You're the most beautiful woman I've ever seen," he whispered. He continued to glare into her eyes, leaning his body into hers until they united. The rain began to pour from the sky. She closed her eyes and he continued to gently stroke her face while pressing his lips to hers, kissing her softly. Her lips trembled. She wrapped her arms around his shoulders, pulling him closer. Pressing his hands against the small of her back, they embraced for a passionate kiss. Catherine felt a twinge run up and down her spine, his touch lingering with every movement.

He opened the door and they went inside. He led her down a dark hallway, into his bedroom. Gripping her hands softly, he led her deeper into the room. Lightening struck, followed by a thunderous roar. It was a wicked night and she felt wicked for being there, but she was following her heart, her passion. Lightening struck again, sending a beam of light through the window, creating a soft glow against their skin. She began to feel flush as a surge of heat raced through her body. Softly and slowly, she instinctively moved closer to him. They engaged in another passionate kiss.

Her heart was pounding and she was sure he could feel it pumping through her chest. *What am I doing here?* she thought.

His hands traveled slowly across her back, and he unzipped her dress.

Gliding his hands to the top of her shoulders, he used his fingertips to slide the straps away from her soft skin. Her body tingled from the softness of his touch.

Closing her eyes, she breathed deeply. Her dress fell to the floor.

The passion that she felt for him heightened. She couldn't turn back.

She unbuttoned his shirt, gently stroking his masculine chest and shoulders, moving his shirt down his arms and off his body. Her head slowly lowered and she gently kissed the wall of his chest. His jaw tightened as she gradually made her way back up to explore his mouth. As they kissed, William reached his hands around her back, unsnapping her bra, gently pulling it down her arms and off her body. Leaning over, he began to stroke her breasts as she slowly unzipped his pants, gliding her hands against his skin. She gently used her fingers to lower his pants. She melted into his arms as he put his arms around her waist, gently slipping her panties over her hips and down her legs. She could feel the rising pressure of his passion as he slowly pulled her down on the bed. Lowering his head, he gently caressed her breasts, exploring her body with his mouth. Her pulse began to quicken with aching and longing for him as she wrapped her trembling legs around his waist. Slowly, he entered her body and their bodies moved together in a rhythmic motion. They moaned in delight, as they continued to engage in slow, passionate kisses, making love over and over again throughout the night, finally drifting to sleep in the early morning hours.

Awakened by the sound of running water, Catherine glanced at the clock on the bedside table. It was quarter to nine. Sitting up, her eyes focused on a white robe laid neatly on the foot of the bed. He had thought of everything.

She got out of bed, put the robe on and went to the bathroom to freshen up. When she finished, she went back into the bedroom. William was sitting on the edge of the bed, dressed in a white T-shirt with a pair of blue pajama pants, holding two cups of coffee.

She moved closer, and he smiled. "Two sugars and a little cream, right?"

"That's right, how did you know?" she asked, taking the cup from his hand.

"I remembered from the coffee shop."

She took a sip, and sat beside him. "Mmm, it's perfect."

"You're perfect," he said, moving closer to kiss her.

Once again, the surge ran up and down her spine. Her lips began to tremble. "About last night," she mentioned.

"What about it?" He moved closer.

"I've never had a one night stand before."

He kissed her neck. "What makes you think it was a one night stand?"

His lips wandered to her mouth.

She took the cup out of his hand, and gently set both cups on the table. Standing in front of him, she placed her hands on his shoulders and leaned down to kiss him. He pushed her back up gently to untie her robe. He glided his hands around her lower back as they engaged in another passionate kiss. Running his hands across her shoulders, he gradually pushed the robe down her arms. She placed her hands on the hem of his shirt, pulling it up, over his head. Slowly, she moved her hands around his waist. She slipped her hands inside his pajama pants, pushing them down his hips to the floor. She began to kiss his neck, gradually making her way down to his chest. She stroked his chest, gently pushing him backwards on the bed as she shifted her body on top of his thighs. Straddling her legs around his hips, she lowered her body to his. She moistened her lips with her tongue and leaned down to kiss him, and their lips melted together. He pulled back. He ran his hands through her thick hair, staring deeply into her eyes. They climaxed together. Slowly, she lowered her body to share a soft kiss. Trading smiles, she moved off of his body and laid beside him.

They rested in each other's arms for a while, then decided to get up, take a shower and get dressed.

While dressing, she mentioned that she had to get home. She had a meeting the following day and had to prepare for it.

They finished, then went into the kitchen for another cup of coffee. Upon entering, she noticed the stainless steel countertops and appliances. The room was light and airy with plenty of windows, but there was no warmth. It was cold.

William watched as she walked out of the kitchen to check out the rest of his space. The living room was decorated with black leather furniture, and had an art deco flair. Quite the opposite of what she would have done.

The ride home turned out to be a quiet one, with each deep in thought. The same thing kept running though her mind over and over. How could she have made love to the man she'd sworn she'd never date, or better yet the same rude man she'd sworn would never see her naked body again. But then again, he was different from the first time they'd met at the swimming pool.

She realized that William was turning down the long driveway leading to her house. He pulled his black BMW into the U-shaped driveway in front of her house. "Well, we're here," he mumbled in a low tone.

She turned to face him. "Would you like to come in?" she asked softly.

"Just for a little while," he replied sweetly.

He got out of the car and walked around to open her door. They walked down the winding path to the entryway. She opened the door and led him through the foyer toward the living room. "Would you like something to drink or eat?" she asked tenderly. "If you like, I can whip up some breakfast for us," she suggested.

Excited, he accepted.

Catherine led William through the living room down the hallway into her spacious kitchen. Together, they cooked a wonderful breakfast and took it out to the pool area.

When they finished eating, William stood. "Well, I know you have some work to finish today, so I'm going to head home."

"Yes, that's probably a good idea," she said.

Taking his hand, she led him around the side gate to the front of the house. When they arrived at his car, he pulled her body close, sharing a warm hug and kiss. "I'll call you tomorrow morning. Maybe we can have lunch together?"

Eagerly, Catherine accepted the invitation, then she watched him get into his car, and waved as he drove away.

When she went back inside, she headed upstairs for a hot shower. Exhausted, she climbed into her soft bed and fell into a deep slumber.

She slept for a couple of hours until she was awakened by the sound of the telephone ringing. Lazily, she leaned over the side of the bed, and picked up the receiver. Finding it hard to open her eyes, she squinted, answering in a low tone.

"Catherine, this is Justin. Did I wake you?"

She sat up. "Yes, but that's all right. I was just trying to catch up on my sleep."

He joked. "That must have been some party. Did you have a good time?"

"Yes, I had a wonderful time after all."

"That's good. I'm glad to hear you had fun." He paused for a moment. "Well, I know you're tired, so I'm not going to keep you. I'm calling to invite you to lunch tomorrow afternoon."

She rubbed her head. "Tomorrow's not a good day," she said, remembering that William said he would call. "How about later in the week? Why don't you call me at my office tomorrow afternoon, and I'll see what my week looks like?"

"I can do that," he agreed.

They spoke for a few more minutes, then hung up.

Catherine got out of bed, and stretched her arms in the air. She put on her robe and slipped her bare feet into a pair of comfortable slippers. She went downstairs to the kitchen and made a sandwich with a glass of lemonade. She took the food to the study to prepare for the meeting.

While she was working the telephone rang. She mumbled to herself, "Could it be William?" She picked up the receiver, and recognized the voice on the other end. Antoinette was calling to find out what had happened with William.

"I don't think you want to know," Catherine stated hesitantly.

"Oh no...You slept with him. Didn't you?"

"Yes, I did...and I enjoyed every minute," Catherine admitted bluntly. "He turned out to be a nice guy after all."

Antoinette's mood changed. "Look, Catherine. I'm not going to tell you what to do. If you think William's the man of your dreams, then so be it. But please be careful. He's been out with a lot of women and I don't want to see you get hurt."

"Don't worry. I'm a strong, independent woman. I can handle any situation."

"Yes, any situation in business, but I'm not so sure about your love life."

"Please, let's change the subject," Catherine whined.

"Okay, let's change the subject. So, what's going on with Justin?" Antoinette interrogated.

Catherine giggled. "Back to the men in my life, huh?…Well if you must know, Justin called a little earlier. He wants to take me to lunch during the week."

"Did you say yes?"

"I told him that I have to check my calendar."

"Have you told him about William yet?"

"No, I can't tell him that—Anyway, we've only been out on one date. I don't think it's necessary for me to say anything right now."

"Well, I think you should because he's really interested in you."

Changing the subject again, Catherine interrupted, "Oh, by the way. I'm sure you noticed that my car is sitting in your driveway."

"Yes. I noticed. So what do you want me to do with it?" Antoinette asked in a harsh tone. "And I have the bag you left at Hugh's too," she mentioned.

Catherine sighed. "Don't worry. Jackson's going to take me there tomorrow morning to pick everything up on my way to the office."

"That's fine," Antoinette replied abruptly.

Catherine could tell that Antoinette was upset, so she decided to end the conversation. "Listen, Antoinette. I hope you don't mind, but I have an awful lot of work to do tonight. Can we talk about all of this some other time? I promise to keep you updated on everything that happens."

With hesitation in her voice, Antoinette agreed.

Setting the receiver down, Catherine shook her head, and went back to her paperwork, finishing a couple of hours later. By then, it was already quarter to ten, so she decided to turn in for the evening.

CHAPTER 6

As Catherine pushed open the etched glass doors to Sheldon Enterprises, she could tell that something unusual had happened. The front desk, normally manned by two receptionists, was unattended and the telephone was ringing off the hook.

Walking up to the counter, she looked down at the blinking telephone lines. "What in the hell's going on here?" she mumbled.

Just then, the sound of laughter erupted from the back of the suite. She stood still, listening intently. Laughter broke out again.

Clutching her briefcase tightly in her hand, she marched down the hall to find out what had happened. As she turned the corner, she saw a group of employees standing in the hallway near her office. Folding her arms across her chest, she stood tall. "What's going on here?" she questioned harshly, startling them with her tone.

Although it was a simple question, no one stepped forward to respond. Instead, they scattered like scared rabbits, leaving Catherine's secretary, Kay, alone in the doorway. "I'm sorry," Kay said quickly, seeing the look of dissatisfaction on her face.

"What's going on? Did something happen?" Catherine asked suspiciously.

Kay smiled softly. "Something happened all right."

Waiting to hear more, Catherine eyed her with curiosity. "What?" she hissed.

Kay smiled again. "You have to see it for yourself."

Confused, Catherine shook her head and walked into the office. Inside, her eyes focused on an unbelievable site. The room was filled with flower arrangements, every type, shape and size imaginable.

Astonished, she cupped her hand over her mouth. Secretly, she guessed that William had sent them, but she asked anyway.

Kay shrugged. "I don't know," she replied from the doorway. The card's attached to the bouquet of red roses on your desk," she pointed.

Sweeping the hair away from her eyes, Catherine walked over to read the card.

Gently pulling the envelope out of the bouquet, her eyes widened. It wasn't one of those small envelopes that people usually receive with flowers. This one was note card size, personalized with the initials W G M printed in the left hand corner.

Running her index finger across the raised gold print of the monogram, she smiled. "It's William all right," she said in a low tone.

Steadying the envelope in her hand, she pulled out the card.

Unfolding it, she read.

Catherine,

I just want you to know how much I enjoyed spending time with you the other night. I would love to see you again. Please say that you'll join me for dinner this evening. I'll call you later.

William

When Catherine finished reading, she looked up to see if Kay was still standing in the doorway, and she was. "Kay, I need a favor," she mentioned kindly. "Can you have all but three arrangements delivered to the retirement home down the street. And if William

Moorehouse calls, put him through, no matter where I am or what I'm doing. I really need to speak with him."

Kay agreed, then left, quietly shutting the door behind her.

Catherine glanced down at the bouquet of red roses in the center of her desk. Smiling, she gently tugged on one of the roses, pulling it out. "I can't believe him," she whispered to herself.

Placing the velvety soft, fragrant petals against her nose, she turned to look out the window, and began to think about the night she'd spent with William. How wonderful it had been to be wrapped in his strong arms. Just the thought of him, caused a rise in her temperature.

Her daydream was interrupted by a knock on the door. Her gaze shifted to the doorway. "Yes. Come in," she called.

The door opened, and Theodore entered. "I hope I'm not interrupting?"

She took a deep breath. "No. Not at all," she replied.

She watched as he peered around the room. "I heard about all the ruckus." He looked around the room again. "Is this what has everyone in such an uproar?" he asked with a devilish grin.

She smiled. "This is it," she replied, placing the red rose that she was holding on her desk. "I was just thinking about opening my own flower shop," she joked. What do you think? Would that be a good move?"

Theodore laughed. "With all of these flowers, you probably could."

Catherine knew that Theodore wasn't the type of man to take time out of his busy schedule for a few silly flowers. There had to be another reason for his visit. "Is there something you need to speak with me about?" she questioned, moving in his direction.

His face lit up, and he grinned. "Tomorrow's the big day," he announced, in regard to the new cosmetic and fragrance line set to go on the market the following day. "I'm here to remind you about the press conference this afternoon."

"Yes. I haven't forgotten," she said. "I wouldn't miss it for the world."

An awkward silence filled the air, and she smiled. She could tell that he wanted to say or ask something, but was apprehensive about doing so. "Is that all?" she asked inquisitively.

He shoved his hands in his pants pockets. "Yes. That's all," he replied, then walked toward the door. He stopped beside a vase of white roses sitting on the table beside the door, then pulled his right hand out of his pocket. Pointing to a rose bud, he looked up at her. "May I have one?" he asked.

"Yes. Please help yourself," she replied, nervously rubbing her hands together.

"This will look nice on my lapel," he commented, pulling the bud out of the bouquet. Holding the bud, he looked around one more time, then gestured to the door. "Well, I better get back to work. I'll meet you in the lobby at three."

"That sounds great," she replied, and he strolled out of the office.

When he left, she took a deep breath, and sat down at her desk. What was he so afraid to ask? She knew that it couldn't have been anything about business. They'd never had a lack of words in that regard. It had to be personal. Then, it hit her. It was the flowers. He probably wanted to know who had sent the flowers, but was afraid to ask. That was the kind of man he was. It had always been his strong opinion that business and personal lives should never be mixed. That was one of the things she liked about him.

After a successful press conference, Catherine went back up to her office to check her messages. The flowers had been cleared away, but William still hadn't called. Moping, she sat at the desk and picked up a pencil. Rolling it in her hands, she stared down at the telephone. "When are you going to ring?" she asked aloud.

Just then, Kay buzzed in. "Mr. Moorehouse is on line two," she announced.

"Finally," she mumbled.

Although she was thrilled that he had called, she didn't want to seem too anxious. She sat back in the chair, counted to twenty, and then picked up the receiver. "William…Hi. It's great to hear from you," she said. "Thank you so much for sending the flowers. They're beautiful."

"Does that mean you've decided to have dinner with me?"

"Yes, I'd love to. Why don't you come by my office around six-thirty?"

"That sounds great…I'll see you then."

The conversation had been short, but Catherine didn't mind. She still had a lot of work to complete before leaving for the day.

Catherine's last meeting concluded around five-thirty, and she headed back to her office. Walking down the hall, she noticed that Kay, and most of her employees, had gone home for the day, the office was quiet.

When she entered her office, she walked to the right side of the room, and went through a doorway leading to her private quarters. She had added the space several years earlier for late night use, or when the weather was so bad that she couldn't get home.

Crossing the earthy limestone floor, she entered the bedroom. In the center of the room, stood a simple umber finished antique sleigh bed, covered with a soft gold and ivory stripe comforter, giving the room a warm, romantic feeling. Directly across from the bed, stood a large matching armoire with a television and stereo sound system, hidden behind the massive doors.

She took her shoes off, and carried them through a cozy sitting area to a dressing area with an attached bathroom. A domed ceiling, covered with exquisite gold leaf designs, and surrounded by recessed halogen lighting hovered overhead, releasing a soft glow, pleasing to the eyes.

Around the room, were golden stucco walls filled with ivory cabinets, with a soft crackle finish. Opening one of the doors, she put her shoes away, then opened another, home to a closet full of elegant dresses.

Knowing that the evening temperature would be chilly, she thumbed through, choosing a simple cranberry dress, beaded and cut low around the neckline, with long sleeves. Pulling it out, she hung it on a brass hook beside the dressing table.

In the middle of the room, was an island filled with drawers beneath a coffee bean granite countertop. She opened the top drawer, which was full of bras. Sorting through, she pulled out a sexy black satin bra, then closed the drawer.

She opened the second drawer, pulling out a pair of silky satin panties, then laid the bra and panties on the countertop. She thought for a moment, then turned around, opening another drawer behind her, filled with black hosiery, each with a velvet pouch of its own. Searching for a pair of lace top thigh-highs, she pulled a pair out, then closed the drawer.

In that dressing room, everything had a special place. And as she had done when she designed her house, space and organization was her top priority, money had not been an issue.

After pulling out a pair of black silk high heel shoes, she went to take a shower. When she finished, she put on a pink chenille bathrobe, then dried her golden brown locks, styling it up. Sitting at the dressing table, she took her time, carefully applying her makeup, then stood up to get dressed. Just as she put on her jewelry, she heard William calling for her.

"I'm in here," she answered loudly, walking back into the bedroom.

She stood motionless as he opened the door. A few seconds later, he appeared in the doorway, dressed in a black tuxedo, minus the cumbersome bow tie.

He grinned. "Wow, you look terrific."

She moved closer. "Thank you. And you look handsome," she said, planting a kiss on his cheek.

As she began to pull away, he smiled, and pulled her close for a hug. He took a deep breath. "You're beautiful," he whispered, gently kissing the tip of her ear, sending a tingling sensation shooting through her body. She could tell that he wanted her, and she wanted him just as much.

Catherine smiled, and took hold of his hand. His gaze shifted to the bed. "Not now," she said in a soft tone.

Rolling his eyes, he smiled, then she led him out of the office.

When they arrived in the lobby, William led her to the parking garage elevator, taking it up to the second floor, where he had parked.

"Where are we going?" she asked inquisitively as they walked out of the elevator, toward his car.

He laughed. "It's a surprise."

"I love surprises," she replied, while he opened the passenger door of his black BMW.

Catherine slid onto the smooth leather seat, then watched as he ran around the front of the car to get in. Once inside, he turned to her. "You look so beautiful," he said leaning forward, softly kissing her on the lips.

He started the engine and drove away.

During the drive, William tuned the stereo to the soft sounds of a jazz radio station. Holding the steering wheel with his left hand, he glided the top of his other hand to her thigh. The heat of his hand raced through her body. Looking down at his hand, she took a deep breath.

"Do you like jazz?" he asked, without taking his eyes off the road.

For a moment, her mind went blank. She turned to him. He was staring straight ahead. "Jazz," she repeated. "Yes. I love jazz," she answered, studying his profile, his dark eyes, freshly shaven cheeks, his strong jawbone. He was perfect.

He turned and smiled, and she melted into the seat.

A few minutes later, they arrived at the marina. "We're here," he stated anxiously, parking in front of a luxurious yacht. He got out, then ran swiftly around to the other side to open the passenger door. Taking his hand, she stepped out of the car, and he led her toward one of the yachts. "Is this yours?" she asked.

He grinned. "Yes, my parents gave it to me for my birthday. Do you like it?"

"It's beautiful," she said, gazing up at the large sleek lines of the vessel.

She turned back to him. "That was some birthday present!" she commented, knowing that they had paid no less than a million for it.

Turning her gaze back to the yacht, she focused her attention on the Captain and three members of his crew waiting on deck to greet them.

William took her hand, and they ascended up the steps.

After introducing her to the Captain, he led her to the sumptuous dining room, where a romantic candlelit table had been set. "What a wonderful surprise," Catherine remarked, setting her sights on the table.

William wrapped his arms around her slender waist, and pulled her close. His eyes burned with desire. "There isn't anything that I wouldn't do for you," he whispered. "I think that you're the most beautiful woman in the world."

Hearing those words touched her heart.

Gently stroking her face with his fingers, he leaned closer. Holding her chin steady, he kissed her soft, supple lips, then pulled away slowly. His eyes didn't wander from her face. "Would you like a glass of wine?" he asked.

Her body shuddered. "That would be great," she answered against his lips.

She watched as he walked over to the bar, and poured two glasses of red wine. She walked to the middle of the room, meeting him halfway, accepting a glass from his hand. As he leaned forward to kiss her again, the chief steward entered the room. Realizing he'd interrupted a private moment, the steward's face turned crimson.

Exchanging smiles, they turned to him.

"Excuse me," he announced politely. "Dinner will be ready shortly," he said, then quickly exited the room.

Sharing a laugh, they went to sit on the sofa, enjoying the wine and each other's company. While they talked, she found it hard to believe he was the same man she'd met at Antoinette's party. He'd changed so much since then.

Catherine sat back against the dark brown leather sofa, and glanced around the room. The interior of the yacht was beautiful, with ornate brass fixtures set against the dark teak and mahogany wood, and the deep green hue chosen for the walls.

She took a sip of wine, then turned back to him. He hadn't taken his eyes off of her the entire time. Using slow movements, he leaned closer, seductively kissing her on the neck. Holding the wine glass firmly in her hand, she took another sip to wet her lips. "I thought that we could talk tonight," she said in a low tone.

"What do you want to talk about?" he asked, his lips drifting to her mouth.

Catherine began to tremble, and her lips gravitated to his. Nibbling his lips between hers, she whispered, "I want to know more about you."

He pressed his lips firmly against hers, his hands wandered to her chest. "Shoot," he said. "I'm ready for your first question."

Pulling her lips away, she rotated her head to the side. His lips wandered just below her ear lobe.

Firmly planting the palms of her hands against his shoulders, she gently pushed him away. "I can't talk while you do this," she insisted, raising the tone of her voice.

He'd finally gotten the message.

He sat back against the sofa. "I'm sorry. What do you want to know?"

Just as she was about to ask the first question, the steward came back into the room. "Dinner is ready," he announced. His timing couldn't have been any worse.

Thanking him, William escorted her to the luxurious dining room. A few minutes later, the staff served dinner, one course at a time, allowing enough time between each serving to enjoy each dish and get ready for the next. She wanted to speak openly, but the steward stayed in the room, standing by silently against the wall while they ate. She did manage to ask a couple of questions, but none were answered in depth.

William spoke vaguely of his family in Boston, saying only that they owned a shipping company, which she had already known. When she asked about his mother, he said that she was involved with several charitable organizations, and a long time member of the local garden club. He mentioned that he had two older sisters, both married with children, one living in Charleston, and the other in Seattle.

Although Catherine was enjoying herself, deep inside, she wanted to see the real man. So he was rich, and he enjoyed the good things in life. What about the man underneath? Was he always so smooth? What about his childhood? Was it a good one? These were questions she had, and she was anxious to uncover the truth.

After finishing their meal, coffee and dessert were served. As the steward filled her cup, Catherine graciously complimented him. "Everything was excellent," she said. "Thank you so much for serving us tonight, and please give my compliments to the chef."

Just as the steward began to speak, William interrupted. "That will be all for now," he said in a stern voice. "I'll call if we need anything else," he said, motioning toward the door for him to leave. Catherine thought that he had been rude, but she decided to disregard his comments.

He escorted her to the upper deck for a moonlit walk. Arm in arm, they walked together, the cool breeze gently kissing their skin. Catherine looked up. The sky was clear, making light of the sundry of stars beaming down. Off in the distance, the bright lights of the city had become faint. She knew they'd traveled far.

Studying the sky, she folded her arms over her chest. "Are you cold?" William asked pulling her close.

She shifted her body to his. "No. I'm not cold. It feels wonderful out here."

Drawing a deep breath, she closed her eyes. "I love the smell of the ocean," she uttered. While her eyes were still closed, William's lips pressed against hers, giving her an unexpected kiss. She could tell that he wanted to make love, and the truth be told, she wanted him too, desperately.

He gazed into her bright eyes, then gently took her hand, silently leading her back to the interior of the yacht. Walking down to the lower deck, he led her to a set of mahogany doors. Turning the brass door knobs, he pushed the doors inward, opening to an impressive master stateroom.

As she walked in, the doors clapped closed behind her.

She took a deep breath, then turned around, her body shivering as she waited beside the bed. He moved toward her, slowly, deliberately inching closer. Closing in on her, he glided his hands beneath her dress, gently stroking her firm thighs, causing them to shake slightly. She closed her eyes, sighing in delight as his hand roamed around her abdomen. With a sense of urgency, she pushed his jacket off his shoulders, down to the hard teak floor. He kissed her neck while she unbuttoned his white shirt, soon after, it fell to the floor. While she tenderly kissed the walls of his chest, he unzipped her dress, pushing it over the soft skin of her shoulders. Then he unsnapped her bra, the dress and bra fell to the floor. He backed away to take a look. There she stood, wearing nothing more than her sexy black satin panties, black thigh-high hosiery, and high heeled shoes.

She licked her lips, then smiled as he moved closer. Wanting to explore further, he gently pushed her against the wall facing away from him. He kissed the back of her neck, then moved downward to the small of her back, and up again. He pushed her hands up against the wall while he continued to stroke his body into hers. Running his fingers through her thick brown hair, he located her hairpin, and gently removed it, and dropped it on the floor. She heard the tapping sound it made as it hit the wood.

    She gently shook her head, allowing her long, silky hair to fall down over her shoulders, then waited in anticipation as he shifted his hands downward, gliding her panties over her hips. Stepping out of them, she turned around, and he gently lifted her body against the wall. Wrapping her legs around his hips, he carried her to the bed, where they made love over and over again, until they were both too exhausted to go on.

    Waking shortly before sunrise, Catherine got up, wrapped the sheet around her body, and then walked over to the window. Through a thick fog, she saw that the yacht was once again docked at the pier. As she stared out, William got up and walked up behind her. "Are you all right?" he asked, gently kissing her shoulder.

    She turned to him. "I'm fine, but I really should get home."

    Agreeing, William showed her to the bathroom to get dressed. From a small closet behind the door, he pulled out a bathrobe and handed it to her. "I'm going to get ready in the other room," he said, then walked out of the stateroom.

    She closed the bathroom door, and stared at her reflection in the mirror. She didn't look at all like the people in the movies, who always woke up looking the same as they had the night before. Having slept without removing her makeup, her face didn't feel fresh and clean like it normally had, it felt dry, soiled.

    She turned on the warm water, and opened the cabinet, finding an unopened bar of moisturizing soap on the shelf. Pulling the bar out, she tore the wrapper open, then wet the bar. Lathering her hands, she smoothed the soap over her face in circular motions, followed by a cool water rinse, bringing the fresh glow back to her skin.

She looked into the mirror again. Her hair was a mess. She brushed through it, but it didn't do any good. Deciding to style it up, she walked back into the stateroom to search for her hairpin. She found the spot where William had dropped it the night before, then stooped down on her hands and knees, hoping to find it. Smoothing her hands across the wood floor, she felt the metal brush against her hand. The hairpin had fallen in the crack between the molding and the floor. She picked it up, then went back to the bathroom to pin her hair up. After she finished, it still looked bad, but at least it was a little neater.

Worse than her hair, was her dress, wrinkled from lying on the floor. Holding it up, she tried to flatten the wrinkles out with her hands, but it wasn't working.

"It's not going to work," William commented, watching from the doorway. She had no idea he was there. She looked up and smiled. Unlike her, he looked great, dressed in a pair of blue jeans, a white tee shirt and black leather jacket.

Noticing that she was upset, he grinned and held his hand out. "Here let me take that," he said.

She handed the dress to him.

"I'll be right back," he said, quickly exiting the room.

"Why don't you take a shower while I'm gone," she heard him shout from the hall. "It'll make you feel much better."

That's a good idea, she thought heading back into the bathroom.

She took a warm shower, making sure not to get her hair wet, since she wouldn't have time to dry it. When she got out, she toweled off, then put the bath robe back on. As she walked into the stateroom, her eyes focused on her dress laying neatly on the foot of the bed. She looked around for William, but just as the wrinkles were gone, so was he.

After dressing, Catherine found William standing outside on the upper deck looking out over the hazy waters of the harbor. He turned around. "You look much better," he said with a huge grin.

She looked down at her dress. "Yes. And I feel much better. Thanks for suggesting that I take a shower. It was just what I needed." She walked closer and put her arms around his waist. "Now, I have a question," she said. "How on earth did you get the wrinkles out of my dress?" She laughed.

"It's a secret," he said kissing her warm lips…"No," he said with a laugh. "We have one of those dry clean machines in the laundry area."

"Ah-huh," she said. "Well, I'm so happy that you do, because I didn't want to put a wrinkled dress on." She wrapped her arms around his shoulders. "In fact, I was thinking about going home in the bath robe," she giggled.

After sharing a laugh, William led her off the yacht.

Walking down the steps, Catherine noticed that the pier was empty of foot traffic, and that made her happy. Being well-known in the community, she didn't want to be recognized by anyone. She wasn't quite ready to see her name in the news, at least not for taking a lover.

The ride back to the office was a slow one, the fog thick and heavy. With both hands planted firmly on the steering wheel, William drove carefully, keeping a constant eye on the road.

Driving farther into the city, the fog began to clear, and William was able to drive faster.

Soon, they were back in the parking garage of Catherine's office building.

Pulling beside her car, William put his car in park, and shut off the engine. "Well, here we are," he said softly, laying his hand against the back of her seat.

She looked around. The parking garage was empty. "Yes. Here we are," she said as though they'd arrived too soon.

Aware of her reluctance to leave him, William smiled, then leaned forward, kissing her softly on the lips. After a long, sweet kiss, he grinned, then got out of the car. As he walked around to open her door, she fumbled through her purse to search for her keys, finding them just as he opened the car door.

Slowly, they walked to the driver side of her car. "Listen," he said. "I have to go out of town for a couple of weeks for a business trip. I'll call you when I get back in town."

"That would be great," she replied, unlocking her car door.

While they shared a warm hug, he reached back and pulled the door open. Taking a deep breath, she kissed him again, then slid behind the wheel. She started the engine, then pushed the button to lower the window. "I'll talk to you soon," she said, waving as she pulled away.

When Catherine arrived home, she headed straight for the bedroom. She took off her clothes, put on a pair of comfortable cotton pajamas, and climbed into bed.

A few hours later, she was awakened by the sun piercing through the bedroom windows. "I really must do something about that," she said covering her head with the pillow. She wasn't ready to get up, but there was no way she could sleep any longer.

She rolled out of bed, glided her feet into her slippers, and went downstairs. She didn't feel up to going to the office, so she went to the study to call her secretary. The phone rang two times, and Kay answered, "Good morning, Miss Sheldon's office."

"Kay, Hi this is Catherine. I've decided to stay home today, so if anything important comes up, give me a call. Oh, by the way, can you fax my telephone messages to me?"

"Sure, Miss Sheldon," Kay agreed.

Shortly thereafter, the list came over the fax machine. One in particular stuck out. Justin had called.

Deciding to return his call right away, she lazily dialed the number. She listened as his phone began to ring, and after two rings, he answered.

"Justin…Hi, this is Catherine. I'm sorry that I missed your call earlier."

"That's no problem. I was calling to invite you to lunch today."

In a sorrowful voice, she responded, "Oh…I'm sorry, but I can't today…"

He thought that she was going to turn his invitation down altogether, but she surprised him. "How about tomorrow?" she suggested.

She could hear the excitement in his voice. "Tomorrow sounds great," he replied. "Can I pick you up at one o'clock?"

"Perfect. I'll see you then."

After she got off the phone, she began to think that maybe Antoinette had been right all along. Maybe it was time she told Justin about William, especially since she planned on seeing William on a regular basis. After giving it some thought, she decided to tell him during lunch.

Still sleepy, she stumbled into the kitchen. She made a cup of coffee and two slices of toast, then went upstairs to watch television in her home movie theater. When she reached the top of the stairs, she walked straight ahead and entered the darkened room. Once inside, she put the coffee and toast down on the table beside a comfortable leather lounge chair. She grabbed the remote control and a soft blanket, then sat down in the chair, adjusting it to the reclining position. She turned on the big screen television, then quickly flipped through the channels. Something on the classics channel caught her eye, but she passed it up. "Oh, wait," she said pushing the down arrow on the remote to go back a few channels.

On the screen, she saw one of her all time favorite movies, a heart wrenching tale of a woman forced to leave her husband and child, only to find a life of loneliness and desperation. Every time Catherine had seen it, she'd hoped the outcome would be different…but of course, it never could. She laid back and watched it again, crying during the same scenes as she had previously.

By the time the movie ended, her eyes were red and swollen, and on the table, an empty box of tissues. She stood up. "Why did I watch that?" she asked herself, stretching her tired muscles. "I wish that someone would remake it, with a happy ending," she mumbled under her breath. How she loved stories with happy endings.

She walked to the corner of the room and pulled a bottle of water out of a small refrigerator, then settled back in the chair to watch the next tear-jerker. She watched the first hour, but unable to keep her eyes open, she fell fast asleep.

When Catherine awoke, her eyes focused on the large round metal clock on the wall. It was already seven-thirty. She'd been sleeping for over six hours. Lazily, she got up, turned the television set off, and then went downstairs to get a bite to eat. After rummaging through the freezer, she managed to find a package of lasagna. She heated it, ate it, and then decided to go for a swim.

After changing into a swimsuit, she slipped into a pair of comfortable black sandals, then went outside. The weather was warm, the sky clear, and the sun was beginning to set in the distance. Because her eyes were still red and swollen, she couldn't wait to dive into the cool water to refresh them. Standing on the side of the deep end, she dove gracefully into the water. As she emerged from the depths, she closed her eyes, and gently threw her head back, keeping her long strands of hair out of her eyes as she ascended. She took a deep breath, then floated on her back.

Taking relaxed breaths, she smiled, thinking about her night with William. What a night it had been. Being with him had been incredible, and thinking of him sent shivers racing through her spine.

Looking up at the sky, a family of birds raced across the sky, followed by another group, then another. She wondered where they were headed. Then figured they were probably on their way back home to their nest.

She floated for a little while longer, the water felt good against her skin, tranquil, relaxing. She took a deep breath, then rolled over, diving beneath the depths of the water, and decided to swim twenty laps, as she tried to do everyday.

Stepping out of the pool, the water rolled off her body. The air was chilly and goose bumps broke out on her skin. Quickly, she paced over to the secluded hot tub, hidden amidst an array of tropical plantings, with a large brick wall enclosing the area. On the wall, she turned a knob, starting the jets, and stepped into the churning hot water.

Relaxing her back against the comfortable side walls of the hot tub, she closed her eyes. The warmth of the water invigorated her spirit, she felt happy, fulfilled. It was just what she needed to end her day.

CHAPTER 7

On a pedestal in the center of the room stood a statuesque model, standing completely still while Catherine pinned the hem on the dress she was wearing.

Hard at work, Catherine was a mess. She'd tucked a pencil in the golden locks of her hair, a measuring tape dangled from around her neck, and she was dressed in a black apron that housed her supplies. "Excuse me, Catherine," a member of her design staff mentioned softly. "There's a man standing in the doorway with a handful of flowers."

She looked up toward the door. Her eyes focused on Justin standing in the doorway, with a handful of freshly picked daisies, with an incredible smile on his face. From across the room, she focused first on his amazing blue eyes, then on his outfit, a pair of old faded blue jeans and a white long sleeved Henley shirt.

Her first thought was that he should have dressed up for the date, but that wouldn't have fit his personality. He was a simple man, with a simple wardrobe, clean and comfortable. For Justin, clothes didn't make him the man that he was, it was the way he carried himself, his cool confidence, that attracted her to him. And with his handsome rugged appearance, he looked sexy in whatever he had decided to wear.

"Oh, my…Justin. Is it already one o'clock?" she asked frantically.

"No. It's only twelve-thirty. I'm early," he said walking toward her. "Do you want me to come back?" he asked, gesturing to the door.

"No," she said. I can finish this later."

His striking blue eyes pierced every inch of her body. "I picked some flowers for you," he said, handing them to her. "I hope that you like them."

Giggles broke out around the room. For a second, she felt like a schoolteacher with a room full of giddy adolescents. "Okay. We'll finish this later," she said, turning back to her team.

Catherine's gaze shifted to a tall, blonde-headed member of her staff who was trying to say something with hand signals. Her mouth was moving, but she wasn't speaking. "What?" Catherine asked. "Go ahead, it's all right to talk in front of Justin."

The model and other members of her staff exited the office, but the tall blonde stayed behind. Smiling, she walked closer to Catherine. "Look at yourself in the mirror," she whispered, then she left the office.

Catherine turned back to Justin and smiled. With flowers in hand, she casually strolled over to the mirror, hanging on the wall above the wet bar.

Justin watched while she looked at herself.

"Oh, my goodness," she said, realizing that she was still wearing the apron, and measuring tape around her neck.

"No. It's all right." He laughed. "You look wonderful."

Grinning, she removed the apron and measuring tape, revealing a navy blue tank dress, then put them away in the drawer below the bar.

Stooping down, she rummaged through the bottom of the cabinet, and pulled a crystal vase out. Standing up, she turned the water on, and began to fill the vase. "So—where did you get the flowers," she inquired.

Justin grinned, then laughed. "I guess it's been a while since you've been out in front of your building, because...that's where I got them," he admitted bravely.

"You have to be kidding?" she replied. She thought about it for a moment, then laughed. "Actually, it has been a long time since I've been out there. I always enter the building through the parking garage."

He shook his head. "What a shame...It's beautiful out there. Your landscapers do a remarkable job. You should check it out one day, it's like a park out there."

"I'll have to do that," she remarked, carrying the vase to her desk.

"Are you ready?" she asked, grabbing her handbag.

"Not yet. There's something that I have to do first," he said walking toward her. Moving closer, he stared deeply into her wide brown eyes, so close that she could feel the warmth of his breath against her face. Her body tensed, and she instinctively closed her eyes. She thought that he was going to kiss her. "Here, let me get this," he said softly, pulling the pencil out of her hair.

Feeling foolish, she opened her eyes, and her face turned flush. She backed away. "Thanks," she said, smoothing her hair down with her fingers. "We better get going," she stuttered, motioning to the door.

She led him out of the office, stopping momentarily at Kay's desk. "Justin, I'd like for you to meet the most wonderful secretary in the world, Kay Stevenson."

Kay stood and shook his hand. "It's a pleasure to meet you," she said, smiling.

"The pleasure's all mine," Justin replied sweetly.

Kay turned to Catherine, listening for instructions. "Kay, we're going to lunch now, if anything important comes up, you can reach me on my cell phone. Otherwise, I'll see you tomorrow morning."

While she listened, Kay studied Justin's boyish charm through the corner of her eye, wondering if he was the one who'd sent all of the flowers. "Okay," Kay replied as Catherine finished speaking.

Then, Catherine turned to Justin, and smiled. "Well, I'm all ready," she said.

He looked at Kay. "It was nice to meet you," he said, then they turned to leave.

Kay had been Catherine's secretary for eight years, and during that time, she'd only seen her with three other men, and they were all big talkers and snazzy dressers, none like Justin. Unlike the others, she liked Justin from the first moment she saw him. She could tell that he was different from the others, and she hoped that he would be the one for Catherine.

When they arrived at the restaurant, they were greeted by the maitre d', who led them to the private dining room. As they entered the room, Catherine's eyes lit up when she saw how elegantly the table looked with a white eyelet fabric placed over the pink tablecloth. In the center of the table was a beautiful floral arrangement, made up of white and pink roses in a crystal vase, and a bottle of wine chilling in a stand beside the table.

Justin pulled her chair out. Exchanging smiles, she sat down.

She couldn't believe how much thought he'd put into making their lunch date special. Everything was perfect, including the view of a beautiful flower garden through the large window beside the table. Right then, she knew there was no way that she could tell him about William. At least not now…

At first, she felt awkward. After all, she was dating two men at the same time. That's enough to make any woman nervous. But once they began to talk, the feeling of uneasiness disappeared completely. She found herself totally relaxed, engrossed with his every word. Just like their first date at the beach, they hit it off right away. She felt comfortable being with him, and she adored his down to earth attitude. There he was, a man of substantial wealth but he didn't flaunt it in any way.

During lunch, he spoke about his work with great passion. His jaw tightened when he spoke about how much he loved being able to make his clients' dreams come true by designing their dream homes. Catherine understood, explaining how rewarding it was to help her clients feel and look their best; not only with her clothing line, but also now with her perfume and cosmetics. It meant a lot to her.

All through lunch, Justin kept the conversation alive and vibrant with fresh, new topics, interesting to both of them. Catherine watched him carefully as he spoke, noticing his gentle mannerisms, high level of intelligence, and cool confidence. And Justin did the same while she spoke. She had all the traits that he was looking for in a woman, especially her unpretentiousness. He couldn't stand pretentious women. And he'd run across a lot of them over the years.

After a long, cozy lunch, they decided to go for a walk in the park. On their way out, she watched while Justin took a minute to stop to shake the maitre d' and the waiter's hands, thanking them for the excellent service, besides leaving behind gratuities for each. That was incredible to her. Not many people would have been as gracious. And at that moment, she knew that he was a true gentleman in every sense of the word.

They strolled through the park, continuing to talk about anything that popped into their heads. As they approached the beautiful pond centered in the middle of the park, Justin said that he had an idea, then rushed to the hot dog stand, a few feet away.

Catherine stopped walking and watched him. After speaking with the vendor for a few seconds, Justin gave him some money, then walked away with a pack of hot dog buns. *What's he doing?* she thought to herself.

Walking back, he smiled. "How would you like to feed the ducks?" he asked, stepping up to her.

"What a wonderful idea," she replied excitedly. "I haven't done that since I was a child."

They walked to the waters edge, and he opened the bag. Within seconds, they saw a family of ducks swimming toward them. Justin handed her two buns, then squatted down, throwing small pieces of buns into the water. It didn't take long for them to gobble it up.

Just as Catherine began to break her two buns into small pieces, three white geese waddled toward her, and a flock of pigeons swarmed over their heads, landing on the ground beside their feet. "Oh, wow," she shouted, throwing the bread. "They're like vultures!" She laughed.

Soon, the package of buns was empty, and the birds immediately set their sites on a group of children, each carrying their own bag of bread.

Justin stood up.

"That was exhilarating," she said, standing beside him, watching as the children opened their bags.

"Do you want to keep walking?" he asked, pointing to the sidewalk.

"Yes. Why don't we walk around the pond," she suggested.

While they walked, they talked about high school. During the conversation, she asked if he had played any sports in high school. He said that he'd been the pitcher for his high school and college baseball teams, taking both teams to the championships. That didn't surprise her a bit. Before she'd even asked the question, she figured from looking at his masculine, slim-lined body that he had to have been either a pitcher or a quarterback.

Justin said that he'd often dreamed about playing in the majors, and several teams were interested, but an injury he'd sustained in his last year of college ended his chances. After telling the story, he tried to hide his emotions, but she could tell that he had missed out on something that had been important to him.

They walked for a while longer, and before they knew it, another hour had passed. They decided to head home.

Driving out of the parking lot, Justin mentioned that he was going to his cabin for the weekend, and he invited her to go along.

Without any thought, she agreed and by the time they arrived back at her office, their plans had been finalized. Justin was to pick her up at six o'clock the following morning. They would stay at the cabin for two nights, and return on Sunday evening.

Catherine knew deep inside that it was wrong, but she couldn't help herself. She loved having him as a friend, and she figured as long as their relationship didn't go any further, it would be all right.

CHAPTER 8

Catherine had just finished washing her breakfast dishes when the doorbell chimed. Laying the dishtowel on the edge of the sink, she looked up at the clock. It was precisely six o'clock...Justin was right on time.

She walked to the entryway, stopping briefly to look at herself in the beveled mirror on the foyer wall. Smoothing her hands over the hair in her ponytail, she wondered if Justin would recognize her in the faded blue jeans and the oversized navy blue sweatshirt that she was wearing.

She took a deep breath, then opened the door.

Justin came into view, standing tall, with the palm of his hand propped high against the door frame. Between his stance and his attire, a pair of blue jeans and red flannel shirt, she could have sworn that he was modeling for an outdoorsmen clothing catalog.

His face glowed, and his eyes were bright. "Hi. You look great," he said. "Are you all packed and ready to go?" he asked enthusiastically.

Sharing his excitement, her big brown eyes widened. "Yes, I'm ready," she replied, with a smile. And she was ready. She'd been up since four o'clock packing for the trip. Since she'd never been to the Sierra's, she had no idea how to dress, so she took her time, filling two suitcases with warm, casual clothes, and a couple of dressy outfits, just in case.

Leading him farther into the foyer, she pointed to the floor near the staircase. "My suitcases are right over there," she said, her voice cracking. Like the other times that she'd been with him, she was nervous, and her stomach felt like it was tied in knots.

Justin could tell that she was feeling uneasy, so he tried to lighten the moment. Leaning over, he lifted the suitcases a couple of inches off the ground, then dropped them to the floor. His body bent at the waist, he reached for his back. "Oh, my back," he cried out as though he were in excruciating pain.

Fearing the worst, Catherine rushed to his side. "Are you all right?" she asked, trying to help him.

From the expression on her face, Justin could tell that she was frightened. His face lit up. "I was just joking," he admitted with a grin.

The joke had been on her. Her face turned red. "Don't ever do that again," she hissed, slapping him twice on the shoulder. "You scared me half to death!" she shouted, unable to resist the urge to smile.

Justin surrendered his hands in the air. "I'm sorry," he said. "I shouldn't have done that to you."

It took a moment for her to regain her senses, but when she did, she found that she wasn't nervous anymore, and her stomach had settled down. Although it hadn't been the best plan to ease the tension, it had worked. And she was happy about that.

Feeling dreadful for what he'd done, Justin picked up the luggage, and apologized three more times before going out the door.

After loading the bags in the truck, he walked back to the house, where Catherine was waiting in the doorway. As he walked up to the entryway, she remembered that she had brewed a pot of coffee for the trip. "I forgot," she said. "I made a fresh pot of coffee for the ride. Would you like a cup?"

"That sounds great," he replied, wondering what she planned to store it in for their journey. She led him to the kitchen, and much to his surprise, she was prepared. Sitting on the kitchen counter, he noticed a thermos, and two insulated coffee mugs.

She went over to get the pot of coffee, while he walked over to check out the set. It looked brand new. "This is nice," he commented, lifting the empty thermos to take a closer look. Flipping it over, he noticed that the price tag was still stuck on the bottom, and he grinned, assuming that she'd purchased it for their trip. As she walked over, he put it down, and turned to her. "Do you want me to fill it for you?"

Agreeing, she put the coffee pot on the counter beside his hand, then watched as he carefully filled the thermos, screwing the top securely on when he was done. Then he filled the two insulated mugs, and they each flavored their own with sugar and cream.

Justin watched as she picked up the coffee pot and brought it over to the sink. She turned on the water, rinsed it, and then dried it with a towel that was lying on the countertop. After she finished, she lifted her hand to a bottle of moisturizer sitting on the windowsill, and pushed down on the top, dispensing some into her hand. As she rubbed the crème into her hands, she turned around. It was obvious that Justin had been watching her. She smiled. "Well, I'm ready now," she said, and they headed out for their weekend adventure.

Shortly after departing, they found out they had the same taste in music, and spent part of the ride listening and singing along with the radio as they drove down the highway toward the rolling terrain of the Sierra's.

The drive to the cabin turned out to be a lot of fun. They spoke about their likes and dislikes, and even had an intimate conversation about their dreams for the future. Justin admitted that his dream was to one day have a house full of children, unlike the lonely life he'd had as a young boy. Catherine understood completely.

Their conversation deepened when she divulged her deepest desire. "What I want," she said, "is to feel needed by someone other than my employees."

"I never would have thought that about you," he said. "I thought that you had many friends in your life."

"Not really," she admitted. "I have my family and Antoinette, and I have some friends that still live in New Orleans, but most of the people that I've met since I moved to Los Angeles are interested in my money more than they are in me." She paused for a moment. "Don't get me wrong," she explained. "I don't think that they do it intentionally. That's just the way it is. Either they have money and they gravitate to me because they have to socialize with people of their class, or they don't have money and they gravitate because it makes them feel good to be around someone who has more than they do." Her face turned sour. "It's like I never know who to trust…"

"That's really sad," Justin replied. "But I'm sure it has a lot to do with the business that you're in."

"It has everything to do with that," she replied somberly.

Catherine's life since her college graduation had been filled with long hours and hard work to become a fashion designer. She had been working toward that goal for so long, that she'd lost sight of the real Catherine. She'd lost sight of the young Catherine who wanted nothing more than to have children and a husband. The girl who dreamed of spending her days carpooling, helping with homework, cheering at little league games. Those dreams had been lost somewhere along the way, and others had taken over, devouring her life, causing a loneliness she'd never imagined.

Justin drove through a woody area. "We're just a few minutes away," he revealed enthusiastically.

Like a child, Catherine became anxiously excited. She couldn't wait to see firsthand what Justin had described so vividly…The rustic cabin…the beautiful lake…the grassy meadow, the deep canyons and the rushing stream.

Looking out over the soothing landscapes of the Sierra's, she found herself lost in a daydream, recollecting memories from her childhood, her camping trips with the girl scouts. How wonderful it had been back then, singing songs around the warmth of a campfire, taking long hiking trips in the wilderness, but mostly having the clear, uncluttered mind of a child.

Her dream was interrupted by the sound of Justin's voice. "This is it," he said.

She blinked to wake herself. Before her eyes stood a white two story cottage with a screened porch.

"This is my home away from home," he said, gazing in that direction.

The cabin wasn't at all what she had imagined. In her mind, she'd pictured a log cabin, like the ones she'd seen in cowboy movies. What she saw before her was not at all harsh or rugged in appearance, it was charming, inviting.

She turned to get a view of the lake, then bolted out of the truck for a closer look, as Justin followed close behind. "Justin, it's just as you described," she exclaimed, staring at the tranquil waters that lay before her.

But there was something that he hadn't described. In the background, she looked up to the heavenly snow capped mountains, staring down over the lake, like God over his people. For miles off in the distance, all she could see were trees and mountains. She hadn't expected such a breathtaking view.

"It's all protected," he mentioned. "No one can ever touch that view. What I don't own is protected by the National Park Service. What you see before you will be there for years to come, no one can ever change it."

In awe, Catherine stood silently drawing a deep breath of the fragrant mountain air, while Justin stood by, swept away by the natural beauty of her profile; her face was perfect, her nose, her jawbone, her cheeks, all in perfect proportion with one another, and her complexion, flawless.

He couldn't believe how much love he found himself feeling for this woman. And so soon. No one had ever affected his heart that way. He knew instantly that she was the only woman for him, the only woman that he wanted.

Oblivious to the fact he had been looking at her, Catherine turned to him, and reached for his hands. "Come on. I want you to show me everything. It's so beautiful here," she cried out, pulling him over the lush green grass below their feet.

Delighted by her blissfulness, Justin laughed. "What do you want to see first?"

"I want you to take me to the stream that you told me about."

"You got it," he replied eagerly. "Why don't you have a seat on the porch while I unload the truck, and then we'll go for our walk," he suggested.

"No...No way!" she answered rather hastily. "I'd rather help you. That way, we can enjoy the view together once we finish."

Justin smiled, and led her to the back of the truck. They unloaded a couple of items, then headed for the cabin. Catherine followed as Justin led her up the brick steps, through a screen door, onto a beautiful wood planked porch, painted green.

She watched from behind while he unlocked the door. As she peered over his shoulder, he felt the warmth from her breath tickling the skin on his neck. For a moment, he closed his eyes, and took a deep breath, trying to control his urge to turn around and scoop her up into his arms. He slowly opened the door, then turned around. "Ladies first," he said softly, moving to the side.

He put his arm around her waist and escorted her inside. As he had described the interior of the cabin was rustic, but not at all like the fishing cabin she'd imagined it would be.

Her attention was first drawn to the large stone fireplace in the living room which nearly covered the entire wall. The second thing that captured her eye was the beautiful wood furniture throughout the room. She stepped in closer, and stroked the sofa table. "Where did you find this beautiful furniture?" she asked.

He walked up beside her. "I made most of it," he replied. "Woodworking is one of my hobbies."

"A hobby," she replied. "This looks like more than just a hobby. You're very skilled. Who taught you how to do this?"

Hesitantly, he responded, "My dad taught me a little before he passed away, then my grandfather, after I went to live with my grandparents. My grandfather was a master carpenter, and he taught my dad when he was a boy. And even though my dad was a devoted surgeon and father, he spent every bit of his spare time in his workshop. He had an extraordinary passion for woodworking."

With sadness in her eyes, Catherine uttered, "It's great that they were able to pass the tradition on to you. And someday, maybe you'll pass the tradition to your children."

Somberly, Justin agreed. "Yes. I will definitely find the time to teach my kids, I'm sure of that."

Silence filled the room.

Justin picked up their luggage. "Come on. I'll give you a tour, then I'll show you to your bedroom."

As they walked around the first floor, Justin explained. "The cabin has three bedrooms and two bathrooms upstairs; and a kitchen, living room, study and bathroom downstairs."

He showed her each room, then took her up the staircase to the second floor. Approaching one of the rooms he commented, "To the left is the first guest bedroom and to the right is the second, and straight ahead is the master bedroom."

She watched intently as he walked into the master bedroom, setting her luggage on the floor just inside the doorway. She began to get concerned. *Why did he put my luggage in the master suite? Does he expect for us to sleep together?* she thought to herself.

Her worries were quickly put to rest when he set his luggage down in one of the guest rooms. "I don't mind sleeping in one of the guest bedrooms," she said without hesitating. "I don't want to put you out of your bed."

"No. I want you to have the master bedroom," he replied sternly. "It's the most spacious, and most comfortable bedroom in the house. And you'll also have your own bathroom." Before she was able to respond, he said, "Now don't try to change my mind, because I won't have it any other way."

As planned, they unpacked their luggage and the groceries, then headed out for their walk. Side by side, they strolled down the rocky path along the lake. After a short hike through a woody area, they arrived at the stream.

They sat on a group of rocks to enjoy the soothing sounds of the water rushing across the rocks. While staring at the water, Justin mentioned that he wanted to take her fishing. "Fishing. How wonderful," she said excitedly. "But I have to tell you. I've never been fishing before, so I need for you to teach me."

Justin grinned and rubbed his chin. "I promise, by the end of the weekend, you'll be a master in the sport of fishing."

"We'll see about that," she giggled.

They sat for a while, silently watching the fish jump in and out of the water. Justin began to talk about how much he loved the area. His mood turned somber when he explained that his mother and father had purchased the property, planning to build a summer home for their family. As he spoke, she realized how deeply he felt about the cabin and the land surrounding it. She'd never met anyone like him. Most of the men she'd dated were only passionate about one thing…Money. But Justin was different, he was passionate about life.

Because it was beginning to get late, they decided to begin their hike back to the cabin for lunch. On the way back, Justin took her through the grassy meadow he'd spoken about. She couldn't believe her eyes. There were wildflowers and tall grasses everywhere, so high in some areas that she actually lost site of him a couple of times. It was one of the most beautiful sights she'd ever seen.

They ran through the meadow, back toward the cabin. When they arrived on the porch, they were out of breath. Flinging themselves into white wicker rockers, they smiled, then laughed. "That was amazing," Catherine said, and Justin agreed.

After taking a few minutes to catch their breath, Justin said that he would make lunch, while she continued to relax.

In a joking manner, Catherine raised her voice and stood up. "Justin Scott. There's no way I'm going to let you wait on me this weekend. Now, what do you want me to do first?"

Leading her inside, he laughed. "All right, Miss Sheldon. I have a huge task for you. Do you think you can handle it?"

"I can handle just about anything."

"Can you cut some lettuce and tomatoes for our sandwiches?" he asked politely.

"No problem. I can handle that," she giggled as they walked into the kitchen.

While she sliced a tomato and tore the lettuce into small pieces, Justin fixed two chicken salad sandwiches. Once that was done, they put the sandwiches on plates, pulled two soft drinks out of the refrigerator and went outside to eat their lunch.

After lunch, Justin said that he needed to go to his workshop to get the gear ready for the fishing trip, and invited her to go with him. But weary from the trip, she decided to stay behind.

When he left, she went to his study to find a book from the collection on the bookshelves. As she entered the room, her eyes focused on the back wall of the study. She hadn't noticed it before, but it was filled with family portraits. Taking small steps sideways, she looked at each and every photograph, especially the ones of Justin when he was growing up. She loved the one of him batting at the batter's plate. He looked adorable in his baseball uniform.

In the center of the portraits, was a picture of him with his parents, sitting on the ground in front of the lake with the mountains in the background. They looked so happy back then. In the picture, Justin looked like he was seven or eight years old, and judging by their clothes, the picture had to have been taken in the early seventies. The lake hadn't changed much since then. Even after so many years, its beauty was unscathed.

Catherine studied the photograph, looking at both his mother's and father's features. Justin had inherited his mother's blue eyes and blonde hair, but his features were more like his father's. He was a handsome man.

She turned around, and looked down at Justin's desk. Unlike the rest of the cabin, neat and uncluttered, the desk was filled with stacks of papers. On top of a stack of papers, she noticed an autographed baseball, enclosed in an acrylic shadowbox, protecting it from harm. Carefully, she lifted the box to examine the autograph, realizing that it wasn't acrylic, it was enclosed in heavy glass. It had to be old. She sat down in the torn brown leather chair, and held it firmly between her palms to see who had signed it. She turned it slightly, and saw the name, Babe Ruth, and she assumed that his father had gotten it when he was a young man.

She put the box down, and looked at the desk. Rubbing her hand across the wood, she realized the desk and torn leather chair had probably belonged to Justin's father. In the corner of the desk, her eyes focused on another photograph of an elderly man and woman. Her eyes focused on the man first. She blinked then took a second look. Justin's resemblance to the man was incredible. She looked at the woman, she had a beautiful smile and she looked kind. Putting the portrait back in its place, she realized they must have been Justin's beloved grandparents.

Standing up, she walked over to the book case, and began to thumb through the titles. Out of the hundreds of literary favorites, one book in particular stood out, an old book of poetry. Pulling it off the shelf, she glided her hand across the cover, then opened the cover. On the inside cover was a handwritten note.

My darling Emily,

In my eyes, you are the most beautiful woman in the world. I knew instantly the day we met that you were the one for me. This past year has been the greatest time of my life and I know it will only get better with every passing year.

You have made me the happiest man on Earth.

All my love, Robert

Reading the inscription, her heart began to beat at a faster pace, and her eyes filled with tears. It was the most heartwarming passage she'd ever read. She assumed the book had been given to Justin's mother by his father on their first wedding anniversary.

Intrigued, she took the book back to the living room, and curled up on a cozy sofa beside the fireplace. Her heart pounded as she read each and every poem. Flipping through the tattered pages, she saw where Justin's mother had marked some of the pages by folding the corners of the pages down. Catherine assumed they were her favorites, and after reading them, she understood why. When she finished, she clutched the book against her chest and fell fast asleep.

Upon waking, she looked around the darkened room, then toward the window. The sun had set, and it was dark. She reached down for the book, but it was no longer in her arms. Rolling sideways, she saw it sitting on the table beside her. She started to sit up, and noticed that Justin had covered her with a blanket.

Glancing around the dim room, her eyes focused on Justin sitting in his big brown leather chair with his feet propped up comfortably on the ottoman. From what she could tell, he was drawing a picture on a sketch pad. She continued to gaze at him. Their eyes met.

Justin smiled warmly, then put the pad in a drawer beside his chair.

She smiled. "How long have I been asleep?" she inquired, her tone soft.

"A couple of hours. I guess you were tired from the trip."

She laughed. "Yes. And I think it might also have something to do with getting up so early this morning." She thought for a moment. "Wait a minute…How long have you been sitting there?"

"About an hour," he confessed.

"Oh no. I'm so sorry. Why didn't you wake me?"

"You looked so peaceful that I didn't want to disturb you," he said, then he changed the subject. "By the way, did you enjoy the book?"

"Yes, I hope you don't mind. While you were gone, I went to your study to find something to read."

"No, why would I mind. That's what they're there for," he said, then paused. "Most of the books in there belonged to my parents. After they passed away, I read their entire collection. They both loved to read. My mom especially. She loved poetry."

He pointed to the book that Catherine had been reading. "My dad gave that book to my mom on their first wedding anniversary. He told me that she'd seen it one day when they were browsing at an antique bookstore. He said her eyes lit up as she read some of the verses. He could tell by her expression that she was interested in buying it, but she didn't dare ask. That was when my father had just started his career as a physician, and they didn't have money for extras."

Justin's eyes began to well with tears. He stood up, and walked over to the fireplace, perching the palm of his hand on the mantle. "Before they left the store, my dad pulled the owner to the side and asked him not to sell it to anyone else. He promised that he'd be back after he got paid to buy it. And he kept his promise. He used to say that the gleam in her eyes when she opened the package was exactly the same as when I was born."

After telling his story, he lowered his head in silence.

Overcome with sadness for what he'd been through, Catherine's heart began to ache. She rose from the sofa, and walked over to comfort him. Gently laying her hand on his shoulder to console him, she whispered, "Justin, I'm truly sorry for your loss."

They stood silently beside the fireplace. He took a deep breath. "What about your parents? Where are they now?" he asked.

Her lips curled into a smile. "My family lives in New Orleans. That's where I was born and raised with my brother and sister. When I was born my dad was an executive in the oil industry, and my mom was an up and coming artist. A few years later, my dad resigned from his company to open an art gallery with my mom. And that's what they're still doing today. They own a beautiful gallery on Royal Street, right in the heart of the French Quarter." She paused. "My mom couldn't stand the thought of putting us in day care, so she decided to stay home to raise us, and in order for her to continue working, my dad built a studio in our backyard. That was where we spent most of our days." Her eyes beamed in the firelight as she went on. "While she worked, she kept us busy by giving us our own art supplies. I can remember sitting on the floor, trying to copy everything that she did. Then, at the end of each day, she would sit on the floor with us to look over our drawings." Catherine laughed. "She framed everything that we drew, then hung our pictures on the walls around the house. She was so proud of our drawings. And they weren't even that good. You know, just kids stuff."

Catherine sighed. "I'm sorry. I'm going on and on about my family. I'm probably boring you to death."

Justin smiled. "Nothing that you say is boring to me. I'd like to hear some more about your family. How often do you see them?"

"I try to visit a few times a year. Unfortunately, not often enough," she divulged. Catherine started to feel homesick. "Now that's enough of my life story. Let's talk about you. What were you sketching when I woke up?"

"Nothing much," he answered hastily. "I was just drawing some preliminary sketches for one of my clients," he said, then quickly changed the subject. "Are you hungry?"

Her stomach made a rumbling noise, and she laughed. "Now that you mention it, I am a little hungry."

"Then why don't you go to take a warm bath and I'll start a light dinner for us. While you were asleep I caught a fish. I thought I'd pan fry it with some vegetables. How does that sound?"

"That sounds wonderful."

Feeling tired, she decided to take him up on the offer.

Thanking him for his hospitality, she headed upstairs.

While undressing, Catherine drew a warm bath. She pulled her hair up with a clip and slipped into the bathtub. Justin was right, a bath was just what she needed. She soaked for a while, then decided she'd better wash up and get out before Justin finished dinner. She toweled off, put on her plush bathrobe and tried to decide what to wear. She pulled out an ankle length brown suede skirt, a matching brown turtleneck sweater, and a pair of black boots. She brushed her hair, and nestled it on top of her head, then hurried to go back down.

Justin was standing beside the stove when she entered the kitchen. He was in the process of pan frying the fish. Silently, she slid beside him to check out his cooking skills. "Oh, wow. The fish smells great," she remarked taking a deep breath.

He kept his eyes on the fish. "Did you enjoy your bath?"

"Yes, the bath was just what I needed to wake me up. By the way, thanks for cooking dinner without me."

"Oh, no problem, I love to cook," he said, then slowly shifted his gaze in her direction. A smile filled his face. "Wow. You look beautiful," he remarked.

Catherine's cheeks reddened. "Thank you," she replied modestly.

Justin put the fork he was holding down, and turned the fire off. "The fish is done," he said, then he shifted his body closer. The look of desire filled his eyes.

She could tell that he wanted to kiss her, and she began to feel awkward. She took a deep breath, then pointed to the dining room. "I think I'll go set the table," she stuttered, then turned to walk away.

For a moment, Justin didn't move. He couldn't understand why she had dodged the kiss. Perplexed, he put the fish and vegetables on a platter, picked up a bottle of wine, then walked into the dining room.

Catherine sat down just as he entered the room, overwhelmed with a rush of emotions. She was tense, and Justin noticed it immediately.

He set the platter down on the table, then filled the glasses. Handing a glass to her, he announced that he wanted to make a toast.

She shifted her gaze in his direction. Their eyes met.

With a comforting smile, he lifted his glass to hers, "To a special friendship. May it last forever." Catherine smiled, and tapped her glass against his.

Justin sat down, and they began to eat. While they ate, they made small talk, but the conversation was tense. He wanted her to look at him, but she didn't. It was like she was afraid of what would happen if she did. Justin knew that something was wrong. There was something on her mind, something that she wasn't telling him. He could feel it. But he didn't know what it was.

After a quiet dinner, they cleared the table, and she washed the dishes while he dried. The tension between them was fierce.

When they finished, they decided to retire to the living room for a glass of brandy. Catherine sat in one of the leather chairs beside the fireplace while Justin poked the red hot wood, causing the fire to blaze. After he finished, he turned around to look at her. He noticed her arms were folded across her chest and she was rubbing them. Concerned, he asked, "Are you cold?"

"Yes, a little bit," she nodded.

He grabbed a blanket that was lying on back of the sofa, and gently laid it across her lap. Then he handed her a glass of brandy. "Here, take a couple of sips of brandy. It'll help to warm you."

She clasped both hands around the glass. "Thanks," she said, without looking up. She took a sip, and instantly felt the warmth of the liquor run through her body. Justin took his seat in the other chair. Quietly, they enjoyed their brandy while staring silently into the flames.

Justin had to break the silence. "Would you like to listen to some music?"

Catherine smiled. "Music sounds great," she replied.

She watched as he walked over to the stereo and turned it on. A radio station that was playing some great songs from the past came on, and an upbeat song began to play. He reached his hands out. "That's a great song. Would you like to dance?"

At first she was apprehensive, but the music put her in the mood. She laughed. "Sure, I'd love to." She stood, gripping his hands. They began to dance, slowly at first, then fast. Laughter filled the room as he swung her around for a dip when the song came to an end. The two of them were close to tears from laughing so much. Justin pulled her up, and they found themselves face to face. A slow song began to play. He pulled her body close. Resting her head upon his shoulder, they swayed around the room. As the song ended, once again they found themselves face to face, hand in hand.

She backed away. "Well, it's getting late. I think I'm going to turn in now."

"That sounds good," Justin said. "We have to get up early tomorrow morning."

"Well, goodnight," she said, and turned to go upstairs.

Justin put his hands in his pockets. "Goodnight," he murmured.

He didn't want the night to end that way, but he didn't have any choice. After turning off the lights, he went upstairs.

Lying in bed, he tossed and turned, unable to fall asleep. He couldn't stop thinking about her. He got up and paced around the room. He wanted to go to her bedroom, but he didn't dare. He stared out the window. A pack of wolves began to howl in the distance, assembling its members. In the night, he often cried the same way, but his cry was a silent one. His was a lonely cry in desperate search of a pack of his own.

Catherine awoke at dawn for the fishing trip. Stumbling out of bed, she opened the window to check the weather. It was pretty chilly so she decided to layer her clothes. She put on a pair of blue jeans, a white thermal undershirt, and a heavy blue and black check flannel shirt. She pulled her hair up in a ponytail, put on a tan khaki baseball cap and grabbed a navy overcoat to wear when she got outside. She was ready to go fishing for the first time ever!

As she walked down the stairs, she could hear the sound of pots rustling in the kitchen. When she walked in, she saw Justin standing beside the stove cooking eggs and bacon. She walked up next to him. "Good Morning," she said softly.

He turned to look at her. "Good Morning. Did you sleep well?"

"Yes, I slept like a baby."

"Would you like a cup of coffee?" he asked, pointing to the pot.

"Yes. I'd love one," she replied walking over to pour a cup.

"Breakfast will be ready in a few minutes. Are eggs, bacon and biscuits all right?"

"Yes. That's fine," she replied.

When breakfast was finished, they sat quietly, still tense from the night before. Soon after they finished, they decided to head out for their fishing excursion.

As they walked on the porch, Justin picked up their fishing poles and the supplies, then led her through the screen door. Catherine followed, while Justin pointed toward the lake telling her what he had planned. They walked down to the dock, where a small boat was tied.

Justin loaded the supplies in the boat, then held his hand out to help her in. As soon as she sat down, he untied the boat, and pushed it away from the pier. He paddled a short distance, stopping at what he called the perfect fishing spot. He pulled out their fishing rods, along with the worms they were going to use as bait. And like the perfect gentleman, he baited her rod.

After a quick lesson on how to cast the line and reel in any fish she caught, he cast his line into the water.

Silently, they waited patiently for a bite. An hour later, Catherine felt a tug on her line. "Justin, something's happening. I think I have one. It feels really big!" she exclaimed.

Scooting over, he coached her while she reeled the line in. Pulling the line above the water, they both laughed at the sight of a tiny bass squirming on the other end.

They cast the lines again, fishing for two hours without any luck. Catherine sighed, then laid her fishing pole down beside her feet to go to the other end of the boat to get a drink out of the ice chest. She began to stand. Justin looked up. "No, Catherine. Don't stand up…You're going to tip the boat—" he frantically called out.

In her haste to sit down, she wobbled the boat. The next thing they knew, they were both floating in the water on opposite sides of the flipped vessel.

Justin hurried, swimming over to make sure she was all right. When he got to her, he found her calmly treading water. "I'm so sorry," she shouted.

"Are you okay?" he asked, concerned for her well-being.

Her lips were trembling. "Yes, I'm fine but the water is freezing cold."

Justin tried to flip the boat back over, but it was too heavy. "We're going to have to swim back to shore. Can you make it?" he asked calmly.

"Yes. I can make it. But we better hurry. I'm really cold!"

When they reached the shoreline, they plummeted to the ground, lying beside one another, gasping for breath. Breathing deeply, Justin got up and hovered over her body to see if she was all right. Water dripped down his face, onto hers, as he spoke. "Are you all right?" he asked.

At first, she didn't respond. Then her blue lips trembled, and she opened her eyes. "I'm…okay…," she stuttered.

"I have to get you inside," he said. Put your arms around my neck."

She did as he instructed, then he helped her to stand.

Although she was a good swimmer, the cold water had taken its toll on her body. Her body was tired, fatigued, and her limbs were numb from the cold.

Justin helped her to the cabin, then carried her up to the master bedroom. Laying her on the bed, he said, "We have to get you out of those clothes," then pulled her coat off.

Her lips were still blue, but she was feeling much better. She stood up. "I'm all right," she said. "I can do the rest. You better get out of yours too," she said.

"Are you sure?"

She smiled slightly. "Yes. I'll be fine," then walked into the bathroom and turned on the shower. As she unbuttoned her shirt, Justin watched for a minute to make sure that she was all right, then he left the room.

When Catherine finished showering, she put on a bath robe to warm her chilled body. Unable to get rid of the chill, she went downstairs to sit beside the fire. As she walked into the living room, she saw Justin sitting in his chair, dressed in blue jeans and a long sleeved tan shirt.

Curiously, he looked up. "Are you still cold?"

Her lips trembled. "Yes. I can't seem to warm up."

He rushed to get up, grabbing the blanket from the sofa, and draped it across her shoulders. Gently reaching for her hands, he pulled her down on the floor beside the fireplace, then wrapped his arms around her shoulders, briskly rubbing her arms with his masculine hands. The warmth of his body transferred to hers.

She began to tremble again, but not because she was cold, but because he was kissing her neck gently and ever so slowly. Using his hands, he shifted her body around until they were staring into each others eyes. He rubbed her arms. "You're trembling again. Are you still cold?" he whispered.

"No, I'm not cold anymore," she replied, gazing into his eyes.

He tugged her closer until their lips united. Closing their eyes, they engaged in a soft kiss. She resisted the passion. "I'm sorry. I can't do this. There's something I have to tell you."

"What is it? What's wrong?" he asked.

Nervously rubbing her hands together, she said, "I think you should know. I've been…I mean…" She took a deep breath. "I'm not ready for this…not now…I hope you understand…

"Sure. I understand," he replied. He covered well, but he was baffled. "Catherine, I hope that you know, I'd never pressure you into anything. I treasure our friendship too much for that."

When she didn't answer, he changed the subject. "Would you like a drink?"

"A glass of wine would be great right now," she replied nervously.

While she waited, he stood up and walked into the kitchen. She thought about what she'd said and wanted to kick herself for not telling him the whole truth…that she was seeing William. But she just couldn't bring herself to do it….Not now. The time wasn't right.

A few minutes later, he came back into the room with a bottle of wine and a large cast-iron pot. "What's the pot for?" she asked curiously.

"I thought you might like a snack. I'm going to pop some popcorn for us."

"Popcorn…How wonderful. What a great idea."

While Justin knelt beside the fireplace, Catherine got up, put on the stereo, and then went over to join in on the fun. She knelt down beside him and poured two glasses of wine. She watched while he shook the kettle over the flames. The kernels began to pop and the lid began to lift off. Holding the pot over the flames, he turned to sneak a peak at Catherine. His eyes followed her every movement as she watched in amazement with a gleam in her eyes and a smile on her face. He couldn't help but feel total love, total commitment for this woman. A woman that in reality he hadn't known for very long, but in his heart, felt he'd known forever.

As the flames crackled in the background, they sat beside the fire to enjoy the popcorn and the bottle of wine. While eating, they reminisced about their memories of sharing popcorn with their families. That was such a wonderful time in both of their lives. They laughed, talking about other memories from their earlier years. They both smiled, agreeing about how wonderful it was to be so young and innocent.

A forgotten song began to play on the stereo. Justin stood, put his glass of wine on the table, and reached his hand out. "This is a great song. May I have this dance?"

Catherine stood, and reached for his hand. "I'd love to," she replied, setting her glass on the table beside his. Dancing cheek to cheek, they swayed around the dim lit room, in perfect synch with one another.

When the song ended, Catherine backed away. "I think I'm going to turn in," she mentioned, waiting for a response.

Justin stepped closer, and tension filled the air.

She waited for him to kiss her on the lips, but instead he kissed her cheek. "Well, goodnight," he whispered, and watched as she turned to walk upstairs.

Justin couldn't see her face, but as she walked away, the skin on her forehead wrinkled, and she bit her lip, trying to comprehend what had just happened. As she approached the stairs, she paused momentarily at the bottom, replaying their movements in her mind. For a second, she thought about turning around, and running back into his arms. But she couldn't do that. He'd kissed her on the cheek for a reason. Maybe he'd lost interest in pursuing her. Or maybe he thought that they should remain friends.

Catherine put her hand on the wooden rail, and slowly made her way up the stairs. She didn't realize it, but Justin was watching her every move. And his thoughts were the same. He wanted to go to her, but he was afraid. Afraid of rejection.

He watched as she disappeared from his view, then he walked over to pick up his glass of wine. Lifting the glass, he turned around to check on the fire, noticing that the flames were beginning to die down. Moving closer, he took a sip of wine, and stooped beside the hearth. One by one, the flames vanished from his sight, leaving the smoldering embers behind.

The following morning, Catherine was awakened by the sound of birds chirping outside her window. Looking toward the window, she raised her head from the pillow and sat up to listen to their pretty song. Stretching her arms above her head, she got out of the bed and walked over to the window to check the weather. The sun streamed over her hands as she lifted the window. Outside, it was sunny and mild, quite different from the last two days.

After showering and changing, she walked down the hall to go downstairs. As she approached Justin's bedroom, she saw that the door was ajar. Walking lightly on the wood floor, she peeked through the crack to see if Justin was still inside. And she smiled when she saw him. Underneath a blanket, he was fast asleep.

She went down to the kitchen, and brewed a pot of coffee. After pouring a cup, she decided to take her cup with her for a hike down to the stream. Before leaving, she wanted to write a note to Justin to let him know where to find her. She rummaged through the kitchen drawers, searching for a sheet of paper and an ink pen, but she couldn't find any.

She remembered seeing Justin put his sketch pad and pencil in the drawer beside his chair two nights earlier. She went into the living room and opened the top drawer of the mahogany chest. Just as she remembered, the pad and pencil were sitting right on top. She lifted the pad out of the drawer and flipped the pages to find a blank sheet. Most of the pages were filled with drawings of some of the houses that Justin had designed. She smiled, then turned the page.

She couldn't believe her eyes. There on the page was a drawing of her…a drawing of her while she was asleep on Justin's sofa. It seemed that Justin was in the midst of drawing a portrait of her, not a house plan, as he had said when she awoke from her nap the day they arrived at the cabin.

Staring down at the drawing, she heard the sound of Justin's footsteps coming down the stairs. *Oh, no,* she thought. *I better hurry.*

His footsteps veered closer.

Feeling his presence behind her, she tucked her hands behind her back and turned around. She felt like a child who had just gotten her hand stuck in the cookie jar. He was standing beside the fireplace wearing white long johns, covered by a burgundy bath robe.

She stood still, quietly closing the drawer behind her. Anxiety set in. Her voice cracked as she spoke. "Hi. I was getting ready to write a note. I thought that I would take a stroll down to the stream for another look before we leave this morning."

Justin hadn't noticed a thing. "That sounds great," he replied, stretching his arms in the air. "If you wait a few minutes, I'll go with you."

She pointed to the door, and smiled. "Terrific, I'll wait for you on the porch," she replied hastily. She stood still while he turned to go back upstairs. And when he was gone, she breathed a sigh of relief.

She turned around and opened the drawer, making sure the pad was in its proper place, then went out on the porch. Closing the door behind her, she moved toward the nearest white wicker rocker and plopped herself down.

Looking out over the lake, she rocked at a steady pace, thinking about what she had seen. Why had he drawn a picture of her? And why hadn't he been honest with her when she asked? After giving it some thought, she figured that he probably hadn't said anything because he was embarrassed. That made sense.

A few minutes later, Justin walked out on the porch. This time, he was dressed in blue jeans and a v-neck heather gray wool sweater, with a white tee shirt underneath. "Are you ready to go?" he asked.

She rose to her feet, and smiled. "Yes. I'm all ready."

While walking to the stream, they made small talk about their weekend adventure, and even laughed about the boat incident. But the conversation seemed different, seemed strained.

When they arrived at the stream, Catherine sat down on a group of rocks, watching while Justin picked up a handful of stones and walked to the water's edge. One by one, he skipped the stones across the surface of the water, while she sat quietly in the background.

She watched him for a minute, then closed her eyes to listen to the sounds of the forest; the water in the stream rushing across the rocks, the birds singing above, the sound of the breeze whistling through the trees. It was so peaceful here.

Catherine could hear the sound of chipping noises coming from the trees above her head. Looking up through the thick branches, she looked for the source, locating the culprit a minute later. It was a woodpecker, pecking on one of the tree trunks. She smiled at the sight of him. She'd never seen one before.

Leaning back against the rocks, she turned her attention to Justin, watching as he continued to skim the pebbles across the stream. She wondered what he was thinking. His thoughts could have been about their weekend, or like her, he might not have been thinking at all, just listening to the relaxing sounds of the wilderness.

Justin threw his last pebble, then turned around and smiled. "Are you ready to go?" he asked, walking toward her.

She nodded, then looked around again. "It's beautiful here," she said. "I'm going to miss it a lot."

Justin reached his hand out. "Then you have to come back with me."

Accepting his hand, she smiled, but didn't respond. Even though she would miss the beauty of the cabin, deep within her heart, she knew it was time to go home.

After breakfast, Catherine and Justin cleaned the cabin, and loaded the truck. They took one last look at the lake before they drove off. The drive home was much quicker than the trip there, and before she knew it they were in her driveway. Justin put the truck in park, then turned to her. "Well, here we are," he said, gently placing his hand atop hers. Her heart began to race, pounding so hard, she was certain he might notice it pumping through her chest. Turning away, she looked out the windshield, and took a deep breath.

Justin could feel her hand trembling beneath his, and he realized that she was nervous. Leaning forward, he kissed her on the cheek, and lifted his hand from hers. "Well, I really had a great time," he whispered, then leaned back against his seat.

Inside the truck, the air was getting warm, and Catherine felt like she couldn't breath. She had to get out. As she turned to him, a tear fell from her right eye. She hoped he hadn't noticed. "Well, I better go," she said nervously. Fighting the tears, she reached for the door handle, and pushed the door open.

Justin watched as she stepped out of the truck. His body felt frozen, unable to move. He wondered what she was thinking about. Why was she so distant? They'd just had a wonderful time together. How could everything have changed? What was she so afraid of?

Baffled by these questions, he pressed his hands firmly against the steering wheel, and shook his head. He wanted her more than life. Why didn't she want him? He was determined to find out.

He got out and walked to the back of the truck where she was standing. He pulled the suitcases out, then followed her to the front entryway, watching silently while she unlocked the door.

She pushed the door open, and turned to him. "Well," she said. "Thank you so much for inviting me. I had a wonderful time."

He smiled. "I did too. I hope we can do it again, sometime?"

She didn't answer.

"Is it all right if I call you later?"

Smiling, she took another deep breath. "Yes, that would be nice," she whispered.

She'd said yes, and that made him feel good. Leaning forward, he kissed her on the cheek again, and began to slowly pull away. He felt her hand on his, preventing him from moving. He watched closely as her lips gravitated to his and they shared a soft, simple kiss.

Stunned by the kiss, Justin released her hand, and stepped back to look at her. He wanted to move closer, and take her in his arms, but he didn't. For he knew that if he pushed too hard, he might lose her forever.

Justin smiled and shoved his hands inside his pockets. "Well, good-bye," he said, then he walked away.

CHAPTER 9

❀

As Catherine shut the door, she dropped her bags on the floor, and closed her eyes. "What am I doing?" she cried aloud. "How can I feel this way about two men?"

"Miss Catherine. Is that you?" a voice called out.

Catherine opened her eyes, and cleared her throat to respond. "Yes. It's me," she stuttered, unable to speak clearly.

As she walked across the marble floor into the den, her housekeeper rushed round the corner, stopping abruptly when she saw her.

Maria noticed the tears in Catherine's eyes. "Are you okay?" she asked.

Catherine wiped the tears away with her fingers, and sniffled. "Yes. I'm fine," she said. "And I'm so happy to see that you're back…How was your trip?"

Maria's eyes softened, and she smiled. "It was wonderful, and I owe it all to you," she acknowledged, having just returned from a two month visit with her family in Mexico.

"You don't know how much I've missed you," Catherine mentioned.

"I can see that you missed me. The refrigerator is empty," Maria laughed.

They walked toward the kitchen. "How about you? Have you been out of town?" Maria asked.

Catherine went to the refrigerator and pulled out a bottle of water. "Yes, I've been on a trip, and I also had a wonderful time," she replied, unscrewing the plastic bottle top.

Maria watched as she took a sip, then put the bottle down on the kitchen counter. Catherine picked up the stack of mail that had accumulated over the last two days, and flipped through the envelopes. "Did anyone call while I was away?" she asked curiously.

"Yes. Someone by the name of Mr. Moorehouse called yesterday," Maria said.

Catherine's eyes lit up. Lifting her eyes from the envelopes, she looked up at Maria. "What did he say?" she asked as she set the mail on the counter. "Does he want me to call him?"

"Yes. He called from San Francisco. I left the telephone number on your desk."

Catherine picked up the bottle of water, and thanked Maria. She wanted to call him, but decided it would be better to wait. What if he asked where she'd been? She had to think about what to say if he did.

Maria followed her to the foyer, and watched as she lifted her two suitcases, and ascended up the steps. "I'm going to go to take a warm bubble bath," Catherine said.

Standing beside the banister, Maria looked up at Catherine. Maria could tell that Catherine was upset, and she thought a cup of tea might help to relax her. "Would you like a cup of tea?" she asked kindly.

"A cup of tea sounds great," Catherine replied in an appreciative manner. "You're the best."

As soon as Catherine got to her bedroom she undressed, put on a bathrobe and went into her large marble bathroom. While she was running the water, Maria arrived with a cup of chamomile tea.

Thanking her, Catherine turned on the Jacuzzi jets, then slipped into the bathtub. The warm water was just what she needed, and the jets relaxed her tired muscles. Leaning her head back against the back of the tub, she closed her eyes, and sipped her tea.

After her bath, she dressed in a pair of comfortable satin pajamas, and went back into the bedroom. Moving closer to the bed, she pulled the decorative pillows off of the bed, and pulled the covers back. Sliding into the solitude of her cozy bed, she turned off the lamp, and closed her eyes.

Her thoughts started to wander back to the trip. Back to Justin. She had been hiding something important from him. Something that he had to know. And she had to find some way to tell him. She wanted it to be easy. But she knew that it wouldn't.

The telephone rang, interrupting her thoughts. After three rings, she decided to answer.

"Hi. It's me," Justin said. "I was just thinking about you."

Catherine was surprised that he had called so soon. "What about me?" she asked softly, afraid to hear the answer.

"I was thinking about what happened between us tonight," he said. "I thought that we should talk about it." He sighed. "I feel like there's something you're not telling me."

She didn't respond, but he could hear her breathing.

"I want you to know that you can tell me anything."

Unable to respond, Catherine bit her bottom lip.

He could tell that she wasn't ready to open up to him. "It's all right," he said. "I'm not going to pressure you. Just let me know when you're ready to talk, and I'll be here to listen."

She still didn't respond, but Justin could tell that she was listening.

"Well, I'm going to let you go now," he said. "Why don't you take some time to think about it, and I'll call you later in the week."

Lowering the receiver, she started to cry. She'd never met a man like him. Most men wouldn't have been so supportive. But Justin was different.

Early Friday morning, an envelope was delivered to Catherine's office. Taking a close look, she saw William's name written in the top left hand corner. Holding the envelope firmly in her hand, she glided the silver letter opener through the side, and opened it. Pulling the letter out, she unfolded it, and read it aloud.

> My dearest Catherine,
>
> I know that you love surprises, and I have a big one. I would like for you to go home, pack a suitcase with an evening gown, a coat, and enough clothes to spend one night with me. A limousine will pick you up at one o'clock this afternoon and take you to the airport, where my jet will be waiting. When you reach your destination, a car will be waiting to take you to your hotel. Enjoy your trip. I look forward to your arrival.
>
> William

It was an invitation that she couldn't resist. How romantic.

Excitedly, she followed his instructions, and went home to pack. Just as the note said, a limousine picked her up at precisely one o'clock, and drove her to the airport. When she arrived, the flight crew greeted her and she boarded the plane. About an hour later, she reached her destination, San Francisco.

As she descended down the steps of the airplane, her eyes focused on the limousine driver, waiting patiently beside the car. Above the sky was clear and sunny, with a stiff breeze blowing in the air.

Making her way down the last few steps, she tightened the sash on her ivory coat, and shoved her hands deep inside her pockets to keep them warm.

As she said good-bye to the flight crew, the driver opened the door, and smiled at her. Before stepping in, she eyed him closely, noticing how young he was, probably in his early twenties, kind of unusual for a limousine driver.

Sliding onto the soft seat, she waited while her luggage was loaded in the trunk. Inside the car, it was warm. She listened as the trunk closed, then watched as the driver ran up to the front and got in. Once inside, he put the car in gear and gunned the engine. The motion of the car's movement jerked her back against the seat as the car sped over the tarmac.

Planting her feet firmly on the floor, she pulled the seat belt over her chest and held on to the leather door handle for dear life. She'd never experienced anything like that before. He was a wild man. And she was terrified.

Catherine watched out of the window as the driver drove down the freeway, then exited, merging into a lane of traffic. Making his way through the hilly streets of the city, he stopped abruptly at each intersection, with a couple of sharp turns along the way.

Catherine was furious.

The sound of a cable car's bell clanged in the distance, and she listened as the sound got closer, and closer. Peering to the side, she watched as the cable car groaned up the steep hill beside the car, full of wide-eyed tourists. Seeing the cable car reminded her of the street cars back home in New Orleans. But it also reminded her of her family, and how long it had been since she'd last seen them.

The car hit a bump in the road, startling her from her memory. Nervously, she looked up to see what had happened. "Sorry about that," the driver said. "They have to do something about that pot hole…It's a big one. And no matter how much I try to avoid it, I always seem to hit it." He laughed.

"Young and senseless," she mumbled beneath her breath.

"Did you say something," he asked loudly.

"Yes. I said that maybe you should try to slow down right before you get to it," she suggested, clutching the leather door handle firmly with her hand.

The driver could tell that she wasn't very excited about his driving skills, or lack thereof, and he hoped that she wouldn't report it to anyone. "That's a good idea," he agreed. "I'll do that next time."

"Sure you will," she whispered to herself.

A minute later, the car screeched to a halt below the canopy of the hotel.

"Thank God," she mumbled, watching as the doorman walked over to open the door.

As he pulled the door open, Catherine unbuckled the seat belt, and stepped out of the car. "Good Afternoon, Miss Sheldon," he said. "Did you have a pleasant trip?"

"No. Actually, I didn't," she replied angrily, sweeping her hand over her hair.

"I'm so sorry," he apologized, casting a set of evil eyes in the driver's direction.

Noticing the doorman's reaction, she realized that it probably hadn't been the first time the driver had given someone a ruff ride. And she figured that it might have been the last.

As she looked up at the prestigious hotel, the driver brought her luggage to the sidewalk, and set it down on the pavement, then stood by to wait for a tip. Pulling a twenty dollar bill from her handbag, she handed it to him. "Get some driving lessons," she suggested, her voice cynical.

Normally, she would have given a lot more, but his poor driving skills and bad manners had ruined his chances. And Catherine wasn't going to give him anything that he didn't deserve.

The bellhop retrieved her luggage, while the doorman led her inside the lobby of the sophisticated hotel. As she walked across the polished floor, she glanced around, noticing how beautiful the lobby was with its elegant furnishings, exquisite artwork and crystal chandeliers.

The bellhop had been awaiting her arrival, so he took her directly up to the suite. As the bellhop opened the door, she paused to catch her breath, then walked inside. Walking across the Italian marble foyer, she was anxious to see William. While the bellhop brought her luggage into the bedroom, she walked into the living area, certain that William would be waiting. But he wasn't there. The suite was empty.

The bellhop came out of the bedroom, and walked toward her. "Do you know where I can find Mr. Moorehouse?" she asked curiously.

"I'm sorry, Ms. Sheldon. I don't know where he is now. He left the hotel about an hour ago and he didn't say where he was going or when he would return. I'm sure he'll be back soon."

Thanking him, she went to give him a tip. "That's not necessary," he said, turning down the gratuity. "Mr. Moorehouse has taken care of that already."

Catherine escorted him to the door, and thanked him for his service. After he left, she walked into the bedroom to unpack.

Just as she finished, she heard a knock on the door.

Her face brightened. "There he is," she mumbled, and rushed to the door.

Pulling her ivory sweater down over her black skirt she smiled, then opened the door. On the other side stood a short lady, dressed in a black uniform.

"Good Afternoon. I have a message for you," she said, handing over a letter sized envelope. Accepting the letter, Catherine asked that she wait while she went to get her purse. But once again, she was told that William had already taken care of the gratuity.

After thanking her, Catherine closed the door. Standing in the foyer, she took a deep breath, and opened the envelope. Inside was another letter. It read.

My dearest Catherine,

I'm so happy you decided to join me. Please dress in an evening gown and go down to the lobby at seven o'clock. A driver will be waiting to take you to me.

William

Though she was disturbed by William's secrecy, she was also intrigued. She couldn't wait to find out what he had planned.

Catherine walked into the living room, put the letter on the coffee table beside a fresh flower arrangement, and then walked back into the bedroom to get ready.

A few minutes before seven, she stepped out of the elevator into the lobby. Walking across the marble floor, she looked simply stunning, dressed in a long black dress with a feminine bateau neckline, and a black cashmere coat hung neatly over her arm. As she walked toward the front door, the doorman met her. He complimented her on how beautiful she looked, then helped to put her coat on. Outside, another limousine was waiting to take her to her final destination.

After a fifteen minute ride, the car pulled up to another building. Reaching for her handbag, she peered out the window to see where they were. Through the glass windows of the building, she could see people dining inside.

The chauffeur opened the door, and she stepped out.

She walked up to the door, where she was once again greeted. This time, by a gentleman dressed in a black tuxedo. Taking her arm, the man led her inside to a dining room full of dinner patrons.

Catherine thought that he would take her to one of the tables, but instead he led her in the other direction toward a winding staircase, carpeted in red. Slowly they ascended up the stairs, through a set of doors into a private dining room.

Through the dim lit room, she saw a set of doors leading to a balcony. The man led her in that direction. As she walked closer, the cool San Francisco breeze blew through the barren space.

The man pointed outside to where William was standing, looking out over the city, dressed in a white tuxedo. As she drew nearer, he turned around. Slowly, they walked towards one another. He smiled, reaching his hands out. "What do you think about your surprise?"

She took his hands, and they embraced. "I'm impressed," she replied.

He kissed her on the lips. "That's not all," he said. "I have another surprise for you later tonight."

Catherine's eyes lit up. "That sounds wonderful," she replied delightedly.

William led her to the other side of the balcony where a candlelit table for two had been set, with a beautiful orchard flower arrangement in the center. The table was draped in white linen with fine china place settings, sterling flatware, crystal glasses and the balcony surrounding the table was decorated with floral arrangements and candelabras. The sound of music filled the air, as the sheer curtains covering the doors danced in the crisp night air.

Her eyes sparkled as William filled two long stemmed champagne glasses. He handed a glass to her, then held his glass up high. "I'd like to make a toast to the most beautiful woman in the world, my darling Catherine."

"And to the most romantic man in the world," she added. "Thank you for giving me a memory that I will never forget."

Staring deeply into each other's eyes, they gently tapped the glasses together, then both took a sip. William led her to the edge of the balcony. In silence, they stood enjoying the view of the city. A moment later, he put his hand out. "Would you like to dance?"

"Yes. I'd love to," she smiled warmly.

He clasped her hands, leading her to the center of the balcony. The music from the sound system stopped, and classical music erupted from the doorway. Catherine turned for a glimpse. An orchestra had set up, and they were beginning to play a beautiful waltz. Amazed, she turned to him. "I can't believe this. Once again, you've dazzled me."

They danced, for what seemed to be forever, until he stated, "I have a special dinner planned for us. Would you like to dine now?"

Agreeing, he led her back to the table and pulled out her chair. "I hope you don't mind," he admitted. "I took the liberty of ordering for us."

"I don't mind at all. I'm having the time of my life."

He leaned over, ringing a bell which was on the table. As the band continued to play, dinner was served. When they finished, Catherine was full.

The waiter entered with a silver platter, containing dessert.

"Dessert," Catherine remarked, reaching for her stomach. "I'm sure it's delicious, but if you don't mind, I think I'll pass on the dessert."

"You have to eat dessert," William said hastily. "Come on," he urged. "I'll share it with you."

Hesitantly, she agreed.

The waiter placed the platter in front of her, then walked away. Slowly, she lifted the lid. Peering inside, her eyes lit up. "What is this? This isn't dessert…this is…Oh, wow…William, it's beautiful." Under the lid, sat an exquisite diamond necklace, shimmering in the warm glow of the candlelight.

She just stared down at it. "Well, aren't you going to try it on?" he asked.

Thrilled, she pulled it out of the box. "Oh, William. This is beautiful," she exclaimed, rushing to the other side of the table. "I can't believe you did this for me. I love it!"

She gently placed it in his hands. "Will you help me with the clasp?"

Stooping beside him, he placed it around her neck. She held it firmly in place as he tightened the clasp. She quickly turned, falling into his lap. "Oh, William, this has been the most remarkable night of my life. You're the most wonderful man in the world!"

They embraced for a moment. "Would you like to dance with me again?" he asked.

"Yes, I'd love to," she answered, firmly gripping his hand.

Looking radiant, she stood up. The orchestra began to play and together they swayed around the balcony in perfect harmony. William held her tightly, gently kissing her sweet, warm lips. With passion in his eyes, he whispered, "Would you like to go back to the hotel now?"

Without speaking, Catherine nodded in agreement as they walked past the orchestra heading to the staircase.

When they arrived back at the hotel, they silently made their way through the lobby and up to the suite. As they approached the door, Catherine began to feel shivers run up and down her spine, just as she had in the past whenever he was near.

William drew her warm body to his as they walked inside. The door shut behind them. They engaged in another kiss. Their bodies united. Catherine could feel the pounding of his heart against her breasts.

Gently, he backed her up against the door, and leaned into her. He set his hands on her shoulders, and glared into her eyes. "I've missed you so much. I've longed for you every night since I've been away."

Their intimacy deepened with every touch. Pressing her lips to his, she whispered, "I've missed you too." They kissed harder and harder. Anxiously, Catherine pushed his jacket over his shoulders and they began to undress one another. They stood naked as he gently rubbed his body up and down against hers, pushing her back against the door. Burying her face against his neck, she put her arms around his shoulders, then wrapped her long legs around his waist. Slowly he lifted her, carrying her to the bedroom. He gently laid her on the bed. With longing in his eyes, he began to kiss and stroke every inch of her body as she quietly watched his every move. She put her arms around his neck, pulling him down atop her. They made hard, passionate love and climaxed together. Resting for a moment, he gently shifted his body to her side as she stroked his chest. "You're wonderful," he praised. "Do you know how much I've missed you?"

She didn't respond. Instead, she shifted her body atop his, and kissed his neck. "Will you show me again how much you've missed me?" she asked eagerly.

With a warm smile, he pressed his lips to hers. "I'd be happy to." Once again, they began to kiss slowly, then more passionately. Throughout the night, they made passionate love, again and again, until they couldn't go on any longer; falling asleep in each other's arms.

The next morning, Catherine woke up feeling the warm rays of sunlight against her face. Rolling over, she checked to see if William was still asleep, but she found herself alone. Stretching, she rose from the bed and put on her robe to go to find him. She went from room the room, but he was nowhere in sight.

The hotel door opened as she walked in the living area. She stood quietly, surprising him as he came through.

"Good morning sleepy head." He laughed. "Wow, you look a mess," he added.

Walking closer, she tried to flatten her hair with her fingers. She giggled. "I had a really rough night. Someone kept me awake all night long."

Kissing her gently, he laughed. "Oh, really…and I guess you didn't have anything to do with that?"

He walked over to the sofa, motioning for her to join him. "Why don't you come to sit beside me. I have something for you." He was holding a white paper bag.

Sliding beside him, she put her arms around his neck. "What is it?" she questioned.

He pulled two cups out of the bag. "Coffee and bagels," he said, setting them down on the coffee table.

"I thought that you were talking about something else," she joked.

"Come to think of it, I have that too. Which one would you like first?" he remarked pulling her onto his lap.

She stroked his face with her fingers. Determined to have him once more, she began to kiss his lips, slowly at first, then more quickly.

William removed his shirt, then as he watched, Catherine dropped her robe to the floor. He looked in wonderment, as if it had been the first time he'd seen her naked. He laid back against the sofa, pulling her back atop him. He gently stroked between her breasts, down to her inner thighs and back up again. A fire burned within her body as he gently stroked her face. She pulled her body upward, watching, as he entered her. With each thrust, he shifted deeper and deeper, until they climaxed together.

Catherine laid her head against his chest, exhaling a shaky breath. "I think I'm falling in love with you," she whispered.

She'd taken him completely by surprise. He didn't respond. The expression on his face said it all, but unfortunately, she wasn't looking to notice.

The last thing he wanted was to fall in love. There were too many other things that mattered more. He had a reputation for being a playboy, and he enjoyed the luxury of having a "no strings attached attitude." He always figured that if he fell in love, he wouldn't lose only his image, but also all of the fringe benefits that went along with it. Having a partner would restrict his lifestyle. And his lifestyle was much too important to him. He liked to live life to the fullest, one day at a time. He figured that most of the women who wanted a commitment were also looking for someone to have children with. He wasn't ready for that yet, and quite frankly didn't know if he ever would be.

After a few minutes of silence, Catherine looked up at him. He was staring toward the window, deep in thought. She knew what he was thinking about, and she wanted to explain. She sat beside him. "William. What I said…I didn't say it for a response from you…I understand if you're not ready to say the same thing. The last thing I wanted was to make you feel uncomfortable."

He continued to look away.

She stood up and put on her robe. "Listen, why don't we just forget about it for now? I'm going to take a shower and get dressed," she stated, then walked away.

Walking down the hallway, she couldn't hold back her tears. She went into the bathroom, and opened the shower stall to turn on the water. While the water heated, she stared into the mirror. Removing her robe, she thought, *Why did I tell him that? It's apparent he doesn't feel the same way. I feel like a fool, but I guess I had to find out sooner or later.*

Lost in thought, she opened the door. She stepped into the shower letting the warm water run down her face and body. She put shampoo in her hair and began to massage it through her scalp, then closed her eyes, rinsing under the stream of water. She could hear the bathroom door open. The shower door opened, "Can I join you," William asked somberly.

Relieved, she sighed, "Sure you can," and watched as he took off his robe and stepped in.

The water flowed down over his head. He looked up, "I'm sorry I reacted that way. It's just that you caught me by surprise."

Preventing him from speaking, she held her index finger against his lips. "It's all right. You don't have to explain," she acknowledged in a soft voice.

She leaned her body into his torso, closed her eyes and kissed him gently on the lips. They engaged in a soft kiss, silently bathing one another.

After dressing, they went downstairs to eat breakfast in the hotel restaurant, then went back upstairs to pack for the trip home.

While packing, William told Catherine that he wanted to talk to her about something. She began to get nervous. She held her breath as he went on, "How would you like to spend Thanksgiving with me in Monte-Carlo?" he asked.

She took a breath. "Monte-Carlo?" she questioned curiously.

"Yes. Monte-Carlo. I think we'd have fun. How about it? We can spend our days lounging on the beach and our nights wandering around the city. It's beautiful there at this time of the year. It'll be great. Please say yes!" he urged.

Hesitating for a moment, she replied, "Well, I was planning to ask you to spend Thanksgiving with me in New Orleans with my family. But I guess Monte-Carlo would be all right. I guess it doesn't matter, as long as we're together."

William cheered up. "All right! It'll be much better than all right. It's one of my favorite places to go. The night life is incredible! You're going to love it!" They embraced. "I'll make the arrangements as soon as we get home," he added.

CHAPTER 10

When Catherine arrived home from San Francisco, she checked the messages on her answering machine. Several people had left messages while she was away. The most important ones were from Antoinette, Justin and her mother. Justin had called three times and seemed genuinely concerned about her whereabouts. She wanted to return his call, but first she decided to make a cup of tea.

Walking out of her study, she saw Maria coming around the corner. "Miss Catherine, I didn't hear you come in. I was in the kitchen and started hearing noises from this direction. You scared me half to death," Maria announced, clutching her hands to her chest.

"I'm sorry, Maria. I didn't mean to startle you. I just got home and decided to check my messages. I was about to return some phone calls, but I want to get a cup of tea first," she said, pointing to the kitchen.

"By the way, how was your trip?" Maria questioned.

Catherine smiled with a dreamy look in her eyes. "Thanks for asking. I had a marvelous time," she said, walking toward the kitchen.

Following her into the kitchen, Maria suggested that she make the tea while Catherine rested.

Agreeing, Catherine headed back toward the study.

Sitting down at her desk, she decided to call Antoinette first. While dialing the number, Maria walked in with the cup of tea. Catherine couldn't wait to take a sip.

Antoinette's telephone rang, but the answering machine picked up. Catherine left a message, "Hi, Antoinette. This is Catherine. I'm sorry we haven't spoken lately, but a lot has been happening. Give me a call during the week and I'll fill you in on the details."

After hanging up, she decided to call Justin before retiring to her bedroom. Dialing his number, she took another sip. The phone rang, and his answering machine picked up. *Where is everyone*, she thought, finding it odd that he too wasn't home.

After the machine beeped, she left a message, "Hi, Justin. This is Catherine. I went to San Francisco over the weekend. I'm sorry that you were worried about me. I'll try to call you sometime tomorrow."

"Huh, that was pretty easy," she mumbled. "Now, for the hardest." She dialed the next number. The telephone rang four times. *Maybe I'll get off easy tonight*, she thought to herself, hoping that her parents weren't home either.

A woman's voice answered.

"Mom. Hi, it's Catherine."

"Hello my darling. I'm so happy that you called. I was beginning to worry about you." No matter how old she got, her mother still worried about her.

"Oh, Mom…I'm fine," Catherine replied fidgeting with her hair. She always fidgeted with her hair when talking to her mom. "I had to go out of town and I just walked in the door a few minutes ago. Is everything okay?"

"Yes, baby. Everything's fine. I was just calling to find out if you're coming home for Thanksgiving."

Catherine took a deep breath and sighed. She hated to tell her mom that she wouldn't be home for Thanksgiving. "To tell you the truth," she divulged, "I just made plans to go to Monte-Carlo for Thanksgiving with a friend of mine."

"What kind of friend?" her mom asked suspiciously.

Catherine rolled her eyes. "What do you mean, what kind of friend?"

"You know what I mean. Are you going with a man or woman?"

"Well, if you have to know...I'm going with a man."

"Is it serious?" her mom pressed.

Catherine smiled softly. "Yes. I guess it's pretty serious. I've only been seeing him for a short time, but I really like him a lot. And I think you're going to like him too."

Excited, Catherine began to tell her mother all about William. And once she started talking, she just couldn't stop. They spoke for over an hour. Just as she had done with Antoinette, she opened up and divulged everything she was feeling about William.

Her mother was happy that she'd finally found someone. She knew all too well, how long Catherine had gone without dating, having put all of her energy into her company.

After Catherine finished talking about William, her mother changed the subject. "Now, about Christmas," she said, then paused for a moment. Catherine waited for the rest. "For the first time ever, your father and I plan to spend Christmas out of town."

Ever since she was a little girl, their family had always spent Christmas together, so Catherine was surprised by the news.

She thought for a moment, then responded. "I think that's great," she said eagerly. "So—where have the two of you decided to go?"

"We're going to Paris," her mother replied in a dreamy tone. "We're going back for a second honeymoon—"

"And when are you coming back?" Catherine interrupted.

Her mother sighed. "We're supposed to stay for two months," she disclosed. She thought that Catherine would be upset.

"I think that's wonderful," Catherine said. "The two of you deserve to be alone for once in your life. In fact, it's probably the most romantic thing you've ever done. You're going to have a wonderful time." Catherine looked at the crystal clock sitting on her desk. "Well, listen mom. I better get off the phone. My ear's getting tired." She laughed.

"Sure. Go get some rest, and we'll talk later," her mother instructed. "I love you," she added.

"I love you too. By the way, say hello to dad for me and give him my love," Catherine said, slowly lowering the receiver.

The following day, Catherine spent her time lazily around the house. She rolled out of bed late, then went into her home gym for a workout.

Later in the afternoon, she decided to relax by working in her flower garden. She slipped into a comfortable sundress, put on a wide-brimmed straw hat and a pair of gloves, and went outside. The white patches of clouds rolled slowly across the blue sky while she sat on the ground beside her favorite flowers; pulling weeds, pruning, and turning the soil.

Catherine had started gardening as a teenager, when one of her science projects had been to start and manage a butterfly garden for an entire school year. Most of the kids dreaded the task, but not Catherine. That butterfly garden was only the beginning. Gardening had affected her tremendously. It not only calmed her, but it'd taken a special place within her heart, giving her the opportunity to see the world from another perspective.

A family of birds chirped from the shadows of the tree above, watching Catherine's every move. She sat tall, wiping the sweat away from her forehead with the back of her glove. The birds chirped louder, as if they were serenading her. She looked up, searching the branches for their bright faces and noticed a newly developed nest they'd built in the safe confines of her property.

"Now, now. Are you hungry? Let me get some food," she said softly. She stood, then walked to the shed to put her tools away. A few minutes later, she emerged with a bucket of seeds to fill the bird feeders.

When she finished, she walked back to the shed to put the bucket away, then headed for the house. The side gate made a harsh grating sound just as she reached the back door. Someone was opening the gate. She stopped, listening intently, then walked over to see who was there.

"Catherine, are you back there?" a man's voice called out. She recognized the voice. It was Justin.

"Yes, I'm here," she called, walking toward the gate.

As Catherine approached the corner of the house, Justin stepped out of the shadows. He smiled brightly, pointing back to the gate. "I hope you don't mind. I knocked on the door, but no one answered. I thought you might be back here."

She stood still and removed her hat. She smiled, running her fingers through her thick brown hair. "No. I don't mind at all. I was just doing some gardening." Slowly, she walked toward him. "I was just getting ready to go inside to get a bottle of water. Would you like one?" she asked motioning to the house.

"Sure. That would be great," he replied.

She led Justin into the kitchen. As he closed the door, she went to the refrigerator and pulled out two bottles. "So—did you get the message that I left last night?" she asked, handing a bottle to him.

He twisted the top off. "I sure did," he replied, smiling softly.

She pointed through the large glass window. "I was thinking about going for a swim. Would you like to join me?"

"I'd love to," he said, "but I don't have a swimsuit."

"That's all right," she waved. "The bathroom closet in the pool house is filled with swimsuits. I'm sure you can find one in your size."

She took a sip of water, and put the top back on. "Why don't you go out to the pool house to change and I'll meet you there," she instructed graciously. Justin nodded, turning toward the door. She watched as he went out, then she turned to go upstairs.

Justin opened the door to the pool house and turned on the lights. Looking around the exquisite, warm colored interior, he walked farther in, then down the narrow hallway to find the bathroom. Just as she'd said, the closet was filled with swimsuits in every size and color imaginable. Gliding the hangers across the rack, he found a pair of black trunks in his size. After pulling them out, he undressed, laying his clothes neatly on the granite vanity beside the closet.

After dressing, he turned to look in the full length wall mirror. Gazing at his reflection, he checked his teeth and nose, then stepped back, flexing his muscles. Laughing, he grabbed a towel off the shelf, then went back outside.

He sat on a lounge chair near the pool to wait for Catherine. Glancing around the beautifully landscaped yard, he nervously rubbed his hands together. He looked up and saw her through the kitchen window. "Wow, she looks incredible," he whispered to himself as she opened the door and walked outside.

Slowly, she strolled across the lawn, her hips moving rhythmically with every step. Through the darkness, he couldn't see her face, but her body looked incredible. He watched closely as the muscles in her thighs rotated beneath her skin as she moved closer. She was dressed in a black swimsuit, high cut above her muscular thighs, holding a towel across her forearm.

Taking a deep breath, he remained seated.

"I see you found a swimsuit," she said, stepping up to him.

Her face came into view. "You look great," he said unable to resist the urge to compliment her.

She laid her towel on top of his. "Thanks," she replied. "Are you ready to go in?"

"Yes, I'm ready," he said, his voice cracking as he stood. He felt like a teenage boy looking at the girl of his dreams.

Catherine walked to the deep end, then gracefully dove in. When she emerged from beneath the water, she saw Justin standing by the side of the pool. "The water feels great," she called out. "Come on in."

Stretching his arms over his head, he dove in, appearing a few seconds later beside her. She smiled. "I'll race you to the other side," she exclaimed getting a head start.

"Hey, that's not fair," he shouted as his body glided across the water.

She moved to the side of the shallow end near one of the pool lights, and he swam closer. "Do you swim a lot?" he asked.

"I try to swim at least once a day," she replied. She looked up at the sky. "I especially love to swim in the evening so I can check out the stars."

"Are you an astrology buff?" he asked, laughing.

Her face turned serious and her forehead wrinkled. "Not at all," she replied, pointing to one of the lounge chairs. "Sometimes, I lay there and just look up at the sky." She laughed. "I know that sounds silly but it helps to clear my mind after a hard day," she explained.

Although Justin was listening intently, she concluded that what she was saying was probably boring to him. She stopped talking. "Well, that's enough of that," she said. "Do you want to race again?"

Always up for competition, Justin agreed. "What do I get if I win?" he asked as Catherine swam to the steps.

She reached the steps and sat down. "What do you want?"

Justin thought about it. "How about dinner? Have you eaten?"

"No, actually, I haven't," she replied. "You're on," she said. "Whoever wins gets to choose where we'll dine tonight."

He swam beside her to get ready.

"On your marks, get set, go," she said loudly, and the two of them started to swim to the other side.

Justin was already there when she touched the side of the pool. "I guess I won," he said with a dazzling smile.

She raised her eyebrows. "That wasn't fair. You swam below the water and I swam above it."

"Hey. You didn't say that I couldn't go under!" he teased.

"You're right," she said with a laugh. "But I'll know better next time. So—where do you want to go?" she asked, lifting herself out of the water.

Justin pulled himself up, and sat beside her. "I thought we might eat in," he said. "How about pizza?"

"Pizza sounds great," she replied, not expecting that he would have chosen pizza.

She stood up and picked up her towel from the chair.

"What do you like on yours?" he asked, reaching for his towel.

Catherine didn't hesitate in her response. "I like everything except anchovies."

"Oh, no. That's one thing we don't have in common. I always make them load mine up with anchovies."

"Yucky," she said. "I don't mind anchovies when they're pureed in my food, but I can't stand to see them laying on top of my pizza," she explained.

Justin laughed. "Okay, I get the message. We'll just order them on the side."

"That's not a good idea either," she mentioned. "They'll probably forget to tell the person putting the toppings on and it'll show up wrong."

"Okay, okay. No anchovies," Justin laughed.

Catherine finished toweling off. "Why don't I go in to order the pizza while you change. Then you can meet me in the house," she suggested.

"That sounds good to me," Justin agreed walking toward the pool house.

Once inside, Catherine ordered the pizza, then went upstairs to change out of her wet swimsuit. She dried her hair, pulled it into a ponytail, dressed in an ankle length black linen tank dress, then went back down to meet Justin. Her bare feet glided across the wooden floor as she walked from room to room to find him.

Entering the formal living room, she saw Justin looking at her family photographs on the mantle. Hearing her, he turned around. "Are these your parents?" he asked softly.

"Yes. That's them," she said, walking beside him.

His eyes shifted from one photograph to the other. "And who are these people?" he asked pointing to another photograph. She smiled. "That's my brother Randall, his wife Paige and their children," she said pointing. Her finger glided across another photograph. "And that's my sister, Camille with her husband, Michael."

Turning to her, he gazed into her big brown eyes. "You have a beautiful family," he commented. Justin started to shift his body closer, and Catherine felt a shiver run through her stomach. "Would you like a drink?" she asked to change the mood.

"That would be terrific," he replied. "Do you have any beer?"

Just as Catherine began to reply, the doorbell rang. She looked down at her watch. "Wow, the pizza's here already. That was fast," she commented.

Walking into the foyer, she grabbed a twenty dollar bill out of her purse. Justin intercepted. "Here, I've got that," he smiled, reminding her of their bet.

Catherine moved to the side to let him answer the door. "Well, I'll get the beer," she said, and turned to walk into the den.

Stooping down behind the bar, she pulled two bottles of beer out of the small refrigerator. She could hear Justin talking to someone, but couldn't understand what was being said. Standing up, she listened intently while she removed the bottle caps from the beer. "Thanks a lot," she heard Justin say, then she heard the door snap shut.

A few seconds later, Justin entered the room, holding a vase filled with pink roses. "It wasn't the pizza man," he said. "Looks like you received some flowers."

Although Catherine figured they were from William, she pretended to look surprised. With the beer in her hands, she walked closer and smiled. "Wow, I wonder who they're from?" she said, setting the bottles down on the coffee table.

Just as she reached for the vase, the doorbell rang again. Justin handed the vase to her. "Ah, now that has to be the pizza," he said, and walked toward the front door.

While Justin paid for the pizza, Catherine brought the flowers into her study. Even though she wanted to, she didn't open the card, feeling that it was better not knowing for sure who'd sent them.

And if it had been William, she was glad he hadn't decided to deliver them personally.

Catherine set the flowers down on her desk, and hurried back into the den. As she entered the room, she smiled, seeing Justin sitting on the floor beside the coffee table with the box of pizza in the middle of the table. "How about if we eat here?" he asked.

Nodding in agreement, Catherine sat down on the floor across from him and reached for her beer. While she took a sip, Justin opened the box, offering her a slice first, then he lifted out a slice for himself. After a couple of bites, he asked the dreaded question. "So—who were the flowers from?"

Setting down her pizza on the inside of the box top, Catherine took another sip of beer. Waving her free hand in the air, she responded. "Oh, they're from one of my friends," she answered as though it was no big deal.

Having lied, Catherine felt terrible.

"Oh," Justin said, and left it at that.

Just as Justin finished eating the last slice of pizza, the telephone rang. Standing up, Catherine excused herself to answer the call.

Hurrying into her study, she picked up the receiver. "Hi beautiful," the man's voice announced. "Did you receive the flowers?"

It was William.

Thanking him, Catherine said that she had received them and they were beautiful. She started to say that she had company, and would have to call him back, but he continued to talk, excitedly telling her about a classic car he had just purchased for his collection.

While William described the car in detail, she looked down at her watch, three minutes had already gone by.

In the den, Justin waited patiently for five minutes, then walked toward the study. He figured she'd gotten stuck with a call about work.

As he entered the room, he saw her standing behind the desk with the large bouquet of roses set on the desk in front of her.

When she realized that he'd entered the room, Catherine looked in his direction and shrugged her shoulders, unable to speak to him. "I'm sorry," she mouthed, without speaking.

Justin used hand signals, pointing down the hall. "I'm going to go," he whispered. "I'll call you later."

Nodding, Catherine agreed, and sat down at the desk.

A few minutes later, William finally stopped talking.

"It sounds wonderful," she said, speaking of the car. "I can't wait to see it."

Before hanging up, William told Catherine that his schedule for the next week would be pretty hectic. He explained that the deadline to finish his project was coming up, and said that he was having problems with the contractors finishing the job in time. That meant he'd have to spend most of his time pushing them to meet the task, and he probably wouldn't be able to see her during the week.

She thought about it for a moment. "That's all right," she said, "I want to finish my spring collection before Thanksgiving, so that will give me extra time. It should work out perfectly for us."

"Good," William said. "I'm glad to hear that…Listen, one other thing. I'm planning a reception to celebrate the completion of my project, and I'd like for you to come with me?"

Catherine didn't hesitate to accept. "I'd love to. When is it?"

"It's this Saturday night at eight o'clock. I can pick you up around seven, and we can go straight there."

"That sounds great," she responded. "Well, if I don't see you before Saturday, I just want you to know that I already miss you," she whispered.

"I miss you too," he answered, lowering the receiver.

CHAPTER 11

By Friday morning, things around the office had settled down considerably, and Catherine was finally able to breath a sigh of relief. Because she still hadn't spoken with Justin, she decided to give him a call at his office.

The receptionist who answered the telephone said that Justin wasn't in, but she thought his personal secretary might know his whereabouts.

Fidgeting with a pencil, Catherine waited for his secretary to pick up.

"Good Afternoon, Mr. Scott's Office, Gwen speaking."

"Hello, Gwen. This is Catherine Sheldon."

"Yes. Hello, Miss Sheldon. What can I do for you?"

"I'm trying to locate Justin, and I thought you might be able to help me?"

"Why, yes. He's been out at a job site all this week. The contractors were short a couple of employees, so Justin told them that he would lend a hand with the construction. He's there right now. If you'd like, I can give you the number to his cell phone?"

Catherine bit the eraser of the pencil. "Actually, I think I'll pay him a visit. Do you have the address of the building?"

"Yes, I have it right here," Gwen said, and gave Catherine the address.

As soon as she hung up, Catherine rolled her chair away from the desk to stare out the window. Unsure of whether she should go or not, she rationalized out loud. "What should I do? I hate to disturb him if he's busy. But then again, maybe he's not. He might just be standing around supervising the men."

She looked down at her watch. It was eleven-thirty. Realizing that he had to break for lunch, she decided to pack a picnic basket and surprise him. Without hesitation, she rolled her chair back to the desk and paged her secretary. "Kay, can you find the telephone number for Lucio's Restaurant and get Lucio on the phone for me?"

"Yes, Catherine. I'll do it right away."

"A few minutes later, Kay buzzed in, "Lucio is on line two."

"Great…Thanks Kay."

Catherine picked up the receiver, "Hi, Lucio. How are you?"

"I'm fine. What can I do for you?" he replied in his heavy Italian accent.

"I need to ask a favor of you," she urged.

"Anything for you, Miss Sheldon."

"Thank you Lucio. You're a dear." She paused. "I want to surprise someone with a picnic basket for lunch. I'm going to a construction site and I'm sure they won't have any type of kitchen set up. Can you put some lunch together for me?"

"No problem. Would like you to pick it up, or shall we deliver it?"

"I'll pick it up in about fifteen minutes. Will that give you enough time?"

"That's perfect. I even have a basket that you can use," he remarked.

"Thanks so much Lucio. You're a sweetheart."

After hanging up the telephone, Catherine went to freshen up. She changed to a pair of blue jeans with a light blue sweater, then grabbed her purse and headed out of the office, stopping briefly at Kay's desk to tell her where she was going.

Upon her arrival at the restaurant, she was greeted at the front door by Lucio, who was holding the basket. In a hurried voice she said, "Thank you so much for doing this for me. I really appreciate it. How much do I owe you?"

Waving her away, Lucio smiled. "We can settle up later."

"That sounds great. I appreciate it!" she said as she grabbed the basket and raced out the door.

When she arrived at the job site, she looked at the clock on her dashboard. It was quarter after twelve. "Damn, I hope he hasn't eaten yet," she mumbled, getting out of the car.

She walked up the steps leading to the main entrance and stepped through an open door. She looked around. A few of the workmen were sitting at a table they'd made with saw horses and a sheet of plywood. They were laughing and joking while eating their lunch. One by one, they stopped to look up.

The room was silent as all eyes were cast upon her. An older man stood. "May I help you with something, Miss?" he asked with a curious look on his face.

"Yes. I'm here to see Justin Scott. Is he here?"

The man gave a friendly smile. "Yeah. I believe he's still here. Last time I saw him, he was working on the fourth floor."

Another gentleman jumped in. "I was just working with him. He's still there. He's working in 410." Pointing behind him, he instructed, "The elevator's right past those doors. Just take it up to the fourth floor, and turn right when you get out. Apartment 410 is on the right hand side at the end of the hall. The doors are all numbered, so you can't miss it."

She smiled, graciously replying, "Thank you so much, gentleman, for your help." She began to walk in the direction of the elevators. And when she was no longer in sight, the workers began to laugh and joke with one another again.

Stepping out onto the fourth floor, she turned right, studying the door numbers as she made her way down the hall. Just as the gentleman had said, she could see number 410 in brass numbers on an open door near the end of the hall. She stepped into the space and glanced around to see if anyone was present. She didn't see Justin, but could tell that the space was still being worked on. The walls had been painted, but the floors were still concrete.

Walking to the middle of the room, she put the basket down on the floor and walked in a little farther. "Justin. Are you here?" she called out. Her voice echoed though the empty space with no reply. Walking around the room, she saw a table in one of the bedrooms with an electric saw on top, and a tool bag sitting nearby on the floor. Once again, she called out, "Justin—"

Justin responded from behind her.

Turning to face him, Catherine saw him standing in the doorway. He was a complete mess, covered in saw dust from his hair to his shoes.

"Catherine, what are you doing here?" he asked suspiciously.

"I called your secretary. She told me that you've been working here for the past week. I figured that you hadn't eaten lunch yet, so I decided to take matters into my own hands and stop by with food for you."

His mouth curled into a grin. "You brought me lunch?" Stroking his chin with his hand, he laughed. "What did you bring?"

"I don't know," she replied curiously. "I asked Lucio to prepare something for us and I haven't had the chance to look in the basket yet."

He walked over to the basket. "You mind if I peek?"

"Not at all. Go right ahead."

He wiped his hand on a towel. She moved closer. "I can't believe you did this for me," he said squatting beside the basket.

"Well, that's just the type of girl I am," she joked.

Catherine watched as he opened the lid and looked in.

She pressed, "So—what is it?"

"I don't know. It's in Styrofoam containers. All I see are two cokes." He stood, pointing toward the window. "We can eat on the window seat right over there?" Looking down at his dirty hands, he suggested, "Why don't you set us up while I go to wash my hands."

Agreeing, she smiled warmly, then picked up the basket and walked toward the window. She placed the basket on the window seat, then called out. "This is perfect. I wasn't sure if there would be any place comfortable for us to eat."

She finished taking the containers and utensils out of the basket, then looked up. Once again, Justin was standing in the doorway, watching her every move with the same boyish grin on his face.

"Oh, by the way, it's lasagna, a salad and bread," she revealed, lifting one of the lids. "I hope you like lasagna," she said curiously.

Justin laughed. "I'd eat anything for the chance to have lunch with you," he said jokingly. His face turned serious. "Yes," he admitted. "I love lasagna."

In the back of her mind, she thought he wasn't talking about lasagna, but about her. His comment should have made her feel uncomfortable, but she didn't feel that way at all. In fact, whenever they were together, she never felt nervous or uneasy. He had a way about him that made her feel relaxed every time they were together.

They sat close to each other on the sunny window seat, enjoying a pleasant lunch. While they were eating, she began to question him about his hands on approach to his job. Interrogating him, she asked, "Do you always help your contractors with manual labor?"

"No, I usually don't. But they were short a couple of men due to illness, so I said that I would help out." Nodding his head, he looked around the barren room. "This place is supposed to be finished by tomorrow morning."

"Really? By tomorrow morning," she repeated, looking around. "The whole building…?"

"It'll be finished before morning, even if we have to work all night," he grumbled, then explained. "The guy in charge of this project is a real clown and everybody just wants to finish so we won't have to deal with the likes of him anymore." He paused, and stared out the window. His jaw tightened. "I've known him for years, but this is the first time that I've ever had to work with him. And believe me, I never will again. The guy has the professional personality of a stick, and he doesn't give a damn about anyone except himself. He's only in it for the money…and the publicity."

She didn't know what to say. "I'm sorry to hear that you're having problems," she responded softly.

"It's okay. You learn from your mistakes. And believe me, I'll never work with him again and neither will any of the other guys around here," he stated firmly.

He turned back to look at her. His eyes softened. "I'm sorry. I shouldn't have clouded your visit with my sad story. It's just that he makes me really angry."

Gently, she reached for his hand. "I don't mind at all. That's what I'm here for. We're friends aren't we?"

Justin didn't say anything, but in his mind, he thought, *Friends, there's that word again. What does she mean by that? Does she mean that I don't have a chance in hell of being more than just friends with her, or does it mean that she just wants to be friends before anything more?*

Catherine broke the silence. "Is there anything that I can do to help?"

Justin smiled. "That's great of you to ask, but I don't think so. We'll get the job done, somehow."

They finished eating and Catherine began to put everything back in the basket. "Well, you have a lot of work to do, so I won't keep you any longer," she said.

He reached for her hand. "Thanks for lunch. It was really nice. And having you here was nice, too," he confided. He held her hand tightly, picking up the basket with his free hand, and guided her toward the door.

Catherine could feel the roughness from the calluses on his palms. She could tell that he'd been working hard, because his hands hadn't felt that way before. They'd always been a little rough from fishing, but never that bad.

Hand in hand, they walked toward the elevator and downstairs to her car. Justin watched as she fumbled through her purse for her keys. Finally, she found them and unlocked the door. Justin waited a moment, then leaned over, kissing her gently on the cheek, thanking her again. She took the basket from his hand and placed it on the passenger seat. Right before she got into the car, he mentioned that he would call over the weekend to plan a night out, and she agreed. He closed the door, then walked to the sidewalk, watching while she put the car in gear and drove away.

When Catherine returned to the office, she sat at her desk to finish some paperwork, but found her mind wandering instead. She neatly stacked a pile of file folders, then got up and walked over to the window.

Folding her arms across her chest, she looked out over the city. She began to think about what Justin had said about the man in charge of the project. She couldn't understand why he wasn't willing to delay the completion by a couple of days. Was it that important to him? What kind of man was he? Glaring out the window, her secretary's voice came over the intercom. "Excuse me, Catherine. Antoinette Drew is here to see you."

Smiling, she kindly instructed Kay to send her in.

She walked over to the door and opened it. In the hall, she saw Antoinette pacing toward her with a huge smile. When she got closer, Catherine held out her hands and hugged her tightly. "I'm so glad you stopped by," Catherine acknowledged.

She led her into the office and shut the door. "Oh, Antoinette. So much has been going on. I don't even know where to begin." She waved her hands in the air. "But let's talk about my problems later. What about you? How have you been? Would you like a glass of wine?" Catherine asked walking to the bar.

Antoinette could tell that something had happened because Catherine hadn't stopped talking since she arrived. "A glass of wine would be great," Antoinette replied, wondering what had her best friend so upset.

Antoinette sat down on the sofa while Catherine pulled out a bottle of Chablis. She pulled out the cork and poured two glasses. She went over and sat beside Antoinette, handing her a glass. "Now, I can't wait to here what's been happening in your life. Tell me everything. Are you still dating Hugh?" Catherine interrogated.

Antoinette's mouth curled into a smile. "Yes. I'm still dating Hugh. In fact, I have some wonderful news." She paused briefly to take a sip of wine.

Catherine leaned closer. "So—what is it? I can't handle the suspense?"

Antoinette didn't respond right away, so Catherine took a wild guess. "Wait. I know. You're getting married. Did Hugh ask you to marry him?" she blurted excitedly.

"Why is it that you're always able to read my mind?" Antoinette asked.

Tears flooded Catherine's eyes. "Oh, Antoinette. I'm so happy for you," she cried, hugging her. Catherine pulled away and smiled. "Have you set a date yet?"

"Yes. We plan to marry on Friday, March second. And how would you like to be my Matron of Honor?" Antoinette joyously asked.

Feeling cheerful, Catherine laughed. "I'd be honored to."

Antoinette changed the subject. "Now, that's enough about me. What about you? You left a message saying that you had a lot to talk to me about." In her motherly voice, she encouraged, "Just take your time and tell me everything that's happened to you since we last spoke." Antoinette got her started. "First, are you still seeing William?"

Catherine's face began to glow. "Yes. I've seen him a couple of times since Hugh's party." Then she went on to say, "You already know that I spent the night with him after the party?"

"Yes. That was the last time we spoke. What's happened since then?"

"When I arrived back in the office the following day, there were dozens of beautiful flower arrangements spread throughout my office. William had sent them along with a note asking me to have dinner with him. Of course, I agreed and later that evening he took me to his yacht."

"You mean his family's yacht?"

Catherine didn't like her tone. "No. It's his yacht," Catherine corrected. "His parents gave it to him as a birthday present." Catherine's face turned serious. "I know you're not happy that I'm dating him, but I can't help myself. There's a powerful connection between the two of us." Catherine held her hand to her chest. "It's there every time we're together. I can't explain it but I have an uncontrollable desire for him."

"So, you slept with him again? Didn't you?" Antoinette asked with a concerned look in her eyes.

"Yes. I did and I'm not ashamed of it," Catherine admitted boldly.

Catherine cleared her throat and continued. "Anyway...when he dropped me off from our date he said that he was going to San Francisco for a couple of weeks. While he was away the most wonderful thing happened, he sent a note instructing me to pack an evening gown and overnight clothes. Then he sent a car to pick me up and take me to the airport. When I arrived, I was whisked away to an unknown destination."

"Which turned out to be San Francisco?" Antoinette interrupted.

Trying to finish her story, Catherine sighed and went on, "Well, yes...and when I arrived, another car brought me to a glamorous hotel and up to a beautiful suite for the two of us. William wasn't in the room, but shortly after I arrived, I received another note. It said for me to dress and go down to the lobby where another car would be waiting for me. I was taken to a restaurant in the city. It turned out that William had rented the private dining room for the evening. A beautiful table had been set up on the balcony, and he had even hired an orchestra. It was wonderful. We had a wonderful dinner and danced the night away. Then he gave me the most beautiful diamond necklace. It was like a fairy tale…I couldn't believe it. We just returned this past Saturday, and yesterday he invited me to escort him to a party tomorrow night. That's pretty much it."

Unsure if she should give her opinion, Antoinette bit her bottom lip. She stood and walked to the window. She was silent for a moment, then she turned around to face Catherine. "You want my opinion, well here it is…You're sitting there telling me all about how William has wined and dined you. How he's taken you to secret destinations, fancy hotels and on and on…but these are all things that you can already do for yourself. Listening to you, you sound like a poor girl who's just been on a great adventure. I'm going to ask you a question, but before you answer, I want you to think long and hard about it."

Catherine's eyes widened as Antoinette posed her question. "Aside from sex and spending money on you, what else has William done for you?"

Catherine was stunned. She didn't respond.

Antoinette walked over and sat beside Catherine. Her voice softened as she spoke. "I'm not trying to hurt you. It's just that I've seen first hand how a woman who's smart and levelheaded can be taken by a man like William." Catherine stared blindly into Antoinette's eyes, and Antoinette continued. "You see, I was married to a man just like him. A man who wined and dined me…and promised me the moon and stars…"

Catherine interrupted. "But Daniel was after your money, William's not after mine."

Antoinette shifted her body close and reached for Catherine's hands. "It's not your money that I'm worried about. It's your heart…which is much more valuable."

With that said, Antoinette backed away and took a sip of wine, then she stood up and walked back over to the window. She knew it was time to change the subject. "So, what else has been happening?" Antoinette asked sweetly.

Catherine gulped a swig of wine. "Do you mean with Justin?"

"Yes. Have you spoken with him lately?"

At first, Catherine didn't want to talk with Antoinette about Justin, but she really needed the advice.

Staring down, Catherine began, "Yes. I have spoken with him. In fact, in between the time that I spent with William, I spent some time with Justin too." She smiled. "He showed up with a handful of daisies, then he took me out for an exquisite lunch. Later, he asked me to go to his cabin with him for the weekend, and I did."

Antoinette was astonished. "Wait a minute…You did what?…Did I hear you correctly? You went to his cabin for the weekend?"

"Yes, he took me on a fishing trip at his cabin and we had a lovely time."

With a happy expression on her face, Antoinette inquired, "What else?"

"If you're asking if we slept together, the answer is definitely not. Nothing happened. We're just good friends. In fact, I just came from having lunch with him and he was a perfect gentleman." She paused, then added, "There was only one really weird thing that happened, and it's probably nothing that I should be concerned about."

Antoinette listened intently. "While we were at the cabin, I was fumbling through a drawer looking for some note paper and I found a drawing of me."

"A drawing of you? You mean he drew a picture of you?"

"Yes. He drew a picture of me while I was sleeping on the sofa. When I woke, he hurried to put it away. Then, when I asked what he was doing, he told me he was working on a house plan for one of his clients."

"Did you ask him about it?"

Catherine's voice softened to a whisper. "No way. There was no way I was going to ask. I guess he just enjoys drawing sketches."

"You mean he enjoys drawing sketches of you. That means that he likes to look at you. Listen, I don't want to sound like your mother again, or be too harsh on you, but I have to tell you, I think he's in love with you."

"I know that you think he wants more, but we've talked about it and we both feel the same way. We're only friends and nothing more," Catherine insisted.

Antoinette sat down and touched the top of Catherine's hand. "Does Justin know that you're seeing William?"

"No. I haven't told him."

"You see, that's my point!"

Catherine sat quietly holding her hands in her lap. Lovingly, Antoinette asked, "Why do you think you haven't told him?"

Catherine didn't have an answer.

Antoinette set her glass on the table and stood. "Well, my darling. You have a lot of soul searching ahead of you, so I'm going to get out of your hair."

The two ladies embraced. Patting her on the back, Antoinette said, "Just think about what I've said. And please, don't rush into anything with William."

Catherine stood silently as Antoinette picked up her purse and walked out the office.

Once again, deep in thought, Catherine walked over to the window to look out. She mumbled, "Could Antoinette be right? Does Justin have serious feelings for me? I guess it's possible. I guess anything's possible."

Trying hard to decide whether there was any truth to what Antoinette had said, she began to think about the times she and Justin had spent together. The flowers, the romantic lunch setting, the way he always held her hands. In agony, she pressed her hand against her cheek, and thought about the night on the beach when he kissed her. Suddenly, it all came back. The way he'd held her close and gently kissed her neck while he warmed her at the cabin, the way he was always staring at her.

Ignoring any feelings she might have for Justin, she decided to tell him about William the next time they spoke.

The following evening, Catherine attended the party with William to celebrate the completion of his project. As they walked into the crowded room, William wore her on his arm like some sporting trophy he'd just won.

Stopping briefly, William kissed her on the cheek.

Glancing around the ballroom, Catherine's eyes focused on Justin standing across the room, staring directly at her. His gaze was sharp. Their eyes locked.

She couldn't believe it. What was he doing there?

While William turned to shake hands with two of his associates, Catherine whispered in his ear that she'd be back in a moment, then she walked away.

Nervously, she walked toward Justin. Just as she approached, she hurried to speak. "What are you doing here? I didn't expect to see you here tonight."

His voice cracked as he spoke. "Apparently not," he said. He looked away, then turned back. "Are you here with William?"

A lump formed in the back of her throat. "Yes," she uttered, finding it hard to swallow. She couldn't believe she'd gotten the word yes out.

Fidgeting with her purse, she waited for him to respond. He didn't speak.

She blinked and a single tear dropped from her long lashes. She stood still for a moment, then turned to see if William was watching, happy to see he wasn't. Not knowing what to say next, she stood silently while Justin's eyes pierced through her. She had never seen him like that before, not even the day before when he was so angry. She tried to explain. "I've wanted to tell you about William, but I couldn't bring myself to do it." She looked away, then turned to face him. "You know…The funny thing about this is that after we had lunch yesterday, I decided to tell you the next time we were together." Fighting tears, she paused for a moment. "Believe me, I had no idea you were going to be here. I didn't want you to find out this way. This was the last thing that I wanted."

Anger filled his eyes. He sipped his drink. "Did you know that William was the guy I was telling you about yesterday?" he questioned softly.

Surprised, she repeated. "William. You mean William's the man you were talking about?"

He put his hands in his pockets. "Yep, he's the one and only."

"Oh, Justin. I had no idea."

He felt deceived. "How long have you been dating him?" He just had to know.

She took a deep breath. "For the last couple of months," she whispered.

"The last couple of months," he repeated loudly. Those words had stunned him. His face turned red, and he shook his head. "I wish you would have told me."

Just as Catherine was about to respond, William walked up behind her, wrapping his arms around her waist. He kissed her on the neck. "Hello, Justin. I see you've had a chance to meet Catherine."

Staring into Catherine's wide eyes, Justin replied, "Actually, Catherine and I have been friends for a while."

William was suspicious. He turned to Catherine. "You never told me that you knew Justin?"

Her voice cracked. "Well, there really was no need to do so. Until tonight, I had no idea that the two of you even knew one another."

As if to send a message to Justin that she was his territory, William laid his hands on her shoulders. "By the way, did Justin tell you that he was my architect on the project we're celebrating tonight?"

Apprehensively, Catherine replied, "Yes. He just told me." Tears flooded her eyes. She looked at Justin. "I hope it came out the way you hoped?"

"It came out all right, but it would have come out much better if we would have had more time," he responded abruptly. He looked at the two of them. "Well, I've put in a lot of hours this past week, and I'm pretty tired so I think I'm going to go home now."

"So soon," snubbed William, "the party just started."

Justin put his hand out to shake William's hand. "Yes, I really have to get going," Justin said. "I just wanted to drop in for a little while to see everyone." He turned back to Catherine. "It was nice to see you again," he said, then turned to walk away.

William hugged Catherine from behind. "That was strange," he said. "Justin was acting as though his best friend had just died."

Catherine fought back the tears. "I don't know. He seemed fine to me. I think he was just tired." Catherine hated what had happened between she and Justin and she knew that somehow she had to explain. Holding her hand against her head, she turned to William. "I'm sorry," she said. "I have a headache coming on. If you don't mind, I'm going to go home too."

"How are you going to get home?"

"I'll just take a taxi."

"If you wait about a half an hour, I'll drive you. I just have to make a speech before we leave."

"No." Catherine replied, kissing him on the cheek. "I'll be all right. I'll talk to you later," she mumbled, then walked away.

Tears streamed down her cheeks as she dashed to the exit. Aware that William was watching her leave, she didn't look back. When she reached the elevator, she frantically pressed the down button. Finally, the doors opened. She rushed in, hitting the lobby button.

The elevator ride seemed to take forever.

When the doors finally opened, she rushed to the front entrance to try to catch Justin. Hurrying outside, she looked around on the sidewalk and on the street, but didn't see him anywhere. The valet attendant approached her. "Did you just deliver a white Land Cruiser to a gentleman with sandy blonde hair?" she asked in a quick tone.

The teenage boy replied, "Yes, he came for his truck, but then decided to have one last drink in the hotel bar before leaving."

"Thanks so much!" she exclaimed and ran back inside.

Walking into the bar, Catherine spotted Justin, sitting in a booth, with a dispirited look upon his face. She paced across the room to his table.

Her voice shuddered. "Justin, I'd like the chance to explain. Can I sit down with you for a few minutes?"

He looked up. "What's there to explain. We're just friends, right?"

Those words hit her hard and she felt as though he'd just stuck a dagger through her stomach. She put her hand on top of his. "I was going to tell you this weekend. It was only yesterday afternoon, after speaking with Antoinette, that I realized you might want more from me than just my friendship. The last thing I wanted was for you to find out this way."

With sorrow in his eyes, he said, "You know, a few months ago, William told me all about this wonderful woman he was dating, but I had no idea it was you. All this time and you never told me. You only said that you weren't ready for a serious relationship. You never said that you were seeing someone. I thought there was still hope for us. I thought something really special was happening between us...I mean, I really enjoy your company and I thought that you enjoyed mine, too."

"I do...I really do, and that's why I feel so bad," she replied in anguish.

Justin took a deep breath and shrugged. "Is it serious?" he asked.

She was hesitant to reply. "Yes. It has been pretty serious. I wanted to tell you so many times, but I was afraid that I would lose your friendship."

Glancing around the bar, he thought for a moment. He raised his voice. "I don't want to lose your friendship either, so I guess I don't have a choice. I'll have to accept it for now, but that doesn't mean I like it. Because I don't." Concerned for her, he continued, "You better go back to the party or William will get suspicious."

"I'm not going back. I told him that I wasn't feeling well, and I was going home. I just want to go home."

Justin reached down, tightly clasping her hand, and together they stood up and slowly made their way to the front entrance of the hotel. When they got to the valet area, he handed his ticket to the attendant, then turned to her. "Did you drive tonight?" he asked sweetly.

"No. I'm going to take a taxi."

"You'll do no such thing. I'll take you home," he demanded.

"Are you sure? I don't want to put you out."

"I don't mind. Unlike William, I want to make sure that you get home safely," he said sternly.

"Thanks," she whispered.

When Justin's truck arrived, the attendant opened the door and Catherine got in. As soon as Justin got in, he turned on the radio.

During the ride, neither said a word. What else was there to say.

When they arrived in her driveway, Justin looked over. Tears were rolling down Catherine's cheeks. He tried to console her. "Are you all right?"

Wiping the tears away with her hands, she turned to face him. "Yes, I'm fine," she mumbled.

It hurt him to see her cry. He leaned over, pulling a white handkerchief out of his back pocket. "Here you are," he said. "You can use this to dry your eyes."

She accepted the handkerchief and wiped her face, then she opened the door. "Thanks for the ride," she said.

Not knowing what to say, Justin got out of the truck and raced around to walk her to the door.

Catherine didn't want this night to end so badly. "Would you like to come in for a cup of coffee or something?" she sniffled as they approached the door.

Much to her surprise, he agreed.

Justin stood by silently while she unlocked the door. After turning on the lights, she led him into the den. "Why don't you have a seat and I'll make a pot of coffee for us," she directed.

He didn't want to leave her side. "If it's all right with you, I'd like to come with you," he said, and she agreed.

They walked into the kitchen and Justin sat at the bar while Catherine put the coffee and water in the coffeemaker. After she finished, she turned around slowly, nervously rubbing her hands together. Justin stood and walked toward her. "How do you like your coffee?" she asked.

He didn't answer. Instead, he took a chance, shifting his body close to hers. She clutched the countertop behind her. Leaning into her, he whispered, "I take mine black," as he softly kissed her on her lips. She hadn't pulled away from him, so he took that as a good sign. *There's still a chance*, he thought.

Justin pulled away from her. "You know what? I think I'll pass on the coffee after all. It's pretty late and I need to get some sleep," he quickly said, then turned to leave.

Catherine followed him to the foyer and watched as he opened the door and left.

Baffled by what had happened, she realized that she had a lot to think about. Her mind had been flooded with a mixture of emotions she'd never felt before.

CHAPTER 12

❁

In order to clear their calendars for the trip to Monte-Carlo, Catherine and William decided it would be best if they didn't see each other during the week, but they did manage to speak each night before retiring to bed.

During those conversations, they talked about the trip and how much they were both looking forward to going. William told her over and over again, how much he couldn't wait. Even though she still had mixed emotions about Justin, she decided to go forward with her plans to travel to Monte-Carlo. And because she hadn't heard from Justin since the night of the party, she found that pretty easy to do.

On Friday, Catherine called William to invite him over for a romantic dinner at her house for the following evening. She suggested having it at her home, not only to be alone with him, but because she wanted to find out more about him. They had never really spoken about their families, dreams, or life outside of the bedroom. She wanted to know more, and it seemed like the perfect time to talk.

Catherine awoke to a beautiful day. She had gone to bed early the night before and felt good. As she sat up in bed, she was blinded by the sun's rays glaring through the windows of her bedroom. Dressed in a long ivory silk nightgown, she stretched her arms above her head, then got out of bed. She put on her matching robe and opened the doors leading onto her balcony. She continued to stretch as she stepped outside taking a deep breath of the fresh morning air. She slowly walked to the edge of the balcony and leaned over gently laying her forearms on top of the stone railing to enjoy the view. She stood motionless, until she was interrupted by her housekeeper's voice calling from the garden below.

Looking down, she saw Maria standing in the middle of the flower garden. "Good Morning, Miss Catherine. I just made a fresh pot of coffee, if you're interested."

Standing tall, Catherine replied, "Thanks Maria, I'll be down in a minute," then turned to go downstairs.

She headed straight for the coffee. Maria came through the back door with a handful of fresh flowers.

"Good Morning, Maria. Isn't it a beautiful day?" Catherine said.

Smiling warmly, Maria agreed. "Yes, and the temperature's perfect this morning. I got up early and went for a walk and then I decided to pick some flowers for the kitchen counter."

"That was a wonderful idea," Catherine replied with a smile. "The flowers are beautiful…By the way, I need your help with something."

"Oh, what is it, Miss Catherine?" she inquired.

"Well, I have a dinner date tonight here at the house and I need some menu suggestions. I know that you have the night off, so I'm planning to cook dinner myself. And as you already know, I'm not the greatest cook in the world!"

In a concerned voice, Maria said, "I don't mind staying to cook for you."

"No way, Maria. I know that you have plans with your family for the weekend and there's no way I would intrude on that. Just pull out a couple of recipe cards and I'll do the rest."

Maria raised her brows. She was worried. "Okay. I guess if you make sure to follow the recipes step by step, you should be all right.

But if you have any questions, just give a me call and I'll try to help you over the telephone."

Waving her hand, Catherine laughed, "Oh, Maria. I'll be fine. How hard can it be? All I have to do is follow instructions on the recipes. I don't think I can mess that up."

Still worried, Maria walked over to her recipe file. She flipped through the cards, then began to set a few aside. "Here we are," she said, gathering the cards in her hands. "You can make filet mignon with rice pilaf and a salad. That would be easy for you to do. As long as you follow my directions exactly."

"Don't I have to light the grill to make steaks?" Catherine asked.

"No, filets are better if you sear them over the stove and then put them in a warm oven to continue to cook. Why don't we sit down and I'll make a grocery list. And if you like, I can go shopping before I leave."

"No, that's all right Maria. I can handle shopping," Catherine insisted.

Sitting at the kitchen table, Maria pulled out three cards, explaining each recipe while she made the grocery list.

After they finished, Catherine quickly stood. "Thanks so much, Maria. I have to get dressed to go to the grocery store and butcher shop now, because I will need the entire afternoon to prepare for my dinner."

Catherine walked Maria to the back door. "Well, I'm going to head home now," Maria said. "Remember, just call if you need any help. I'll be home until eight o'clock."

They shared a giggle as Maria walked away. "Have a great weekend with your family," Catherine shouted from the back door, then turned to go upstairs.

Catherine went to the grocery store and the butcher shop as planned, purchasing everything on the list. On the way home, she stopped by a local flower shop to order flowers to be delivered in the afternoon.

As she drove through the city running errands, she couldn't help but feel excited about the evening she had planned. It had been a long time since she had invited anyone for a romantic candlelit dinner at her house, and an even longer time since she cooked without anyone's help.

Arriving home, she unloaded the groceries, prepared the kitchen for cooking and set the dining room table with her best china, silverware and crystal glasses. She pulled out two bottles of wine, setting them aside on the table.

She went upstairs to take a bath and get dressed. After she took a bath, she put on her terry cloth bathrobe and went through her closet to find something to wear. She pulled out a pretty lavender sweater set, a black crepe skirt, and a nice pair of black pumps. She dried and set her hair and put on her makeup, then finished by dressing in her outfit and pinning her shiny brown hair up into an elegant twist.

William was supposed to arrive at seven, so she only had an hour and a half to cook. Rushing downstairs, she heard a knock on the door. It was the delivery man with the flowers that she'd ordered. When she opened the door, she couldn't believe her eyes. The florist had done an amazing job. They had made three arrangements with roses in a variety of beautiful shades of pink; one for the center piece, one for the den and one for the buffet table in her dining room.

After the delivery man left, she set the flowers on the tables and hurried to the kitchen. She cooked, following each recipe card, step by step, word for word. She seasoned and set the filets out on the counter, she cut vegetables and seasonings for the rice pilaf, putting it on the stovetop to cook, then tore lettuce for a Caesar salad. She grated some fresh Parmesan cheese, made her Caesar dressing, and cubed bread to make homemade croutons. Everything was perfect, with one exception, it was now quarter after seven and William still hadn't arrived.

While waiting, she opened a bottle of the wine, and poured herself a glass. Sipping her wine, she walked into the den. Although it wasn't cold outside, she decided to light a fire anyway to set the mood. When she finished, she looked at her diamond watch again. It was seven-thirty and William still hadn't arrived. She called his house, but there was no answer. Figuring he was on his way, she went back into the kitchen to sear the filets in butter, then did exactly what Maria had said by putting them in a warm oven to continue to cook. A few minutes after she put them in the oven, the telephone rang. Thinking it was William, she rushed to the phone.

She picked up the receiver, hearing the voice of a woman on the other end. It was Maria calling to check on her.

"Dinner's going great," Catherine said. "The rice and salad are finished and they taste wonderful. I just seared the steaks and put them in the oven to continue to cook. Everything's going great with the food, but unfortunately, my date hasn't arrived yet…"

Maria didn't respond immediately. "Your date isn't there yet…oh my…when do you expect him?"

"Any minute now, I hope. I haven't heard from him."

"I hope he gets there soon. The filets won't take long to cook, and if he likes his close to rare, his might overcook," she pointed out.

"Overcook?" Catherine repeated. "Should I have waited to cook them?"

"Yes, I always wait until the last minute because they don't take long to cook." Reassuring her, Maria added, "But I'm sure they'll be fine."

"I hope so," Catherine said eagerly. Just at that moment, the doorbell rang. "I have to go," she told Maria. "He's at the door now."

They hung up, and she rushed to the door. Upon opening the door, she was surprised to see that it wasn't William. It was Justin. He looked handsome, wearing a pair of black slacks and a white polo shirt. He smiled. "Hi, I just got back in town and decided to take a chance on your being home." Nervously putting his hands in his pockets, he commented, "Wow, you look beautiful. I hope I'm not intruding on anything?"

Catherine stood motionless. She blushed. "No, you're not intruding. I'm alone right now, but I am expecting William for dinner," she mentioned.

She backed away from the entrance, and opened the door for him to enter. "I'm sorry. Where are my manners? Please come in. I was just having a glass of wine, would you like to join me?"

"Sure," Justin replied as she led him to the den.

Walking down the steps, Justin stopped. "Do you think it's all right that I'm here?" he questioned. "I don't want to stir up any trouble between you and William."

"No. It's fine. William won't mind," she said, walking toward the bar. "So, tell me about your trip," she said. "Where did you go?"

"I went skiing and hiking in the Cascade Mountains with a buddy of mine. We had a pretty good time."

"You can't ask for anything more than that. I'm glad you had a good time. You deserved to relax after all the work you did on those condominiums."

Curiously, he asked, "What about you? What have you been doing?"

Catherine sighed. "I've been putting in a lot of hours at the office. I'm going out of town for Thanksgiving and I'm trying to clear my calendar before I leave."

Throughout their conversation, Justin noticed that she kept checking the time on her watch. Rubbing his hands together, he popped the big question. "So, when's William suppose to get here?"

Catherine stood and paced. "He was supposed to be here an hour ago. I hope he's all right," she said in a concerned voice.

He tried to ease her mind. "He's probably just stuck in traffic."

Just as she began to reply, the telephone rang. Excusing herself, she went to answer in the hallway. The call turned out to be William explaining that something important had come up and he couldn't make it after all.

Catherine angrily raised her voice. "Something important, huh? I've been waiting for an hour now. Why didn't you call me sooner?" she asked firmly.

"I was on my way to your house when I got the telephone call. I'm sorry for not calling sooner." In a loving voice, he said, "I promise to make it up to you."

Nothing that William could say would make her feel any better. "Listen," she remarked, "a friend of mine just stopped by. Why don't we talk about this tomorrow?" She hurried to say good-bye and hung up.

She didn't realize it, but Justin was able to hear part of the conversation. From what he could tell, he knew that William wasn't coming, and she was pretty upset.

Walking back into the living room, she said, "That was William. It seems that something important came up and he can't make it after all." She took a sip of wine. "Are you hungry? I spent the afternoon cooking a wonderful meal and it would be a pity to throw it away."

"Yes. I'm pretty hungry. I'd love to stay. As long as you're sure you don't mind."

"Not at all. I just hope that the filets aren't overcooked. They've been in the oven for a while now."

Catherine led Justin into the dimly lit dining room. He noticed how beautiful the table looked with the exception of the candles. She'd lit them earlier, and they'd already burned halfway down. The wax was dripping down the candlesticks, so he walked over and blew them out.

With her glass of wine in hand, Catherine walked to the kitchen and Justin followed close behind. She immediately walked to the oven, pulling out the tray to check the filets. Maria told her to use her finger to check their doneness, so she did. Pressing down firmly with her pointer finger, the meat didn't budge. It was as tough as a piece of leather. Justin watched as her eyes flooded with emotion.

Reassuring her, he said, "It's all right. We don't have to eat meat. What else did you make?"

She pointed to the stove. "I have rice pilaf on the burner and a Caesar salad on the counter."

Justin walked over to the pot and opened the cover. He could tell by looking, the rice had turned mushy, but he decided not to tell her. "This is fine," he said in an encouraging tone. "We can have the rice with a salad. That's perfect."

He picked up the pot of rice. "Why don't you take the salad and I'll carry the rice," he said, and then he walked into the dining room. Catherine paused for a moment, then grabbed the bowl of salad. When she walked into the dining room she saw that Justin was already seated at the table. "Now, this isn't so bad," he said.

She smiled slightly, and sat down beside him, setting the salad beside the pot of rice. She picked up Justin's plate and scooped a spoonful of rice out of the pot. It stuck to the serving spoon as she tried to release it onto his plate. "Oh, Justin, this rice is really gooey," she said grimly.

"I like gooey rice," Justin replied in an upbeat tone, hoping to make her feel better. He took the spoon from her hand, and used a knife to scrape it off of the spoon. He put a spoonful in her plate, then served the salad.

Catherine took a couple of bites of salad and a sip of wine. The corner's of her mouth curled up in a smile; but at the same time she broke out in tears. "I'm sorry. I don't think I'm hungry after all," she said. "I did so much work to prepare for tonight, and it's ruined. Everything is ruined. How could he do this to me?" she cried out.

Consoling her, Justin shifted his chair closer. He reached for her hand. "I'm sorry. I'm so sorry that he did this to you," he whispered.

While he held her hands, she put her head down on his shoulder, crying even more than before. Wiping the tears from her eyes with her napkin, she looked up. "I'm sorry, Justin. I don't want to get you involved. I'll be okay. I think I just need to be alone."

"Are you sure you're going to be all right?"

"I'll be fine," she said quietly. "I'm sure he has a good reason. I didn't give him the chance to explain," she added, making excuses for William's behavior.

Justin didn't feel the same way, but he decided to agree with her. "Maybe there's a good reason," he said, then stood up. "Well, I guess I'll head out. Is it all right if I call tomorrow to check on you?"

"Sure. Give me a call tomorrow. I'll be here," she said, leading him to the front door.

As she opened the door, she kissed him softly on the cheek. "Thanks for listening. You're such a good friend," she said.

Justin walked to his truck, got in, and started the engine, but he didn't drive away. He wanted desperately to walk back inside to make things right. He knew that if given the chance, he could show her the true meaning of love. He wanted her to see that William wasn't the right man for her. He wanted her to see that he was. Those were the things he wanted to do, but he couldn't. Leaving William would have to be her decision.

Catherine put the dishes in the sink and went upstairs to take a hot bath. When she stepped out of the tub, she heard the doorbell ringing. It was late in the evening, and she wondered who it could be.

She hurried to put her robe on, then walked down the hall to look out the window. Peering through the sheer draperies, she saw William's car parked in the driveway.

She went downstairs and opened the door. He was holding a handful of long stemmed roses with a "little lost boy" expression on his face. Handing her the flowers, he gently kissed her. "I'm so sorry for wrecking our evening," he said.

She led him into the den. "What happened?" she asked.

Hastily, he explained. "It was my mother. My mom and dad are in town visiting. She started to have chest pains, and we thought she was having a heart attack. We had to rush her to the hospital." His voice settled down. "It turned out to be a bad case of indigestion but it scared us half to death."

Catherine interrupted, "Wait a minute, your parents are in town?"

"Why yes. Didn't I tell you?"

"No. You didn't tell me. How long are they staying?" she asked.

"Actually, they're leaving tomorrow morning," he answered as if he'd done nothing wrong.

"I wish you would have told me. I would have liked to meet them," she pressed angrily. He didn't respond. He stood back, smiling with that same "little boy" look on his face. "Well, I do have some good news," he said.

Catherine scowled. "Oh, yeah. What's that?"

It didn't bother William that she was annoyed. "Earlier today, I told my parents all about the wonderful woman I've been seeing. And they were happy for me." He smiled and walked closer.

Catherine didn't want to stir up a fight, so she decided to drop the subject. "Well, I'm glad your mom's all right," she said kindly.

"Me too," he said, pulling her close. He encircled his arms around her body. "Did you miss me tonight?" he asked.

Catherine could see where the conversation was leading. Still angry, the last thing that she wanted was to make love. She pulled away. "You know," she explained. "I'm really tired. I think I just want to get some sleep." She walked over to the bar and poured a glass of water. "Were you planning on spending the night?" she asked coldly.

"Yes, I thought I would," he replied. "My bag's in the car. I'll run out to get it and meet you upstairs."

Tired, she nodded in agreement, and walked toward the winding staircase.

When she got to the bedroom, she took off her robe, put on a nightgown and slipped into bed. She heard William's footsteps when he walked into the room. She listened carefully as he went into the bathroom. A few minutes later, he came out. She didn't want to talk, so she pretended to be asleep when he crawled into bed.

Early the following morning, Catherine was awakened by the clapping of thunder from an approaching rainstorm. She rolled over, and felt for William, but he was gone. She got out of the bed and went to the bathroom to brush her teeth and comb her hair. Then she put on her robe and went downstairs.

When she walked into the kitchen she could hear the sound of water running. She peeked around the corner, noticing William standing beside the sink filling a slender crystal vase. She walked to the coffee pot. "Morning," she mumbled without looking at him.

He turned around. "Good Morning. I was just getting ready to bring breakfast up to you. I thought you might enjoy eating in bed this morning." He walked over to kiss her.

"Thanks, that was sweet of you," she said without smiling.

She was being cold and William took notice. "I hope you're not still angry with me?" he pressed.

"No. I'm not angry. I'm just disappointed that it took so long for you to call last night." Once again, she wanted to refrain from starting a fight so she kindly asked, "Are you going to the airport with your parents this morning?"

"No. We said good-bye last night," he said. "I'm yours for the day. What do you want to do?" he asked.

"I guess we can't really do anything with the bad weather," she replied. She took a sip of coffee. "I have some work that I have to finish today, then I thought I would just curl up with a good book."

William pulled her closer. "A good book," he repeated. "I had something else in mind," he said while kissing her neck.

Normally, she would have melted in his arms, but somehow his kiss didn't have the same affect. And, he too, could tell that something had changed. His face darkened, and he pulled away.

She didn't want to look into his eyes. "I think I'm going to go upstairs to take a shower," she said while turning away.

"What about breakfast?" he asked inquisitively.

"I'm not really hungry. I'll get something a little later," she said as she paced down the hall.

While she was upstairs, the telephone rang. Catherine didn't answer, so William did. "Sheldon Residence." For a moment, silence filled the telephone line. "William?" the man on the other end asked.

"Yes, this is William."

"Hey, Will. This is Justin Scott. Is Catherine around?"

"She's taking a shower right now. Can I give her a message?"

"Just let her know that I called."

"I'll tell her," he snubbed, lowering the receiver. *Why in the hell is he calling*, he thought. He knew that Catherine and Justin were friends, but he didn't know that they spoke over the telephone. He thought they just socialized at parties.

When Catherine returned downstairs, she walked into the kitchen, and called out for William. He didn't answer. From across the room, she saw one of his famous notes taped to the refrigerator. It simply said;

∞

Catherine,

I had to run out for a meeting. I'll call you later.

By the way, Justin Scott called for you.

William

She couldn't believe it. First, he hadn't called to cancel dinner, then he didn't tell her that his parents were in town, and now he left without saying good-bye. Although she was furious that he had left so suddenly, somewhere in her mind, she was also relieved. Even though she said she wasn't, she was still angry with him.

When the rain finally ended, Catherine picked up her cordless telephone and went outside to call Justin. His line rang three times. Just as she was getting ready to hang up, he answered.

"Hi. It's me," she said in a low voice.

"Hi, me. How are you feeling today?" he asked enthusiastically.

"A lot better. Thanks for asking."

"I called earlier and William answered. I guess he finally showed up last night?"

"Yes, he did."

"What was his excuse this time?" he asked bitterly.

Against her better judgment, she divulged William's excuse. "He said they had to rush his mother to the hospital. They thought she was having a heart attack."

"Was it a heart attack?" Justin questioned.

"No. It only turned out to be a bad case of indigestion."

"That figures. She probably faked it to keep him away from you."

"What do you mean?" she asked curiously.

"She's always done those kinds of things. I didn't tell you, but William and I lived in the same frat house in college."

"I had no idea."

"Well, anyhow. His mom was always doing things like that whenever he was dating anyone. You know…no one was ever good enough for her baby. He moved all the way across the country to get away from her, but he still couldn't." Justin stopped talking. "I think I've said enough," he said realizing he'd probably said too much.

"Well, I'm glad everything turned out okay after all."

After a moment of silence, Catherine changed the subject. "What's going on with you today?"

"Not too much. The weather is so dreary, I thought I'd read a good book."

Catherine giggled. "I was thinking about doing the same thing," she admitted. "But listen, I have a better idea. How would you like to go to see a movie with me instead? I heard that there are some good ones out right now."

"A movie sounds great. What if I pick you up in about an hour?" Justin said eagerly.

Catherine was ready to get out. "If you like, you can come right now."

She didn't have to ask twice. "Then, I'll be over in a little while," Justin said.

A half hour later, Catherine heard a knock on the door. Peeking out the sidelight, she saw that it was Justin. *Boy, he didn't waste any time. He must have flown*, she thought.

She saw his bright smiling face when she opened the door. She'd been feeling depressed about what had happened with William, but Justin's smile always made her feel better.

She swung the door back. "Hi. Come in. I just have to grab my purse," she mentioned walking toward her study.

Justin stepped into the foyer to wait. The phone began to ring as she paced toward him. "Don't worry about that," she waved, walking out the door. "I'm going to let my machine pick up. I'm sure it's nothing important."

As Justin locked the door, he heard William's voice over the speaker. He was stunned when she didn't run back inside to talk to him. He wondered what had happened. For her to not pick up, they must have had an argument.

They spent the rest of the day together. They saw a movie, then decided to go out for Chinese food. The evening was perfect. Justin was such a gentleman and a great conversationalist. Unlike she and William, they always found things to talk about.

On their way back to her house, Justin asked if she wanted to spend Thanksgiving with him. Her face turned sour. She was scared to tell him the truth. But she had to.

She swallowed hard, then in a sorrowful voice said, "I'm sorry, Justin. I'm supposed to spend Thanksgiving with William in Monte-Carlo."

"Monte-Carlo!" he blurted. "Who spends Thanksgiving in Monte-Carlo?"

She could tell that he was upset so she tried to lighten the moment. "Well, I guess I will be this year!" she answered jokingly, as he pulled his truck into the driveway.

Justin didn't laugh.

Discouraged, he stared forward, shifted into park, and turned off the engine. He waited a moment, then turned to look at her. She sunk into the seat, feeling like a child waiting to be reprimanded by an adult. Unable to look him in the eyes, she pulled the handle to open the door. Quietly, she pushed the door open. Justin touched her shoulder. "It's all right," he said. "We can plan to do something together when you get back from your trip."

Relieved that he understood, tears welled in her eyes. She turned to him, and smiled, then she stepped out of the truck.

Justin got out and walked Catherine to the front door. They looked at each other, but neither said a word.

Catherine broke the silence, thanking him for the splendid day. Then without any warning, she moved toward him, surprising him with a gentle kiss on the cheek.

He started to say something, but changed his mind at the last minute. "Well, have a good time on your trip," he said sweetly, and turned away.

Once again, Justin had allowed her to slip away with another man.

CHAPTER 13

❀

Catherine stepped out of the elevator and made a turn down the hall toward her office. Her secretary, Kay, was standing in the doorway with a strange expression on her face. "What is it?" Catherine asked suspiciously.

Kay shook her head. "You're not going to believe it," she said.

Passing Kay, Catherine entered the office. "Oh, my. He did it again," she said in amazement, walking into an office filled with flower arrangements. Stepping closer, she noticed that each arrangement had an "I'm sorry" note attached. She gently tugged a pink rose out of one of the bouquets and lifted the soft petals to her nose. Breathing deeply, she closed her eyes. The fragrance softened her heart.

She opened her eyes and glanced around the room. A single tear fell from her lashes and streamed down her cheek. "I can't believe he did this again," she said.

"I'm happy to see you like them," a voice announced from the doorway.

Turning around, she saw William with a "lost puppy dog" expression on his face. "I'm sorry," he said, walking inside. "Is there any way you can find it in your heart to forgive me?" he asked, shutting the door behind him.

She slowly moved toward him. Laying her hands on his masculine shoulders, she gave him a big hug. As she pulled away, he shifted closer, kissing her slowly at first, then more passionately. "Yes, William. I forgive you," she whispered against his lips. "I've been thinking about what happened, and it was foolish of me to get that upset. Can you forgive me?"

"There's nothing to forgive you for. I'm the one who screwed up. I should have taken an extra minute to call you. I know that now, and it'll never happen again. I promise."

William embraced her tightly. "I'm so glad we're okay," he said. "I was afraid I was going to lose you. And I don't want to lose you. You're the best thing that's ever happened to me."

Once again, they shared a passionate, wet kiss, causing Catherine's body temperature to rise. She was ready to make love to him right there in her office, but William surprised her by asking if she wanted to take the day off to go to his loft.

Willingly, she agreed.

Catherine thought that going to his home, instead of hers, was a huge step in their relationship, and it meant a lot to her. He was finally ready to open his life to her.

When they arrived at his loft, William snapped the front door shut and gently pushed Catherine's back against the door frame. His hands wandered up to her thighs, beneath her skirt. She was hot, moist. Kissing her neck, he moved his hands across her firm buttocks, up to her waist. He slid his hands into her panties, and lowered them to the floor. His lips melted against the skin on her neck while he unzipped her skirt, it fell on the floor. He gripped her hand and led her toward the bedroom. In the hall, they stopped for a moment. Now it was her turn. Never losing eye contact, she unbuttoned his shirt, then pushed it over his masculine shoulders. He smiled while she stooped down to unzip his pants, lowering them to his ankles. Taking her hands, he pulled her up, and gently pushed her back against the other wall while he stepped out of them. Taking her hand once again, he continued to lead her into the bedroom. Once inside, William watched intently as Catherine walked backwards to the bed and sat down, never once losing eye contact with him. With sultry eyes, she slowly unbuttoned her blouse and gently pushed it off her shoulders. With nothing more than her thigh highs and her bra on, she eyed him and he moved closer. Kneeling down beside the bed, he lifted her legs, one at a time, taking his time to roll the hosiery off of her long, lean legs. When he finished, she smiled. Her body burned for him.

Aware of each others desires, they made love, savagely, over and over again, both clinging desperately to one another. Their passion was unlike any other time they'd been together, every touch more tantalizing than the one before.

That afternoon, Catherine gave herself completely to William, her whole self, body and soul. Now it was clear, she belonged with him. Her future was with him.

After their last bout of love making, Catherine fell asleep cradled in William's arms. When she awoke, she looked over, noticing that he had fallen asleep. Rolling close to him, she studied his face. She hadn't noticed it before, but he had crow's feet around the corner of his eyes, probably from being in the sun so often. She smiled, thinking they made him look distinguished. She kissed the top of his shoulder, and he moved slightly. Trying not to disturb him, she slithered out of the bed and walked to his closet. Pulling out one of his white dress shirts, she put it on, then she sat in the leather chair beside the bed to watch while he slept. He looked relaxed, peaceful.

Her stomach started to make rumbling noises. She was hungry.

Standing up, she tiptoed out of the bedroom, following the trail of clothes leading to the front door, picking up hers as she went along.

They'd been so busy undressing one another when they had arrived, she realized she hadn't even had time to look around his apartment. She decided to take a tour.

It was a spacious apartment, an old converted warehouse, with beautiful wood floors, brick walls and high ceilings. It was clean, with plenty of light shining through the large uncovered windows.

She went into the kitchen. Rooting through several cabinets, she stumbled upon a jar of peanut butter and a loaf of bread. She made a peanut butter sandwich, then opened the refrigerator to get a glass of milk. He didn't have any. The refrigerator was empty, with the exception of a couple of beers and two bottles of spring water. She pulled a bottle of water out. She sat down on one of the metal bar stools and continued to browse around the open space while she ate.

When she finished, she went into the living room. She caught a glimpse of his CD collection neatly arranged on a stand in the corner of the room and walked over to where it was. She fumbled through the jewel cases, trying to find out what type of music interested him. She continued to walk around the loft, studying his fine art collection hanging on the walls.

She'd always heard that you can tell a lot about a person by looking at their home. And that proved to be right. By just glancing around, she discovered that he was a modern art enthusiast, he loved opera and classical music, and he kept his space neat and uncluttered.

Her eyes were drawn to a beautiful impressionist painting of a nude couple entwined in a sexual position. She decided to take a closer look. Leaning closer to the painting, she heard his voice from behind, "Do you like it?" he questioned.

Slowly, she turned around to face him. "Yes. It's beautiful."

She watched intently as he walked closer, dressed only in a pair of blue jeans. His brown eyes sparkled. His voice became intense. "It's my favorite. I found it on one of my trips to Italy and I just had to have it," he explained.

They stood beside one another eyeing the painting. "Did you sleep well?" he asked softly.

"Yes. Very well," she replied staring forward, then she turned to him.

He pointed to the kitchen counter. "I see you found my stash of peanut butter."

"Yes. I hope you don't mind."

"I don't mind at all," he said, then he walked over to the window, leaving her behind. She studied his movements while he stared out the picturesque window. Walking up behind him, she gazed out. The sun was setting over the city.

"It's pretty, isn't it?" she whispered against the back of his neck.

He turned to face her, boxing her in with his arms. Grinning, he pressed his chest against hers. "Yes. It is," he said in a low tone. Their lips melted together. "By the way, what do you want to do tonight?" he asked.

Without giving her a chance to respond, he wrapped his arms around her waist, and they engaged in a soft, warm kiss. "I was thinking that we could stay in tonight?" he suggested, pressing his hard, hot body against hers. Without answering in words, she stroked his arms with her fingertips and pressed her velvety lips against his. Gently, she nibbled at his lips, his mouth opened and their tongues entwined in a soft, delicate kiss. "I see you found one of my shirts," he whispered against her lips, his tone low, soft. His hands wandered beneath it. Her heart pounded through her chest while he gently stroked the soft skin of her hips. Closing her eyes, he glided his hands up to her firm stomach, then across her soft skin to her breasts. Anxiously anticipating what was to happen next, she took hold of his hand and guided him back into the bedroom. Once again, she surrendered to him.

Over the next four days, Catherine practically moved into William's loft. And by the end of the fourth night, her heart was filled with new and wonderful emotions where William was concerned.

She'd never been so happy.

William's limousine pulled up to Catherine's house to pick her up for their trip to Monte-Carlo. Excited, she ran out to greet him while his chauffeur loaded her luggage. "I can't believe we're going to Monte-Carlo," she exclaimed, sliding onto the leather seats of the limousine.

"I can't believe you've never been there," William said as the car pulled away from her house.

"No," she said. "But you have to understand, I usually mix my personal trips with business, and I've never had any business in Monte-Carlo."

William began to reminisce. "I made my first trip to Monaco right after I graduated from high school and I've gone there every year since then," he boasted. She listened to every word as he described Monaco to her in vivid detail. "It's my favorite place in the entire world!" he added happily.

The trip was a long one, taking a full twenty-four hours, with a connecting flight in New York that took them to Nice, France. When they arrived in Nice, they took a five minute helicopter flight to Monte-Carlo, giving them a picturesque view of the heart of the Riviera.

When the helicopter landed, they were whisked away in a black stretch limousine. As the car approached the hotel, the driver entered a narrow, winding driveway surrounded by palm trees towering over the well-kept lawns and shrubbery. Catherine looked up, seeing the large white building decorated with frescoes set against an infinite blue sky.

Entering the hotel lobby, Catherine was overwhelmed by its beauty. "It's like a palace!" she exclaimed, seeing the grandeur of the marble columns and crystal chandeliers. The atmosphere, intimate, unforgettable.

While William checked in, Catherine strolled around the lobby, taking pleasure in viewing the exquisite paintings that graced the walls surrounding her. A few minutes later, they were escorted up to their spacious suite.

Catherine should have been weary from the trip, but she was full of energy. William watched as she rushed over to open the doors leading out to the terrace. She walked to the edge of the balcony and drew a deep breath. "The view is breathtaking," she remarked, looking out over the deep blue waters of the Mediterranean. William put his arm snugly around her waist to point out other sites of interests. Off in the distance, her eyes were captivated by the Prince's Palace, and the old town of Monaco. She looked to the left, seeing the mountains in the background. And down below, the luxurious yachts docked in the harbor. "I've never seen anything this incredible." She looked up at the sky. "I'm trying to decide what color the sky is," she pointed out. "It looks like a mixture of indigo and turquoise."

Seeing how happy she was, William laughed. "I'm happy you like it," he said, then he turned to go back inside to get the bottle of champagne and the two glasses that had been delivered prior to their arrival.

Under the shade of the terrace, Catherine and William relished in the panoramic view of the Riviera while drinking their champagne.

After drinking half a glass of champagne, Catherine started to get lightheaded. Jet lag had caught up with her.

Excusing herself, she went to unpack and unwind while William ordered lunch from room service. Both tired, they ate, then spent the remainder of the afternoon catching up on their sleep.

When they awoke, they showered, dressed and headed out for a late supper at one of the restaurants close to the hotel. Following a romantic, gourmet dinner, they went to one of the casinos to try their luck at gaming before turning in for the evening.

William had traveled to Monte-Carlo every year since his high school graduation, but he'd never toured the sites around the city. And that made Catherine happy, because they were able to explore the sites together. Over the next two weeks, they spent their days exploring the city; strolling its beautiful winding, cobblestone streets and taking pleasure in viewing its towering cliffs and lush landscapes. And their nights, relishing in the dazzling night life; dining at elegant restaurants, gaming in the casino, and dancing in the discotheques.

Catherine felt closer to William than she ever had. And no matter what anyone said about him, she was determined to keep him in her life.

During their flight home, William invited her to spend Christmas with him and she agreed. "I'd love to," she said. "But since you planned this trip, why don't I plan our Christmas trip? My parents told me about a lovely Victorian Inn in Connecticut. I'd love to take you there." She smiled. "I know that it can't compare with Monaco, but it's close to home."

William leaned over and kissed her on the cheek. "That sounds great. I'd love to," he said.

They arrived in Los Angeles shortly after nine in the evening, both exhausted. Though they wanted to remain together, they decided to go back to their separate homes to catch up on some much needed rest.

When Catherine got home, she went straight to bed. She woke up around eleven the following morning, feeling much better. Stretching her hands in the air, she got out of bed and immediately went downstairs to get a cup of coffee and check her messages. The most important message had been from Justin. Since it had been over two weeks since she'd spoken with him, she called him first. She dialed his number and he picked up on the first ring.

After a few minutes of cordial conversation, Justin made the mistake of asking about her trip to Monte-Carlo. Without any thought, Catherine excitedly began to tell him about the marvelous time she'd had, oblivious to the fact that he wasn't really interested in hearing about the fun she'd had with another man.

"I'm happy to hear that you had such a good time," he said grimly.

Realizing that she'd said too much, Catherine changed the subject, inquiring about how he had spent Thanksgiving, finding out that he'd spent the day with Antoinette and her family. A part of her felt guilty for not being with him.

During the conversation, Justin asked how she planned to spend Christmas. She hated the thought of telling him about her plans with William but decided to tell him anyway. The one lesson she'd learned over the last few months was to tell Justin the truth at all cost. "William and I plan to spend Christmas in Connecticut," she divulged.

Silence filled the telephone line.

"Did you hear me?" she asked.

"Yes. I heard," Justin replied. "That's great," he said, then he cut her off from speaking. "Well, listen," he said, "I'm in the middle of some house plans right now. I'd better get back to work."

"All right," Catherine mumbled, "then you better get back to work."

Although she was upset that he didn't want to talk to her anymore, she realized it was her own fault for talking to him about William. Just the mention of William's name was taboo where Justin was concerned. And although she knew it, she had done it anyhow.

Moping, she started to feel even more dreadful. She'd been so wrapped up in making plans with William that she hadn't even thought about Justin spending Thanksgiving alone. She was tremendously grateful to Antoinette for having the heart to think about him. Right then, she decided that whatever she and William did for Christmas, she would somehow celebrate Christmas with Justin, too.

Over the next two weeks, she and William spent most of their time together. During that time, she arranged their trip to Connecticut with her travel agent. They would leave on Saturday, the twenty-third and stay through the twenty-ninth, arriving back in Los Angeles just in time for the New Year's Eve extravaganza that she and William were invited to attend.

After finalizing the plans, she called Justin to make plans with him. They decided to have Christmas together at his house on the twenty-second, the day before she was scheduled to leave. She was happy he had agreed to see her.

A few minutes after she and Justin hung up, William called to say he was going out of town, and didn't know when he would return.

"Where are you going?" she inquired.

He jogged her memory. "Remember the job I told you about in San Francisco?"

"Yes. I remember."

"Well, they want me to start the job right after the first of the year, so I have to go there to start the planning phase."

"Okay. But will you be back in time for our trip?" she asked, worried that he wouldn't make it back in time.

"Yes. Most definitely," he reassured her. "There's no way I'm going to miss spending Christmas with you. Just pack your bags and meet me in your driveway at eight o'clock on the twenty-third."

CHAPTER 14

❀

Catherine arrived at Justin's house shortly after five in the evening. Driving through the iron gates, she studied the exterior of the home, a magnificent two story Tudor with stately peaks, surrounded by carefully tended grounds.

Shifting the engine into park, she looked down at the note paper where she'd written his address, and double-checked, making sure she hadn't gone to the wrong house. "This is it," she mumbled, seeing that she hadn't made a mistake.

Holding a gift, she stepped out of the car and walked across the flagstone pavers toward the front door. Taking a deep breath, she nervously smoothed her hands down the sides of the red dress she was wearing, and then she rang the doorbell.

The door opened, and Justin's face came into view.

Overwhelmed by her beauty, Justin smiled and took two steps backwards. "Wow, you look gorgeous," he complimented. He wanted desperately to kiss her, but after everything that had happened between them, he was afraid to push his luck.

"Thank you," Catherine replied gracefully.

Inviting her inside, Justin led her through the large foyer to a dimly lit great room where a fire was burning in the fireplace. "Justin, I can't believe that you live here. You're home is exquisite!" she remarked, impressed with what she saw.

Justin chuckled. "What—did you think that I lived in a "tiny dilapidated shack?" he asked jokingly.

Sharing a laugh, she tried to explain, "No, that's not what I meant at all...I meant...that you're so down to earth...so into nature, I just thought—"

Stroking his chin with his fingers, he grinned.

She shook her head. "What I meant to say isn't coming out that well. Let me begin again. I just figured that you lived in a more modest home."

With a solemn expression, Justin put his hands in his pockets and looked around. "Actually, this was my parents home," he said. "I inherited it when they passed away." Then he laughed. "But you were right about me. If I didn't have this place, I'd probably live in a beach shack, that's more my style. But there's no way I could ever sell this place. It means too much to me." He reached for the gift. "Here let me put that under the tree for you."

In the corner of the room stood a beautifully decorated blue spruce Christmas tree with colorful lights and exquisite glass bulbs. Catherine watched as Justin stooped down, placing the gift on top of the tree skirt, beside the only other gift under the tree.

Standing up, he turned to face her. "Would you like a glass of wine?" he asked.

"I'd love one," she replied, watching as Justin walked to the bar.

She drew a deep breath and nervously rubbed the palms of her hands together. "It smells like you're cooking a feast," she said. "Is there anything I can do to help?"

Pouring the wine, Justin replied, "No. Everything's under control. Why don't we just relax for a while beside the fire and then we will have dinner?" Pointing to a table near the fireplace, he continued, "If it's all right with you, I thought we would dine right there."

Catherine's face glowed in the fiery light as she walked closer to the fire. "That's fine with me," she said, sitting down on the brown leather sofa.

Eagerly, Justin walked over and handed her a glass of wine. He watched as she glanced around the room. "You're furniture is beautiful. Mahogany isn't it?" she guessed.

His eyes lit up. "That's right," he said. "My dad made most of the furniture in this house," he pointed out.

"You have to be kidding? When did he find the time?" she asked, remembering that his father had been a surgeon.

Taking a seat beside her, Justin laughed. "He started when he was really young."

They sat for a while enjoying the warmth from the fire and the wine until the oven's timer sounded from the kitchen. Justin stood up. "It sounds like the tenderloin is ready," he said. "Would you like to come into the kitchen while I check on it?"

Agreeing, Catherine followed him into the kitchen. As she entered, she noticed the beautiful Italian stone floor, granite counter tops and copper pots hanging from the ceiling over a large island. "I love your kitchen," she said. "It's incredible."

Justin grinned. "Thanks," he said. "I just remodeled this room a few months ago. I'm really pleased with the way it turned out." He walked to the oven, and pulled the roast out. "It looks like everything's ready. All I have to do is carve the tenderloin and set the table," he noted.

Catherine walked up beside him. "I can set the table," she volunteered. "Just point me in the direction of your place settings."

"Here, I'll show you," he said, leading her through a set of double doors to an elaborate dining room.

Catherine followed Justin past a long dining table and three large china cabinets, watching intently while he opened one of the glass doors. "I think you can find everything you need in here," he said. He started to say something else but then he suddenly stopped talking. "These were my mom's special occasion place settings," he said somberly, lifting one of the plates out of the cabinet.

Catherine could tell that he missed his parents very much, and her heart went out to him. "They're beautiful," she said, watching as he set it down on top of the others.

He looked up. "Well, I'm going to go back to the kitchen," he said, and then walked away. "Just let me know if you need help," he called from the doorway.

"No. I see everything that I need," she called back.

After gathering what she needed, Catherine headed back into the great room to set the table. When she was finished, she went to see if Justin needed help. He had finished carving the tenderloin and was in the process of transferring the side dishes to serving bowls.

Together, they enjoyed a delightfully cozy dinner. After they finished, Justin eagerly suggested they open gifts, and she agreed.

Grabbing six large pillows from the sofa, he laid them on the floor next to the Christmas tree. Sitting down beside Justin, Catherine looked around the room. The mantle looked gorgeous, strung with fresh green garland, colored lights and pretty red bows. It reminded her of Christmas with her family in New Orleans.

"The house looks beautiful. When did you find the time to decorate?" she asked, continuing to look around.

"To be honest, I just decided to decorate yesterday," he admitted.

With a curious look, she asked, "You decorated the house just for tonight?"

His blue eyes softened. "I wanted this evening to be special for us."

Catherine could feel her cheeks turning red. "Thank you," she whispered. "No one has ever gone through all this trouble for me before." She set her hand atop his. "You're such a great friend," she said earnestly.

There's that word again, Justin thought miserably.

Reaching behind his back, Justin pulled out a beautifully wrapped gift and handed it to her. "Why don't you open your present?" he coaxed.

Accepting the package, Catherine laughed, "It's so beautifully wrapped. I hate to open it."

Taking her time, she tore the paper, revealing a square shaped burgundy gift box. Opening the top, she peered inside. "Oh, my," she said, pulling out a rich multi-colored brocade jewelry box with a gold rim around the edges. As she opened the hinged box, music began to play while a ballerina twirled round and round. "Justin, it's beautiful. I love it," she exclaimed.

"Wait. There's more," Justin said. "You'll find the rest if you reach your hand down a little farther in the box."

Like a child at Christmas, Catherine reached inside and pulled out a strand of pearls. Her face blushing again, she smiled in delight. She thought for a moment, then held the strand up in the air. "Justin, they're beautiful. But I can't accept these. They're much too expensive," she whispered.

Justin's smile turned into a handsome grin and he gently took hold of her hands, locking them around the pearls. "I want you to have them."

Silence filled the room while she stared down at the strand. Her eyes began to tear. "Thank you. They're beautiful," she said. "I'll treasure them forever," she added as she shifted her body to his, kissing him gently on his lips.

Slowly, she pulled away. "Now, you have to open your gift," she said softly, handing the package to him.

Catherine wanted to see his eyes when he opened the gift, so she watched eagerly as he tore the paper open. As he pulled the last of the paper away, his blue eyes lit up. In his hands, he held a book of short stories by famous authors.

"Where did you find this book?" he questioned, stroking his hand over the worn front cover. "I've been trying to get my hands on this book for years. How did you know?"

Her expression turned serious. "I hope you don't mind," she said. "When I was at your cabin, I saw a list of book stores on your desk with a note referencing the book. I could tell that you were trying to find a copy. When I got home, I called a friend of mine who's an antique dealer. She checked around, and we were able to coax a man from Europe into selling his copy."

Excited, he said, "Mind, why would I mind? This is the best present anyone has ever given me. It means the world to me!"

Without any thought, he leaned over, kissing her on the cheek. Staring deeply into her dark eyes, his lips migrated to hers. Her heart started to race, pounding through her chest. Although she was surprised by what was happening, she didn't pull away. Her lips parted, encouraging him to kiss her again. He touched her shoulders, lightly pressing her down atop the pillows. Their eyes locked while he softly stroked the back of her neck below her hairline. Swallowing hard, she melted into his arms. Drawing a deep breath, she held him close while he kissed her neck. His hands wandered beneath her dress, exploring her thighs. His lips gravitated to hers, melting together, entwined. Their passion ignited, every touch was electric. Ravaging in each other, they fiercely sped up, kissing harder and harder, their bodies gliding together, harder and harder. She couldn't stop. Desperately, she searched for the bottom of his shirt and when she found it, she tugged it out of his pants. Gripping his muscular back, she gradually moved her hands up to massage his strong shoulders, drawing him closer to share in another hard, hot kiss. His hands glided up to her soft shoulders, beneath the straps of her dress, sliding them down, off of her shoulders. Thoughts of William rolled through her head, and she stopped kissing him. "I'm sorry," she cried out, pushing him away. At first Justin didn't stop. She pushed harder, shifting his body to the side. "I don't know what I was thinking!" she said, and she rose to her feet.

Concerned, Justin stood up. "What's wrong?" he asked, his tone loud.

"What's wrong," Catherine repeated. "I'm in love with another man, yet I'm here with you. That's what's wrong. Do you know what this would do to William if he found out?"

"What about what it's doing to me?" he said forcefully, reaching out to her. "Every time we're together I have to hold myself back from revealing my true feelings. I don't just want to be your friend. I want much more than that." He looked away, then turned back to face her. "There's something I have to tell you."

Fighting back tears, she looked away, eyeing the room for her belongings, realizing that she'd entered with only the gift. "I'm sorry, but I can't hide my feelings anymore. I just can't do it! I'm in love with you!" he shouted.

Not wanting to hear what he was saying, Catherine slowly backed away from him, lifting her hand so he wouldn't come any closer. "No. Justin, please stop…You don't understand, I'm in love with William!" she cried.

He walked closer, backing her into the wall. As she stared to the side, he gently pulled her face to his. He wanted to look into her eyes. He calmed down and spoke. "You say that you're in love with William, but I don't think you are. I think you're so blinded by passion that you can't see clearly."

Tears steamed down her cheeks. "I'm sorry, Justin, but you're wrong. I do love him and I need for you to accept it," she said, then pulled away. "I really have to go," she mumbled, looking down. "William and I are leaving for Connecticut tomorrow morning and I have to pack."

She started to walk toward the door, then stopped to turn around. "What happened tonight was a terrible mistake. And it must never happen again," she urged.

Overcome with grief, Justin stood still. His eyes filled with tears as she walked out the front door. Coming to his senses, he raced after her and grabbed her arms. "Do you really think that William's interested in spending his life with you?" he asked, forcefully.

She struggled to get away.

"Look, I can't stand by and see you get hurt by this guy!" he said loudly.

She fought to break free.

Holding her tightly, he lowered his voice, "Just give me a minute. I'll let you go in a minute." Loosening the hold on her arms, he continued calmly. "Just think about what I've said. Or better yet, why don't you ask him if he's ready to make a commitment to you and see what he says."

Pulling away one last time, Catherine freed herself and ran to her car.

Justin wanted to go after her, but what would he do? He couldn't force her to love him. Loving him had to be her idea, and hers alone. And he knew that if he pushed too hard, he'd probably lose her forever.

He punched the air. "I'm not going to wait for you," he yelled angrily as the taillights of her car faded in the distance.

CHAPTER 15

❃

As planned, William's limousine pulled up to Catherine's house at precisely eight o'clock on the morning of December 23rd.

Looking out the window of the limousine, William spotted three suitcases sitting on the driveway with a black leather jacket draped over the top of the largest suitcase.

Anxious to see Catherine, William glanced around, finally locking his sights on her as she walked out from behind a group of jade plants near the front entryway.

Excited, William opened the car door and stepped out. "Hi. It looks like you're all ready to go," he said cheerfully, pointing down at the suitcases.

Behind a pair of dark tinted sunglasses, Catherine responded with a nod.

William's eyes followed the curves of her slender body as she moved closer, from her head to her feet, scrutinizing the way she had dressed, the ragged pair of blue jeans, the wrinkled ivory linen shirt, totally the opposite of how she normally dressed. And those dark tinted sunglasses. The sun wasn't even out.

Smiling slightly, Catherine walked down the cobblestone driveway toward him. He watched carefully as she picked up her leather jacket, leaving her luggage behind on the ground. She veered closer.

He thought she was going to stop to kiss him, or at the very least say hello, but instead she passed him by.

"Yes. I'm all ready," she replied somberly, slipping into the car.

Shaking his head in disbelief, William turned and walked toward the car. "What, no kiss," he said sarcastically, staring in her direction.

She was acting weird and he wondered why.

While the driver loaded the luggage in the trunk, William joined Catherine inside the car. As he slid across the seat to be near her, she clutched her forehead. "You'll have to excuse me this morning. I had a little too much to drink last night and I'm paying for it now," she explained.

In reality, it hadn't been the amount of liquor she had consumed the night before that was afflicting her, but instead the lack of sleep. Having spent most of the night crying after her argument with Justin, she had finally managed to drift to sleep in the early morning hours. When she woke her eyelids were red and swollen and she had an enormous headache.

Rather than interrogate her about what she'd done the night before, William pulled her close. "That's all right," he said tenderly. "You can sleep during the flight and get cleaned up right before we land."

On the way to the airport, William began to talk about their trip, but realized that Catherine wasn't the least bit interested in what he was saying. Eyeing her with curiosity, he paused for a moment to collect his thoughts. He was curious to know what she had done the night before, but wasn't sure if he should ask.

After flip flopping with the idea, he decided that he should. "By the way," he said, "what did you do last night?"

Evading the question, Catherine curled up beside him and shut her eyes. "I hope you don't mind, but I really don't want to talk about it. It's a long story and my head is pounding," she said impassively, nestling her head deeper into his shoulder.

Feeling sorry for her, William reluctantly dropped the subject. Although he was disappointed with her, he hid his feelings, hoping that her mood and headache would pass by the time they arrived in Connecticut.

Shortly after they boarded the plane, William gave Catherine Tylenol to ease the pain in her head, and when they were airborne, he put her to bed.

Catherine spent most of the flight asleep, awaking only when she heard the pilot announce that the plane would land in fifteen minutes. Holding her head in agony, she crawled out of the bed and walked to the laboratory to wet her face.

"How are you feeling?" she heard William ask from the doorway.

Turning on the taps, Catherine splashed her face with water, then looked up at him. "I'm okay," she replied in a low tone, her face pale.

Moving closer, William reached for a towel and handed it to her. "You better get cleaned up, we're getting ready to land," he said in an indignant tone.

Catherine took offense to those words.

"Get cleaned up," she snapped. "What does that mean? Don't I look good enough to be seen with you?"

William could tell that she was trying to pick a fight, and he decided to back off. He started to leave, but having second thoughts, he stopped and turned around. "What's wrong with you today?" he asked angrily.

Catherine didn't respond. Folding her arms across her chest, she stood still.

He moved closer. "I want to know what you did last night?" he demanded.

Interrupting the conversation, the captain buzzed in on the intercom asking them to buckle in their seats. Catherine had been saved from having to respond.

Frustrated by the interruption and perplexed by Catherine's dismal mood, William hurled his hands in the air, then silently followed her toward the front cabin. Once there, they buckled into their seats.

Before they knew it, the plane had landed and they were whisked away in a Rolls Royce to take them to the inn.

The drive turned out to be quiet, with both of them sitting apart, looking out of separate windows. For Catherine, the silence gave her the opportunity to calm down and to think about what had happened. She realized how cruel she had acted towards William, and she knew that she owed him an apology. She also knew that she had to change her mood if she planned on staying in Connecticut.

Taking a deep breath, she scooted over to him.

Ignoring her presence, he continued to stare out the window.

Reaching for his hand, she leaned her head against his shoulder. Teary eyed, she whispered, "I'm so sorry, William."

William nodded without answering, then he turned to look at her. She expected him to accept her apology, but he didn't. Instead, he looked at her with a pained expression. "Why don't you get some sleep tonight, and we can start over in the morning?" he suggested.

Agreeing, she kissed him on the cheek.

A few minutes later, the car pulled up to the stately inn, which Catherine thought resembled a gingerbread house. Her eyes focused on the sidewalk leading to the front door, lined with lanterns, burning brightly in the night. On the porch, Catherine could see a woman with fiery red hair, dressed vibrantly in an ankle length purple dress and a short white fur coat.

When the car stopped, Catherine watched as the woman hurried down the steps to greet them.

Pulling the car door open, she introduced herself as Mrs. Pauly, the owner of the inn.

As soon as Catherine stepped out of the car, the chilly Connecticut air hit her. Putting on her leather jacket, Catherine breathed deeply, smelling the air filled with the aroma of the fireplaces, burning cedar. She loved the scent. It reminded her of back home in New Orleans when every once in a while the temperature would dip into the low twenties, giving everyone the opportunity to light their fireplaces.

While the bags were being unloaded, Mrs. Pauly led Catherine and William down a paved walkway across the lawn to where they would stay in the guesthouse of the mansion.

Mrs. Pauly was pleasant, but also proved to be very talkative.

As they walked, she gave them the history of the inn, how it had been built by her great-grandfather in the early 1880's as a family home, and converted to an inn in the mid 70's when she inherited the property. She explained that since she had never married, nor had any children, she decided to renovate the inn and share it with the public.

When they reached the entranceway of the guesthouse, Mrs. Pauly unlocked the door. "I'm sorry," she said. "I must be boring you to death."

Catherine and William looked at each other and smiled.

"Well, here it is," Mrs. Pauly announced, pushing the door open.

Just as Mrs. Pauly started to enter the cottage, William stepped in front of her, stopping her in her tracks. "We can take it from here," he said boldly.

The smile on Mrs. Pauly's face faded and she looked at him suspiciously. "Well, all right," she said hesitantly, handing the key to him. "I think that you will find everything you need inside, but if not, please call me." She started to turn away, then turned back. "I know you must be weary from your trip. Could I have someone deliver dinner to you a little later, then you wouldn't have to leave the guesthouse. How does that sound?" she asked in a motherly tone.

Feeling badly for the way William had blocked Mrs. Pauly's entry into the cottage, Catherine stepped forward to answer. "That sounds wonderful," she replied with a smile. "Thank you."

They assumed that would be all, but Mrs. Pauly went on. "That's what I'm here for. To make your stay a pleasant one. If there's anything you need, day or night, just dial the operator and ask for me," she said as the chauffeur passed with their luggage.

Once again, Mrs. Pauly started to walk away, then she turned around again. "By the way, breakfast is served between seven and ten in the main dining room," she informed them.

Catherine and William watched as Mrs. Pauly walked down the sidewalk toward the main house. Trading gazes with William, Catherine chuckled. "She really likes to talk, doesn't she?"

William grinned. "She definitely does. She's pretty annoying."

"I don't think she's annoying," Catherine replied, defending the kind lady. "In fact, I think she's rather charming."

Stepping back inside the cottage, Catherine glanced around. Beneath a ceiling of exposed beams, she focused on a Christmas tree, brightly lit with white lights and a variety of gold ornaments, standing gracefully in front of a decorated fireplace. She turned to William. "Oh, look how pretty," she said, speaking of the Christmas decorations. Moving closer to the fireplace, she ran her fingers across the carved oak of the mantle and casing. "Look at the fine detailing of this wood," she said. "Can you believe this has been here since the 1800's?"

Cocking an eyebrow, William nodded. "Yes. It's really nice," he replied nonchalantly, shoving his hands in his pockets.

William hadn't said anything, but Catherine could tell he'd rather be someplace else...Monte-Carlo, Paris, Spain. He liked action and Connecticut didn't have very much. But for Catherine, she liked the peacefulness and quaintness of the small town.

Sensing the disappointment in his voice, Catherine turned around. "Won't you give it a chance," she said, aware that William could care less about the Christmas tree or the history surrounding them. "I know it's not extravagant like Monte-Carlo or some other far away land that you've visited, but don't you think it's much more charming?" she asked abruptly.

Jolted by her comments, William started to walk around the room, which had been painted in a deep red hue and filled with exquisite antique furniture.

"Where did you say you heard about this place?" he asked, opening a set of doors leading outside. Catherine had told him while they were in Monte-Carlo, but he didn't remember.

Catherine smiled. "My mom and dad came here a couple of years ago for their anniversary and they've talked about it ever since," she said. "They said that it was the most romantic trip they'd ever taken." Catherine crossed the room to join William outside. "And I can see why," she said, pointing at the spectacular view of the ocean.

Although the temperature outside was nearly thirty degrees, Catherine was unaffected by it. Looking up at the moon, she stretched her hands in the air and took a deep breath. "I love the smell of the ocean," she exclaimed.

Catherine glanced to the right of where she was standing. "Oh, look at that lighthouse," she said, seeing the steadily flashing light in the distance. "Why don't we take a walk there tomorrow," she suggested merrily.

As Catherine looked out over the ocean, William stood by quietly, studying her perfect profile, the smoothness of her complexion, and the highlights in her hair as they glimmered in the moonlight. That, together with seeing how her mood had changed made him smile.

Without turning to look at him, Catherine continued to speak. "Now I know why they liked it so much. It's quite enchanting here," she said, and then she turned to go back inside. "And look at this," she pointed out gaily. "The fireplace is open to the bedroom on the other side."

Catherine walked into the bedroom where a hand carved four poster bed was arranged in the center of the room, draped with tapestry and lace bedding. And on the wall above the bed, a magnificent stained glass window. The detailing of the room was incredible. The serene surroundings made her feel relaxed, calmed her emotions which had been running rampant.

Standing within the door frame, William watched as Catherine kicked her shoes off and tossed herself on the bed. He was getting ready to join her when someone knocked on the door. "I hope that it's not Mrs. Pauly again," William commented.

Catherine remembered what Mrs. Pauly had said about having someone deliver their dinner and she mentioned it to William.

"I hope it's something good," he said, realizing that Mrs. Pauly hadn't asked what they wanted to eat.

While Catherine stayed in the bedroom, William went to answer the door. Listening closely, Catherine could here the voice of a young man talking to William and she could tell he was delivering dinner to them.

After the young man left, Catherine got out of bed and joined William in the dining room. She watched quietly while William transferred the food, place settings and silverware from the cart to the dining room table. After he finished, he motioned for her to join him and she did.

Once seated, William and Catherine lifted the lids of the silver platters to find out what Mrs. Pauly had ordered for them. "Oh, wow," Catherine said, getting a whiff of the broiled fish topped with fresh herbs. "It smells delicious."

William lifted the bottle of wine out of the ice bucket and studied the label. "Good stuff," he commented about the white wine, as he pulled out the cork and poured two glasses.

Silence filled the air while they concentrated on eating. Catherine broke the silence first. "By the way," she said in a low tone, "after we finish eating, I think I'm going to take a hot bath then go straight to bed."

"Sure," William replied, agreeing without lifting his eyes from his plate. "That's a good idea," he said, shoveling a fork full of baby greens into his mouth.

Silence filled the room again. Catherine could tell that he was still sort of angry with her, and she hoped things would be better between them in the morning.

After they finished eating, Catherine stood up and walked into the bedroom while William picked up his glass of wine and went back on the balcony. Then just as she had said, Catherine took a bath and went straight to bed without even looking for William.

The following morning, Catherine woke to the sound of the waves crashing against the shoreline, and to what sounded like thousands of birds chirping just outside the window. She rolled over to wake William, but noticed he had already gotten up.

Lazily, she made her way into the bathroom to shower and get dressed. Her mood had changed considerably since the night before, and she felt in control of her life once again. She hadn't thought about what had happened between she and Justin since the prior morning and had no inclination of rehashing it during the trip. Instead, she only wanted to relax and enjoy William's company.

Dressing in a pair of brown suede pants and long ivory wool sweater, Catherine decided to set out to find William. She checked the main house and then the grounds, but he was nowhere in sight, so she decided to inquire at the reception desk.

The desk was being manned by a young girl who had her head buried in a book. As Catherine approached, the girl looked up. "Good Morning, Ma'am. Can I help you?" she asked politely.

"Yes, maybe you can. I'm looking for one of your guest, Mr. Moorehouse. Have you seen him this morning?"

"Yes. I saw him a little earlier. He said that he was going to the post office."

"The post office?" Catherine repeated. "Why was he going to post office?"

The girl shrugged. "I'm sorry, but he didn't say," she replied.

After thanking the girl, Catherine turned to go to the main dining room for a late breakfast. A few minutes after she was seated, she looked up and saw William standing across the dining room grinning brightly.

Walking up to the table, he leaned down to kiss her on the cheek. "Good morning sleepy head," he said happily. "Isn't it a wonderful day?"

Catherine took a sip of coffee. "You're pretty cheerful this morning," she said, sweeping her hair behind her ear.

Surprised by his mood, she watched as he sat down across from her.

"By the way," Catherine began uncertainly, "why did you go to the post office?"

William's lips curled into a smile and he leaned across the table. "I have a surprise for you, but you have to wait until tomorrow to find out what it is," he whispered.

Catherine was getting ready to inquire more about the surprise, but was interrupted when the waitress stepped up to take their order.

After a delightful breakfast, Catherine and William went for a stroll down the beach toward the lighthouse. Because December was not a popular time for tourists to visit the area, the beach was barren with the exception of a flock of seagulls taking advantage of the serene coastline.

Walking close to the water's edge, being careful not to get their feet wet, they walked for miles, stopping along the way several times while Catherine searched for seashells in the sand. Finally, just beyond a patch of tall brown grass and set high on a rocky point, the red roofed lighthouse came into view.

While William stayed behind, Catherine ran up the hill to get a closer look. As she ran, she could feel a fine mist of water from the ocean sprinkling against her skin and she could taste the salt from the water. She found it refreshing.

"Come on," she called out to William. "Let's see if we can go inside!"

William tried to catch up to her, but she made it there before him. Walking closer, he noticed that Catherine was talking to an elderly man with gray hair.

As soon as Catherine saw William, she gestured for him to come closer. "Come on," she said, "this gentleman is the lighthouse keeper. He said that we can go up."

Saying hello, William smiled and shook the old man's hand.

"Just follow me and I'll take you upstairs," the old man said delightedly. "I don't get many visitors at this time of the year," he explained, leading them into the stone tower up a winding iron staircase. "In fact," he added, "I was getting ready to close up to spend Christmas Eve with my family in the village."

"But what about the tower?" Catherine questioned. "Doesn't someone have to be here to man the lighthouse?"

"Oh, no," the old man waved. "These days everything's automated. The Coast Guard handles all of that now. The only reason I'm still here is to show visitors like you the tower." He laughed. "And occasionally, when the system shuts down, I have to do it the old fashioned way by using my lantern to light the way. But that doesn't happen very often."

When they made it to the top of the lighthouse, the old man led them to the lantern deck overlooking an exhilarating view of their surroundings. Looking down, they could see the waves crashing against the rocks below, to the right, they saw the quaint New England village, to the left, the wooded area around the inn where they were staying. They could see clearly for miles.

"Isn't it beautiful," Catherine asked, admiring the view. Catherine felt William's fingertips gliding across the skin on the nape of her neck. Although his touch surprised her, it was nice. Turning to look at him, she smiled and reached her hand out for his.

Gripping her hand gently, William smiled back.

It seemed that all was well once again.

Thanking the old man for allowing them to go to the top of the lighthouse, they said good-bye and headed down the stairs. Since it was getting late, they started their journey back to the inn. Because they didn't stop to search for sea shells, the walk back was much quicker. As they walked, Catherine looked around the beach, noticing it was no longer barren of people. She saw one man jogging, an elderly couple walking through the tall brown grass of the dunes toward the beach, and even a man with his young son fishing in the surf.

Before long, they found themselves back in the gardens at the inn and they could see Mrs. Pauly headed their way. "Here we go again," William whispered.

Laughing, Catherine slapped William on the arm. "Now, don't start," she instructed jokingly.

As Mrs. Pauly approached, Catherine smiled gently in her direction. "I don't mean to bother you," Mrs. Pauly said. "I just wanted to let you know that we're getting ready to serve Christmas Eve dinner in the main dining room." Mrs. Pauly looked at William slyly, "That is…if you're interested in dining with us."

Catherine laughed. "Oh, yes we're interested," she replied, speaking for the two of them. Because they had missed lunch, they were both quite ravenous. "What time should we arrive?"

"Any time you're ready, dear. I'll have someone set a table for you." As she had done before, Mrs. Pauly started to turn away, then turned back. "By the way, we're having chutney-glazed Cornish hens, an herbed stuffing, some wonderful fresh green beans and for dessert your choice of apple or pumpkin pie…How does that sound?"

Just thinking about it made Catherine's mouth water. "That sounds wonderful," Catherine said. "We'll get changed and see you in a little while."

After taking showers and dressing, William and Catherine headed to the main dining room. When they arrived, they saw Mrs. Pauly across the room talking to a table full of diners. Looking up from her conversation, she saw them and walked over. "I'm so happy you made it," she said. "We're getting ready to begin serving."

As Mrs. Pauly led them to their table, Catherine looked around the dimly lit room. There were more people dining than she'd expected, the room was quite full.

The table Mrs. Pauly had set was in the corner of the room. Mrs. Pauly stood by while William pulled out Catherine's chair, then sat across from her.

"Your server will be with you in a minute," Mrs. Pauly said. Excusing herself, she hurried toward the kitchen.

"This is really nice," William said, acknowledging the warm, festive surroundings.

Less than a minute later, the same young man who had delivered their dinner the night before, stepped up to the table carrying a bottle of sherry. After allowing William to look at the bottle and taste the sherry, giving it his approval, the young man poured two glasses, and then discreetly disappeared.

Taking a sip of sherry, Catherine stared into William's brown eyes over an elegant beveled glass candle lamp aglow in the center of the cozy table. For the first time since they'd left Los Angeles, she saw him in a different light. Seeing the strength in his eyes, she remembered what she'd seen in him all those months ago. Deep within his masculine body and brash attitude there was another side of William struggling to get out. And every once in a while, he let that part of him show. The side of him that was kind, loving and gentle. The part of him that she loved.

William could tell she was thinking about him. "What—?" he asked, flirting with his smile.

Catherine set her glass of sherry down on the table and reached for his hand, gripping it gently. Beneath the table, she felt his leg rub against hers, arousing her desire.

Looking up, she saw the waiter headed their way with a tray filled with food. "Here comes our dinner," she informed him, releasing his hand gently.

Dining on a delightful dinner, Catherine and William continued to flirt with their eyes, blocking out everything and everyone around them. For a while, they were the only people in the room. That is, until Mrs. Pauly chimed in on their romantic interlude as she gathered her guests around the piano to sing Christmas carols.

Catherine figured that William wasn't interested, but he surprised her. Standing up, he reached his hand out for hers. "Would you like to join them?" he asked with a smile.

Agreeing, Catherine stood and followed William to the piano. And for the next hour they joined in singing a medley of Christmas carols.

After that, Mrs. Pauly had everyone join her around the hearth while she read *The Night Before Christmas*. Catherine and William laughed when she started reading, but Mrs. Pauly turned out to be an excellent story teller.

As soon as she finished the story, William and Catherine took another glass of sherry, said goodnight to everyone, and headed out of the dining room to go back to the guesthouse.

Once inside the solitude of the cottage, William tuned the stereo to a soft music station, while Catherine watched from the sofa. Taking his last sip of sherry, he set his glass down on the fireplace mantle and crossed to her. Although he was only five feet away from her, the walk seemed to take forever as she waited patiently for him to arrive. Her thighs tingled, she took a deep breath and exhaled a shaky breath. As he approached he reached for her hand. "Would you like to dance?" he asked, his tone, soft.

Licking her lips, she smiled and took his hand.

Together, they swayed to the soothing sounds of *Nat King Cole*. It seemed that William had forgotten all about her mood swings, and for that Catherine was grateful.

As they danced, William inhaled the scent of Catherine's hair, smiling as he detected lavender amid her curly brown locks. It was his favorite. Their cheeks rubbed together, his face was smooth. His hands glided across her back, stroking it as his lips wandered to her neck. Catherine's body shivered with every touch, her breathing labored. Moving together to the music, William's hands glided down her back and to her thighs beneath her dress. Aware of what would happen next, she froze when she felt them. Exhaling a shaky breath, Catherine shut her eyes and lowered her hands, gliding them atop his as he stroked her thighs. Their lips joined and she melted in his arms.

Unable to control the power of her desire, Catherine led him into the bedroom and gently pushed him down on the bed. With his elbows propped on the bed, he laid back to watch while she undressed. Although this wasn't the first time he'd seen her body, it felt like the first. He grinned as she climbed on the bed, her body above his. Without losing eye contact with him, she slowly unbuttoned his shirt, kissing the wall of his masculine chest as she went along. Still watching him, she glided her hand to his waist unbuttoning his pants, and unzipping them slowly. Eyeing her with desire, he lifted his body, allowing her to remove his pants, one leg at a time.

Just as he had given her pleasure in the past, she wanted to do the same for him. It didn't take long before William reached the state of euphoria and he gripped her arms and muttered, "I love you," as he pulled her up to him.

Grinning, he buried his fingers in her thick hair, pulling it back away from her face while they shared a kiss, long and hard.

Had she heard him correctly, had he told her that he loved her. She didn't even want to think about it. At that moment, she just wanted to be with him. Without words, one on one. She was in bliss and she didn't want it to end.

Shifting his body atop hers, William's lips wandered from her mouth, down her chest, to her navel and back up again. Entwining his fingers with hers, they became one and their bodies moved rhythmically with more intensity than ever before. When they climaxed together, Catherine clenched his back with her fingers. Breathing deeply, she took pleasure in the moment.

When it ended, they were exhausted, wet with perspiration and unable to move. As they caught their breath, William rolled on the side of Catherine and held her tightly in his arms, tracing the skin on her arms with his hand. Feeling wonderful, they fell asleep in each other's arms.

Waking to the sound of Christmas music, Catherine sat up in bed and listened closely. At first, she wasn't sure if it was a dream or reality. Realizing that it was real, she got out of bed and wrapped a sheet around her naked body, then strolled to the living room. She laughed when she saw William standing beside the Christmas tree dressed in a Santa costume. Rubbing her tired eyes, she giggled, "Oh my goodness, William. Where did you get that costume?"

"Ho, Ho,Ho," he said in his best Santa accent. "I'm sorry young lady but you must be mistaken. My name is Santa Claus not William."

She veered closer. "My, my Mr. Claus," she said in a sexy tone, and dropped the sheet to the floor.

Delighted by the view, William's eyes widened.

Moving closer, she naughtily pressed her body against his, while her hands gradually made their way down the front of the red jacket. "May I ask what you have under that red jacket?" she asked.

"Why not at all, Missy. Why don't you take a closer look," he suggested, still talking like Santa.

Enticing him with her lips, she kissed him while her long fingers wandered around his mid-section, unbuttoning the jacket, one button at a time. Her lips wandered to his neck. Breathing heavily, their lips met. As it had been the night before, the heat between them was intense.

Caught in the rapture, they made love all day long, finally falling asleep wrapped in each other's arms. Having missed breakfast and lunch, when they woke, they ordered Christmas dinner from room service.

After they ate, they decided to exchange presents.

Sitting on the floor beside the tree, Catherine handed William his gift, then watched eagerly as he held the package up to his ear and shook it. "What can it be?" he wondered aloud, ripping the paper off.

Opening the box, he pulled out a gold Rolex watch with a mother of pearl face. "It's beautiful," he exclaimed, leaning over to kiss her. "What a wonderful gift."

Smiling, William put the watch on his wrist, then handed a small package to Catherine. "Open it," he directed eagerly.

Jokingly, she put the box against her ear. "It's a piece of jewelry," she guessed.

William studied her face while she leisurely removed the wrapping paper, revealing a small jewelry box. "I knew it," she said with a laugh. "It is jewelry," she proclaimed as she flipped up the lid.

Her face lit up. Inside the box was an exquisite emerald cut diamond ring, sparkling in the candlelight. She smiled, then her expression turned sad. "Is this what I think it is?" she questioned.

Moving closer, William knelt down and gently gripped her hands. "Catherine Sheldon, will you make me the happiest man alive—Will you marry me?"

Astonished, she sat still. She'd been hit totally out of the blue. A marriage proposal was something that she hadn't expected.

Still on bent knee, William waited patiently for a response.

Her voice shuddered. "I don't know," she said.

William's face saddened while she explained. "I know that we've had a terrific time together over the past few months, but marriage. I'm just not sure."

Shocked that she hadn't accepted immediately, he lifted the ring out of the box and stood up. "I thought this was what you wanted," he said, waving it in the air.

"What about what you want?" she asked calmly. "Are you sure you're ready? I mean, your whole life would change. Are you ready for that? Because to be honest with you, I'm not sure if I'm ready." She lowered her head and went on, "There's still so much I don't know about you. And what do you really know about me? Do you know what my favorite color is…or my favorite food?" She paused for a moment. "And what about my dreams for the future? Do I want to have children? Or better yet, do you want to have children?"

"Those are all things we can learn as we go along," he replied optimistically, sitting down on the floor beside her.

Sitting quietly, she looked up at him. Before she had a chance to respond, he put the ring in the palm of her hand and cupped his hands around hers. "Why don't you keep it for now. You can take as much time as you need to make a decision," he encouraged. "But I want you to know that whatever you decide, I'll understand."

Catherine clasped the ring in her hands, close to her heart, and looked him directly in the eyes. "Thanks for being so understanding. I just need some time to think about this."

William pulled her close. "Whatever the outcome, I just hope that we can remain the way we are now," he whispered against her ear. "The last thing that I want is to lose you over this. And maybe one day, in the near future, you'll surprise me by putting it on your finger."

Shifting her body close, she held him tightly, clenching the ring in her hand behind his back. She drew a deep breath. "I do love you," she said and they exchanged a warm kiss.

William stood up and reached out to help her up from the floor. "Why don't we go for a walk on the beach?" he suggested, and she agreed.

Hand in hand, they walked along the darkened beach, speaking only briefly in short questions and one word answers. And their moods, definitely somber.

After walking for an hour down the secluded beach, they decided to head back, agreeing it was best to turn in for the evening.

When they climbed into bed, William stared up at the ceiling as he spoke. "Tomorrow morning, I want us to wake up as if nothing out of the ordinary happened today. And I promise that I won't talk about marriage again until your ready."

For the next four nights, they didn't make love. Instead they spent their nights snuggled in each other's arms and their days taking long walks on the beach and strolling through the village shopping in quaint little shops. And just as he had promised, William never once mentioned the ring or marriage. But Catherine could feel it. Everything had changed.

By weeks end, their visit to Connecticut was over. It was time to go home. Time to get back to reality. Just in time for the big New Year's Eve extravaganza.

CHAPTER 16

❦

Back home in Los Angeles, Catherine took one last look at the engagement ring William had given her before putting it away in the table beside her bed.

As the drawer snapped shut, she thought about the time she'd spent with William in Connecticut. Despite the fact she'd turned down his marriage proposal, their trip turned out pretty pleasant after all.

Over the next two days, Catherine kept wandering back to the table where she'd stored the ring, each time promising herself it would be the last time she would look at it until she'd made a final decision.

One time, she even put it on her finger to see how it would feel. Staring down at the sparkling diamond, she wondered what their life would be like if she married him. She fantasized about having children with him and even tried to imagine how they would look. Would they have her features or his. She laughed when she thought about William trading in one of his sports cars for a mini van. She couldn't even picture him doing that. Funny thing was, she'd give up her Mercedes in an instant for the chance to car pool a van full of kids around town.

Although Catherine spoke with William several times over those two days, she didn't see him again until New Year's Eve when she went to the suite he had reserved for their big night at the extravaganza.

Followed by the bellman, Catherine walked out of the elevator toward the suite. Her hands started to tremble and her heart began to race. Oddly, she was nervous about seeing him. She thought for a moment, then turned to the bellman. "If you don't mind, I can take that from here," she said, pointing to the luggage cart. The last thing she wanted was to show up at the door with the bellman watching her every move.

The bellman nodded in agreement, and she reached down in her purse and pulled out a twenty dollar bill. "Here you are," she said, handing it to him. The bellman thanked her, then quickly headed toward the elevator.

Wheeling the luggage cart down the hall, Catherine proceeded toward the suite.

Stepping up to the door, she took a deep breath and shook her hands to stop the trembling. She knocked, and a moment later, William opened the door, wearing nothing more than a white bath towel wrapped snugly around his waist. His eyes softened and he smiled. Her heart melted, her anxiety faded.

Seeing the luggage cart beside her, William looked around in the hall. He wondered where the bellman was, but didn't ask. "I was just thinking about you," he said sweetly.

Eyeing him with curiosity, Catherine walked past him into the living room. "And what were you thinking?" she asked coolly, flirting with him.

Pulling the cart inside, William snapped the door shut and turned to look at her. His gaze was sharp.

Beneath her skirt, her upper thighs started to tingle. She knew what he was thinking.

Slowly, he moved closer.

Staring at his body, muscular and tan, she swallowed hard.

Closing in on her, he glided his hand around her waist, circling her slowly. Feeling the warmth of his breath against her neck, she closed her eyes and reached down, cupping his hands with hers. He was behind her now. He kissed her softly near the back of her ear. "Make love to me," he whispered. "I want us to be the way we were before."

Slowly and steadily Catherine turned around and their lips met. Cupping his cheeks with her hands, she nipped her lips between his. His hands wandered to her blouse, unbuttoning it, then slipping it off her shoulders.

Standing before him, Catherine looked down at the towel around his waist, then up again, smiling at him. Her eyes turned serious, and she took his hand and led him into the bedroom, to the bed.

Once inside, their passion exploded and they made passionate love. There hadn't been that much heat between them since before he'd proposed to her in Connecticut. And that made Catherine happy. It finally seemed their relationship was headed in the right direction.

When they finished making love, they ordered a light dinner from room service, then started to get ready for the party, which was to begin at eight o'clock.

For the occasion, Catherine dressed in a navy blue sequin top velvet dress and William in a black tuxedo. When they finished dressing, they looked like the perfect couple, a perfect match.

Catherine and William went downstairs to the hotel ballroom. As they walked inside, Catherine looked around to find Hugh and Antoinette, finally seeing them sitting at a table near the dance floor. She turned to William and smiled brightly. "There they are," she pointed.

Veering close, she noticed something else…Justin was sitting with them. And sitting beside him, a woman. Catherine was stunned. Not only had she not expected to see him at the extravaganza, she certainly hadn't expected to see him with another woman.

Trying not to be obvious, Catherine caught of quick glimpse of the woman to see if she could identify her. She'd never seen her before.

As they neared the table, her heart fluttered. Why was she feeling so nervous? Why did seeing Justin with someone else make her feel so heartbroken?

She caught Justin's eye and he turned to look at her. His eyes pierced every inch of her soul. Their gazes met, and they smiled politely at one another.

When they stepped up to the table, Catherine stood by motionless, watching as Justin stood up to shake William's hand. Then Justin did something totally unexpected. Leaning close, he gave her a long, sweet kiss on the cheek while whispering how beautiful she looked in her ear.

The tension between the three of them immediately began to rise. William's face turned red in anger, while Justin's date looked on, unaware of what was happening.

Antoinette could tell that William was furious and she tried to ease the tension. Just as William started to confront Justin, Antoinette pulled Justin on the dance floor, leaving his date sitting at the table with Hugh.

Once Justin was gone, Catherine cordially said hello to Hugh and Justin's date, then led William to the patio for some fresh air, grabbing two glasses of champagne from one of the servers along the way.

Outside, Catherine reached for William's hand and led him to the edge of the balcony. She didn't look at him, for if she would have, he would have seen the tears welling in her eyes.

She took a sip of champagne. "Look how beautiful the city looks," she said, staring off in the distance.

Taking a deep breath, she tried to clear her eyes. She hoped he wouldn't mention anything about what had happened with Justin.

"So, Catherine, what's up?" William asked softly.

Catherine turned to him. "What do you mean?" she asked, playing dumb.

"I mean, what's going on between you and Justin. The guy hasn't taken his eyes off of you since we got here. And what was that kiss all about?" Pausing, he took a long breath. "And you haven't taken your eyes off of him either." He raised his voice. "Do you think I'm blind? Do you think that I don't see that something's going on between the two of you?"

Wanting a response, he pushed on. "Why don't you enlighten me on the subject?"

Smiling slightly, Catherine couldn't look him in the eyes. "Nothing, Justin and I are just good friends. That's all," she said in a low tone and she turned away.

William gripped her arm and pulled her back to him. "Are you sure that's all," he pressured.

"Yes, I'm positive," she said turning back. "Why, are you jealous?" she joked.

"That's not the point!" he responded, his face reddening in anger.

Catherine stepped closer and hugged him. "Well, let me put your mind to rest," she whispered. "There's no reason for you to be jealous."

Smiling, she took his hand and led him back inside to the dance floor.

Uncertain of his suspicion, he decided to drop the subject. Maybe she was being honest, maybe they were just friends. He still wasn't sure.

During the evening, Catherine used her charm to convince William that there was nothing going on between she and Justin. Making sure she stayed away from Justin, she spent the evening laughing and dancing with William, while Justin watched from across the room.

At eleven-thirty, the band director announced there was only a half an hour until the stroke of midnight. The caterers began to pass out confetti, noise makers and party hats to all of the guests. Catherine and William continued to dance on the crowded dance floor but their fun was soon interrupted when another man crashed into William, spilling a glass of red wine all over him. After the man apologized, they quickly made their way off the dance floor. Catherine tried to get it off with club soda, but it only made it worse. "Maybe you should go upstairs to change," she suggested.

Hesitantly, William agreed.

Eyeing Justin, he kissed her on the cheek. "I'll be right back," he said, then he hurried away.

William took the elevator to go upstairs. As soon as he stepped in, he rushed to push the button. The doors began to close and a woman called out. "Wait, please hold the elevator," she said, stepping inside.

William didn't look at her.

"What floor?" he asked, looking down at his stained shirt.

"I'm going wherever you are," the woman announced in a soft, sexy voice.

His ears perked up, and he slowly shifted his gaze in her direction. He was sure he'd heard wrong. "What did you say?"

Batting her eyelashes, she moved closer. "Don't you remember me?" she asked.

William's forehead wrinkled, and he tried to think back. She wasn't familiar. "I don't think so," he said. "You must be mistaking me for someone else."

She smiled. "William, it's me, Tammy Myers from back home in Boston. We dated for a while in High School."

He took a step back and stroked his chin. It was her. "Wow. You look so different," he commented, looking her over from head to toe.

Old memories began to come back. While in high school he was talked into dating her by his persistent mother, who was friends with her parents. In order to get his mother off his back, he took her out on a couple of dates, then discarded her. After he graduated, his mother always seemed to bring up Tammy's name, telling him how much she'd changed. But he had no idea. She'd gone from a lanky, flat-chested girl with frizzy red hair to a tall, full-figured woman…And her red hair wasn't frizzy anymore.

"I can't believe it's you," he said. "Do you live in LA?"

"I'm here with some friends of mine," she explained vaguely.

The elevator reached the third floor. "Well, this is my floor," he said, looking at the numbers above.

"Can I use your telephone?" she asked, inching closer. "I have to call my friends to let them know I'm here."

William nodded in agreement and she followed him to the door of the suite, entering behind him. He gestured to the telephone, "Well, there it is," he said. "Why don't you use the phone while I go to change my shirt."

"Sure," she replied, lifting the receiver.

As soon as he walked out of the room, she put the receiver down. She strolled down the hall, and entered the bedroom. Across the room, William had taken his shirt off, and was getting another out of the closet.

When he turned around, he saw her standing in the doorway. She dropped her handbag to the floor and began to unbutton her top.

"Whoa…What are you doing?" he questioned nervously.

"What do you think I'm doing?" she replied, moving closer.

Slowly, she pushed the shirt over her shoulders, and it fell to the floor. Mesmerized by her, he watched intently. She walked over and began to stroke and kiss his masculine shoulders, making her way up his neck to his mouth. She put his hands on her hips while she unzipped her skirt. He grinned as she took his hands, leading him to the bed. He couldn't resist the temptation. One by one, their clothes dropped to the floor. She pushed him on the bed. He couldn't fight the urge.

Downstairs, Catherine managed to stay away from Justin by mingling with some of the other guest. When Hugh and Antoinette realized that she was alone, they decided to leave the dance floor to check on her.

As they approached, Antoinctte pulled her aside. "Catherine. It's already eleven forty-five. William hasn't come back down yet? Do you think he's all right?"

Catherine shrugged. "I don't know what's taking him so long."

"Do you want me to have Hugh go up to check on him?"

"Oh, no. That's not necessary. Why don't you stay here and enjoy the party and I'll go," she insisted, and walked away.

Catherine took the elevator upstairs. When she approached the door to their suite, she could see that the door had been left ajar. Slowly, she opened the door and walked through the darkened suite. Peering down the hall, she could see the light on in the bedroom but she couldn't hear a peep. *He probably fell asleep*, she thought as she veered closer. A whimpering sound came from the room. Her hands began to tremble. Slowly, she pushed the door open. She couldn't believe her eyes. Standing motionless in disbelief, her eyes filled with tears. Through blurred vision, Catherine saw William and the other woman turn to look in her direction, startled to see her. Catherine was in shock. Her legs felt like lead and she couldn't move to turn around.

The woman hurried to the bathroom while William jumped to his feet. Once again, Catherine tried to turn around, but she still couldn't move. He walked towards her. "I can explain everything," he said, stooping down to pick his trousers up from the floor.

Catherine tried to control her voice. "Explain. What are you going to explain?" she cried. "Do you think you can explain how you ended up in bed with another woman?"

As he pulled his pants up, her legs finally started to move. "I don't give a damn how it happened!" she cried out as she backed up. She glared at him, furious. "Do you expect me to understand how you could do this to me?" she shouted.

He walked closer. She pointed to him. "Don't even try to explain because I will never understand." Tears rolled down her face. "I want you to stay away from me," she demanded. "I don't want to see you. And I especially don't want to ever talk to you again!"

She turned around and headed for the exit. Struggling to dress while he followed her, William called for her to stop, but it was too late. She was already running toward the elevator. She knew he was going to try to stop her. She banged on the elevator button. Finally, the doors opened. The elevator was empty.

Once inside the safety of the elevator, she reached down for her purse. "Oh, no. I left my purse in the ballroom," she mumbled. "Damn, I don't want to go in there," she said, using her hands to wipe the tears off of her face.

When the elevator doors opened in the lobby, she rushed to the ballroom to collect her belongings. Opening the door, she could hear the crowd of revelers in the midst of singing, *Auld Lang Syne*. People everywhere were throwing confetti and exchanging kisses as colorful balloons fell from above. When she got to the table, she could see Antoinette hugging Justin a few feet away.

Happy to see they weren't looking in her direction, she grabbed her purse from the chair and turned around, only to find herself face to face with Justin.

Surprised to see him, she stopped abruptly. Their eyes locked. "I have to go," she muttered as the tears once again flooded her eyes.

"What happened?" he asked in a concerned tone.

Feeling foolish, she didn't respond. She walked around him, but he followed close behind waiting for an answer. When they got to the lobby, Justin could hear William calling Catherine's name. Justin turned around and grabbed him. "What did you do? Why is she crying?"

Looking over William's shoulder, the other woman appeared and Justin knew exactly what had happened. William tried to go after Catherine, but Justin prevented him from moving. The two men struggled. "I don't have to explain anything to you," William said sternly.

Justin held his ground.

"You better get out of my way right now!" William commanded, forcefully pushing Justin to the side.

William paced to the front entrance and Justin tackled him, throwing the first of many punches. As the word of a fight made its way through the ballroom, Antoinette and Hugh hurried to the hall where they witnessed the scuffle.

Crying, Antoinette urged Hugh to break up the fight before anyone sustained serious injuries. With the help of a security guard, Hugh didn't waste any time. Hugh pulled Justin off of William. With all his strength, Hugh held Justin, while the officer held William.

Struggling with the guard, William managed to free himself and he ran out the front door.

Because it was New Year's Eve, the valet was having a hard time trying to find a taxi for Catherine. After flagging down several, a taxi finally pulled up to the curb.

The valet opened the door, and Catherine slid into the car. Someone tugged on her arm. It was William, pulling at her, apologizing for what he had done. The valet asked William to leave her alone, but he didn't listen. He just kept tugging at her arm.

William didn't realize it, but Antoinette had followed him outside. Together, she and the valet pulled him away from Catherine. "Haven't you done enough?" Antoinette yelled. "Let her go!"

Catherine yanked the door closed. "Just go!" she instructed the driver in a frantic tone.

As the car pulled away from the curb, she could hear the sound of William's voice calling out to her, fading in the distance. The driver looked through his rear view mirror, "Where to, Miss?" he asked in a gentle tone.

Unsure of where to go, Catherine thought about it for a moment, then gave him her home address.

William knew that he somehow had to explain. Flagging down another taxi, William jumped in, demanding that the driver speed to Catherine's house.

As the taxi approached Catherine's home, William noticed that the house was in total darkness. He knew there was a possibility that she hadn't gone home, but decided to try anyway.

When the car stopped, he bolted out, yelling for the driver to wait for him. Rushing to the front entrance, he banged on the door persistently, calling her name, but there was no answer.

On the other side of the door, Catherine sat quietly on the foyer floor. In tears, she clutched her ears. She didn't want to hear him.

A few minutes later, the yelling was replaced with silence and she listened intently as the sound of the car's engine moved away. With her back against the door, she crossed her arms over her chest and stood up. She was devastated.

The telephone rang several times, and the answering machine picked up. She stood silently listening as Antoinette and Justin plead with her over the intercom to pick up the telephone. But she refused. Knowing how they felt about William, she couldn't bear the thought of having to explain what had happened.

Wiping the tears from her eyes, she turned and slowly ascended up the staircase.

Wanting to escape the madness, Catherine packed her suitcases to leave immediately for her home in New York, where she could hide away until the dust settled.

CHAPTER 17

❀

Catherine spent New Year's Day alone at her estate on the outskirts of New York City. She tried not to think about what had happened with William, but couldn't help it. She had so many feelings running through her head. She couldn't stop the emotions. She spent the entire day moping, refusing to eat.

After taking a warm bath, she broke down and called Antoinette. It was the first time Antoinette had ever been speechless. The two ladies spent nearly two hours on the phone, and Antoinette listened as Catherine, for the most part, cried.

Antoinette couldn't stand to hear it anymore. "Catherine, I know that you're upset, but you have to pull yourself together for me. You must pick up the pieces of your heart and go on."

Crying, Catherine said, "I know that's what I should do, but I don't know if I have the strength right now. I feel so numb." She ran a tissue over her face to wipe away the tears. "I'm so sorry to lay all of this on you right now."

Heartbroken by her friend's sadness, Antoinette replied, "Sweetie, I don't mind. I love you like a daughter. Your happiness is important to me." Antoinette paused. "I can take the next flight, and stay with you for a few days?"

"No. It's the holidays and you need to spend time with Hugh and your family."

"What about you? When are you going to come home?" Antoinette questioned

"I don't know. I think I'm going to stay here for a few weeks." Catherine gently blew her nose. "Don't worry about me. I'll be fine." Silence filled the phone line. "Antoinette, before we hang up, I need you to promise me something."

"Sure dear. Anything."

"You have to promise not to tell anyone where I am. I need some time to sort through my feelings."

"Okay. I promise. But only if you promise to call me anytime day or night if you need someone to talk to."

Once again, Catherine wiped away the tears. "I promise," she agreed.

After Catherine hung up, she poured a glass of brandy and headed for her comfortable oversized sofa. Snuggling under a blanket, she watched the flames from the fireplace until she fell into a deep slumber.

What seemed to be a short time later, she was awakened by a chipping noise. Opening her swollen eyelids, she could see Mr. Schultz, the elderly groundskeeper, responsible for taking care of her property. He was leaning beside the fireplace, poking the firewood. Lazily, she sat up and rubbed her eyes.

Hearing her move, he turned around. "I'm sorry, Miss Sheldon. I didn't mean to wake you."

"Oh, that's all right. What time is it anyway?"

"It's ten-thirty," he said as he stood.

"Ten-thirty in the morning?"

"Yes, ma'am."

"I can't believe I slept that long."

"Yes, ma'am. You've been sleeping like a baby for a while now. I spent the night at my daughter's house and when I got home early this morning, I noticed the light from the fire through the window. At first, it startled me, because no one was supposed to be here."

"I'm sorry. I decided to come at the last minute. I should have called first," she explained.

"I don't mind. In fact, it feels good to have you here. It gets pretty lonely out here, so I was happy to see you. I hope you don't mind that I tended to the fire while you were asleep."

Catherine stretched her arms in the air. "No. I don't mind at all. I really appreciate it."

As she looked on, he turned to leave, then he turned back. His eyes softened, "By the way, Miss Sheldon, Happy New Year."

"That's right," Catherine muttered. "Yesterday was New Year's Day, wasn't it?"

"It sure was and if you don't mind, I have plans to visit my family again today."

"No, not at all. You go ahead and enjoy yourself. I'll be fine."

"Okay. If you need anything, just call me. I'll leave my daughter's telephone number on the notepad beside the telephone."

"Thank you," Catherine said, smiling graciously, and Mr. Shultz left.

Catherine had no idea what was in store for her next…She had no idea that Justin had coaxed Antoinette into confiding her whereabouts, and was planning a surprise visit.

Justin arrived shortly after nine the following morning and was immediately greeted at the gate by Mr. Schultz. After some intensive questioning by Mr. Schultz and a lot of persuading by Justin, Mr. Schultz hesitantly let him through, pointing to where Catherine could be found.

As Justin walked around the side of the house, he could see Catherine in the distance. It was a blustery cold, gloomy day and she was sitting on a blanket in the snow, beside the pond. Not knowing what he was going to say, he slowly walked down the hill toward her.

Walking up, he noticed she wasn't wearing a coat. She was dressed in an oversized gray cashmere sweater, a pair of blue jeans with her golden locks of hair nestled on the crown of her head. Her legs were pulled up to her chest with her arms wrapped around them. He stopped to watch her for a moment as she focused her silent gaze on the slow moving water of the pond, not realizing he was there. Silently, he sat beside her.

Feeling his presence, she turned to him. He could tell she had been crying. The white of her eyes was painted red and the tender skin around them swollen. For a moment, neither said a word.

As he turned to the side to look out at the pond, she was astonished to see the bruises on his face. Lifting her hand to his face, she gently examined his swollen eye and cheek with her soft hand. "What happened?" she asked in a melancholy tone.

"I had a little accident," he replied with a boyish grin.

The look of worry filled her eyes. "Were you in a car accident?"

He lifted his hand, sweetly rubbing it against hers and smiled warmly. "No. It wasn't a car accident. I'll tell you about it later. Right now, I just want to get you out of the cold before you catch pneumonia."

Standing up, he held his hand out for hers. She hesitated for a moment, then gave her hand willingly. When they got inside, they went into the great room, where Mr. Schultz had lit another fire.

Leading her close to the fireplace, Justin rubbed his hands briskly up and down her shivering arms. To lighten the moment, he joked, "You know, this isn't the first time I've had to save you from the ravages of nature. You really have to learn to stay warm and dry."

Remembering the day she fell into the lake at his cabin, her mouth slowly curled into a smile, "I don't know what I would do without you?" she said.

"I don't know either, and I don't want to find out," he confided in a serious tone. He stared into her eyes. "I know what happened between you and William," he mumbled.

She began to interrupt.

"No. Wait," he said. "There's something I have to say."

Staring into the fire, he sighed. "Look. I'm not here to say I told you so. You know I'd never do that to you. I'm here to say that I am always going to be here for you. I want you to know you can always count on me."

With that said, Catherine stepped forward, wrapping her arms around his strong shoulders. "Thank you for coming," she whispered, pulling him close. She drew a long breath. "The last few days have been pretty tough and I can use some company right now."

Catherine gestured for him to sit with her on the sofa and they snuggled in each other's arms. "Please tell me how you got that black eye?" she asked curiously.

"I got into a fight with William," he admitted.

Surprised, she pulled away. The intensity of her voice changed. "You didn't?"

His blue eyes turned from blue to green in the firelight. "Yes. I did," he whispered with a solemn nod.

"I want you to promise that you will never do anything like that again," she insisted.

Grinning, Justin promised, then he gently pulled her close, cradling her while they silently watched the fire. The more they snuggled, the more secure Catherine felt in his strong arms and soon she fell fast asleep.

Catherine awoke the next morning, still in the same position, feeling wonderful. As she raised her head from Justin's chest, she realized she'd slept in his arms.

Quietly, she got up from the sofa and went to the kitchen to make a pot of coffee. After it was finished, she poured two cups and headed back to wake Justin.

As she entered the room, she walked over to him. The fire crackled in the background and she watched while he slept. Having an urge to be near him, she leaned over softly kissing him on the cheek and he smiled.

Slowly, his eyes opened and her face came into view. "Good morning," she said.

Because Justin's muscles were stiff from the position he had slept in, he struggled to sit up.

"I thought you might like a cup of coffee," Catherine said, offering the cup to him.

"A cup of coffee sounds great. Thanks," he said as he reached for it.

Catherine sat beside him. "How long do you plan to stay?"

His eyes softened. "I'm going to stay for as long as you need me," he divulged.

"Then, how would you like to stay for the rest of the week?"

"That sounds wonderful," he answered eagerly.

Justin watched as she stood up and walked over to one of the windows. For the first time since she had arrived, she opened the draperies allowing the sun's rays to stream through the room. Although she hadn't forgotten about how badly William had hurt her, she was beginning to realize that life does go on. People get hurt all the time and somehow they manage to survive the pain.

After opening all of the draperies in the great room, Catherine took Justin to one of the guest rooms to settle in.

Because it was Justin's first time in New York, they spent the next four days exploring the city. By week's end, Catherine had taken Justin to see the statue of liberty, two shows on Broadway, and an opera at the Met.

Having survived the trauma, Catherine felt alive once again. And she realized for the first time how much she truly loved having Justin with her. No matter what the future had in store for her, she knew that Justin would always remain a true friend.

For their last night in New York, Justin didn't want to go out. Instead, he planned to surprise Catherine with a candlelit dinner for two. While she was upstairs getting dressed for the evening, he slipped away to the grocery store.

When he returned, he overheard a telephone conversation between she and Antoinette. They were in the midst of discussing how her feelings for William had been diminishing day by day. She told Antoinette that she was having a glorious time with him. That put a huge smile on his face. It was all he needed to hear. Not wanting to eavesdrop any longer, he rushed to the kitchen to start cooking.

Catherine could hear the clanging of pots and pans as she finished her conversation with Antoinette. As soon as she hung up, she went to the kitchen to see what was happening.

Peering through the broad doorway, she stopped to watch Justin hard at work washing dishes. It made her smile. He looked so handsome, dressed in a navy blue flannel shirt and a pair of blue jeans. He had rolled up the sleeves of his shirt, and had his hands buried deep within the bubbles of the sink.

As she watched, she was surprised to hear Mr. Shultz's voice from the corner of the breakfast nook. "Good evening, Miss Sheldon. I just came over to give the two of you a weather report," he said.

As she walked toward Mr. Schultz to say hello, Justin turned around to look at her.

"I was just telling Justin that a snow storm is on the way," Mr. Schultz informed her. "Looks like we're going to be in for a rough night."

"Oh, no. You have to be kidding?" she replied in disbelief, turning to Justin.

"I wish I was," Mr. Schultz said.

Distressed by the news, Catherine's forehead wrinkled. Her serious eyes had told Justin that she was worried, and with quickness in his step, he rushed to her side as Mr. Schultz continued, "It's supposed to get pretty bad. We may even lose power."

"How long is it supposed to last?" she asked quizzically.

"Just overnight from what the weatherman says. This one should clear out by morning."

Relieved, Catherine sighed. "That's good news."

Mr. Schultz stood up and put a pair of ear muffs on. "Well, I'm going to go now," he said, and turned toward the door.

Just as he started to open the door, Catherine called out for him. He turned around. "Would you like to join us for dinner?" she asked graciously.

"Thanks for the invitation, but I've already eaten," he replied. A thought came to him. "Oh, by the way," he said. "I chopped some extra wood. It's right outside the door under the tarp, if you need it. I'm going to be home all night. Just let me know if you need anything."

Catherine and Justin walked over to the door to see him out. The cold wind blew through the kitchen as Mr. Schultz opened the door. "Thanks for coming over," Justin told Mr. Schultz as he firmly gripped Catherine's hand in reassurance.

They waved good-bye, then closed the kitchen door. Grasping her shivering arms, Catherine turned to Justin. His strong jawbones tensed, then relaxed and he changed the subject. "Guess what? I have a surprise for you."

The look of worry slowly disappeared from her face. "What kind of surprise?" she asked.

His eyes twinkled as he spoke in an Italian accent. "Tonight, I plan to wine and dine you with a very special cuisine. First, you will enjoy a mixed green salad, followed by my specialty, spaghetti and meatballs. For dessert, a chocolate mousse pie. And to top it all off, two wonderful bottles of Chianti."

Catherine giggled. "How'd you know spaghetti was my favorite food?"

His stare turned intimate and he leaned closer. "I know a lot more about you than you think," he admitted.

The tension between them began to grow.

Catherine's legs weakened and her pulse quickened as he wrapped his strong arms around her. Pulling her body close, they shared a tender kiss. Unable to go any farther, she held her hands firmly against his chest and pushed him away. Nervously, she walked over to the stove.

Turning back, she gazed at him. "It's too soon. I'm not ready for this yet," she explained calmly.

Justin watched as she removed the cover to the pot and stirred the spaghetti sauce. He was disappointed, but knew deep within his heart that one day she would be ready to share herself with him. It was only a matter of time.

Trying to lift the somber mood, he walked beside her. "It looks like our dinner is ready. Why don't we sit down to eat?" he said cheerfully.

She turned to him and smiled. "That sounds great. What can I do to help?" she asked kindly.

Justin threw the dishtowel over his shoulder, and once again spoke in an Italian accent, "Not a thing, Madame. The preparation is complete. For your pleasure, I took the liberty of setting the table in the dining room." He reached his arm out. "Please come with me and I'll show you to your seat."

Giving her arm willingly, Catherine giggled. "That sounds lovely. Please lead the way."

Entering the dining room, Catherine's eyes detected an amazing site. Just as he had done for Christmas, Justin had decorated the dining room with twinkle-lights and set an exquisite table. Her eyes filled with tears and she turned to him. "Oh, Justin. I can't believe you went through all the trouble!"

Justin laughed. "I'm glad you like it." His voice softened. "You know Catherine, there isn't anything that I wouldn't do for you," he mentioned tenderly.

Stroking her tears away with her fingertips, she cried, "I know that. In fact, I think I've known it all along. You've been so wonderful, and I've been so awful to you over the last few months."

He reached his hands out. "No. You haven't been awful at all. I think you've just been confused."

Gripping his hands, she stared deeply into his eyes as he continued, "You deserve the best that life has to offer. And I'm not talking about material things. I'm talking about what really matters. I'm talking about the things that can't be bought…"

Her eyes wet and red, Catherine fell into his strong arms and laid her head upon his shoulder. After cuddling with her for a moment, Justin pulled away slightly, using his fingertips to gently pull her chin upward. He wanted to look into her eyes. She tried to look away but his grip was too strong. His blue eyes turned serious. "You know, if you give me the chance, I'll show you how love is supposed to feel."

Catherine's body became feverish, her soft lips drawn to his. Slowly, they got closer. Frightened, she pulled away. "It's too soon. I hope you understand. I'm just not ready."

Although Catherine yearned for Justin, her heart still ached from the pain she had suffered at William's hands. Before proceeding with any new relationship, she had to be certain that she was over William.

Justin broke the tension again. "Why don't I open a bottle of the wine, while you take your place at the table?" he suggested thoughtfully.

"That would be great," she said and she sat down.

During dinner, they tried to make small talk, but it just wasn't working. There was too much tension in the air. Later, while they cleaned the kitchen, Justin told her that he had decided to leave the following morning for Los Angeles. She too decided that it was time to return. She had been hidden away for much too long. She knew in order to put William behind her, she had to go home. It was time to take her life back.

When they finished cleaning the kitchen, they decided to turn in for the evening. It had been a long day, and they were both ready for a peaceful night of rest.

When Catherine got to her bedroom, she realized that the snow storm that Mr. Schultz had spoken about was beginning to move through the area. While putting on her flannel pajamas, the wind began to howl. She walked over to the window to look out. The snow began to pound against the window. Startled, she stepped back and jumped into bed.

After turning out the light, Catherine snuggled beneath two layers of blankets. Her thoughts turned to Justin. She tossed and turned, but just couldn't get him out of her head. A big part of her wanted to get out of bed and go to him, but she was afraid. An hour passed. She still wasn't able to fall asleep. Finally, she decided to go to him, not for sex but for comfort.

As she made her way down the hall to his bedroom, she noticed that the door to his room was closed. Stooping down, she peered under the door to see if the light was on, but the room was dark. She hesitated for a moment, then gently tapped twice on the door. He didn't answer, so she turned to walk away.

When she got back to the end of the hall, the door opened. As she turned around, she saw him standing in the dim glow from the bedroom light, wearing a pair of pajama pants, without a shirt.

Her hands trembled as she walked closer. "I couldn't sleep. I hope I didn't wake you?"

"No. Not at all. I've just been lying in bed listening to the sound of the snow hitting my window."

Catherine smiled. "I know. I've been doing the same thing. I just can't seem to go to sleep."

For a moment, they stared awkwardly at one another without speaking. Her heart was pounding so much it felt as though it was going to explode. "Do you want to come in? I promise to be a gentleman," he added, easing the tension.

"That would be great," Catherine said as she entered the room.

Realizing it was probably a bad idea for her to be there, she turned to leave, but found herself face to face with him. As she nervously pushed her hair off her shoulders, he leaned over and kissed her softly on the lips.

This time, she didn't pull away.

Before things got out of hand, Justin made a suggestion. "Why don't we sleep together?" he said.

Stuttering, he clarified what he was trying to say. "I mean...we don't have to do anything…"

Agreeing, Catherine sat on the edge of the bed while Justin pulled a white tee shirt over his head.

Without any pressure from Justin, they spent the remainder of the night wrapped in each other's arms, waking to the sound of a snow plow driving down the street.

Sitting up, Catherine could see Justin staring at her.

"What? Is my hair a mess?" she asked.

He laughed. "No. You look beautiful."

She started to get out of bed, then turned to face him.

"Thank you for being here for me last night. That was exactly what I needed."

She started to feel awkward about being there. "Well, I better go to get dressed," she said nervously. "Then, I think I'll pack for our trip home."

Justin nodded in agreement as she left the room.

After packing, Catherine went downstairs to find Justin. As she entered the living room, she saw him sitting on the sofa, watching the weather channel.

"Hi," he said, cheerfully, turning in her direction. "I was checking the weather. Looks like everything's clear now."

Sitting beside him, Catherine fidgeted with her hands. "Yes. I just got off the phone with my pilot. He said the storm wasn't as bad as they thought it would be. We have to meet him in a couple of hours."

Justin turned the television off and stood up. "How would you like pancakes for breakfast?" he asked.

Catherine smiled. "That sounds great," she replied, then she stood up and led him to the kitchen.

Once in the kitchen, Catherine removed the cover to the griddle and began heating it, while Justin mixed the pancake batter. Working as a team, Catherine retrieved the butter and maple syrup while Justin cooked the pancakes. Then she set the table.

After enjoying a home-cooked breakfast, they cleaned up the house and packed Justin's rental car. An hour later, they were at the airport boarding Catherine's private jet for the trip back to Los Angeles.

When they arrived in Los Angeles, a car was waiting to take them to the airport's parking garage where Justin had left his truck. At first, Catherine was going to let the driver take her home, but after a little coaxing from Justin, she decided to ride with him instead.

The drive home turned out to be a quiet one, with each, deep in thought. In silence, she stared out the truck window. She realized that New York had been a turning point in her life.

After all of the pain, she'd finally made the decision to forget about William. She wanted nothing more than to put what he had done in the past, and move on with her future. It seemed like the man to do that with was Justin, but she needed a little more time to make a decision. And time was what Justin was willing to give.

Pulling into Catherine's driveway, the truck halted. Justin stared at her. Taking a deep breath, he leaned over, gently kissing her. "Well, I guess I better get you inside now," he whispered against her lips.

"Yes, that's probably a good idea," Catherine acknowledged.

While Justin unloaded her luggage from the truck, she unlocked the front door. Carrying the luggage, he stepped up behind her. She invited him inside but since they were both weary from the flight, they decided to say good-bye at the door.

"Well, I had a great time," Catherine said nervously.

Justin smiled. "I did, too. Thanks for the tour of New York."

Catherine's eyes turned serious and she moved closer. "Thank you," she whispered softly against his cheek. Closing her eyes, she searched for his lips. Wetting her lips with her tongue, she kissed him delicately, then slowly opened her eyes. They traded smiles.

"I'll call you later," he said and she watched as he walked to his truck.

Waving good-bye, she turned and went inside.

Snapping the door shut, Catherine leaned back against the door, and smiled.

Realizing that she better check her messages, she walked to her study. Much to her surprise, there weren't any messages from William, however, several from Antoinette. And from the sound of her voice she sounded pretty stressed.

Catherine picked up the phone and walked into the kitchen to brew a cup of hot tea. After finishing, she dialed Antoinette's number. The telephone rang several times, and Antoinette finally answered.

"Hi, it's me," Catherine said, swallowing a sip.

"Oh, Catherine, I'm so happy to hear from you. Did you just get in?"

"Yes, I just got home a few minutes ago. Your message sounded urgent."

"It's William. He's been hounding me everyday."

Anguished, Catherine replied, "Oh, Antoinette, I'm sorry you had to be bothered with him. That was the last thing I wanted." Pushing the hair out of her eyes, she continued, "If he calls again, just tell him that I'm home, but I'm not interested in seeing him."

"Are you sure you want me to let him know you're home?" Antoinette questioned in a concerned tone.

"Yes. I'm positive. I finally feel strong enough to deal with him if he calls. While I was away, I realized what a fool I've been over the last few months. I don't think he's capable of caring for anyone except himself."

Antoinette's tone changed. "I'm so happy that you're back to your old self. I was really worried about you."

"I'm fine now. It just took a couple of weeks for me to see my life clearly. But now I'm back, and I'm ready to face the world."

Antoinette knew that Catherine's battle with William wasn't over yet, but she was glad to see that Catherine was up to the task that lay ahead. "If he calls again, I'll give him the message. But I think you should know. He looks just awful and he's been drinking a lot lately. So just be careful. After that incident at the New Year's Eve party, Lord only knows what he might do."

"Thanks for the warning," Catherine said. "Now, why don't we change the subject? What have you been doing lately?" she asked cheerfully.

"Well, I have good news. Hugh and I have been planning our wedding," Antoinette revealed.

Catherine frowned. "Oh my, the wedding," she whined. "I was supposed to help you with that."

"Don't worry about it. Hugh and I have everything under control. But we can talk about that later. How about you? What happened in New York?"

Catherine sat back in her chair to tell the story. "Well—as you already know, Justin came to visit," she began.

"So—did anything happen between the two of you?" Antoinette inquired.

"Do you mean, did I sleep with him?"

For a moment, Antoinette remained quiet. "Well, did you?" she asked.

Catherine's voice became stern. "No, I didn't. I'm not ready for that yet. So, back to you," she said, trying to change the subject. "What else have you and Hugh been up to?"

"While you've been away, Hugh and I also planned a party to introduce our families before the wedding."

"That's wonderful," Catherine exclaimed, reaching for her calendar to mark the date. "When is it?"

"We planned it for two weeks before our wedding, here at my house."

"Perfect," Catherine said, making a notation on the calendar.

Weary from the trip, Catherine decided to cut their conversation short. "Well, listen, Antoinette, I'm pretty tired. Is it all right if I call you tomorrow?"

Without hesitating, Antoinette agreed.

After hanging up the telephone, Catherine went upstairs, changed and went straight to bed.

Lying in bed, she began to reflect on her time in New York. She had such a great time with Justin and she was already missing him. She especially missed the way that he'd held her snugly in his strong, warm arms. She'd taken his friendship for granted for so many months. And he was right, she hadn't been seeing clearly. For if she had, she would have noticed that the man of her dreams was standing right before her eyes the entire time.

Justin had been so wonderful. He'd tried so hard to protect her from getting hurt.

Deep in thought, she was stunned to hear her telephone ring. She listened as it rang three times. Finally, on the fourth ring her answering machine picked up. She waited for the voice to come over the speaker, "Catherine. It's Justin. Are you there?"

Relieved that it wasn't William, she hurried to pick up. "Justin, Hi."

"I'm sorry. Did I wake you?" he asked.

"No. In fact, I was just thinking about you," she admitted.

Lovingly, he responded, "Tell me more. What were you thinking?"

She grinned. "I was thinking about how much I miss you."

He laughed. "Well, if you'd like my company tonight, I can make it to your house in record time."

"Why don't you make it here safely instead," she replied, giving him permission to come over.

Justin didn't waste any time in responding. "All right, I'll be right over," he said, and they hung up.

CHAPTER 18

A half an hour after Justin called, Catherine heard a knock at the door. Looking down at her watch, she rushed to greet him. "That was fast," she said with a smile, pulling the door open.

Taking an involuntary step backward, she cupped her hand over her mouth. William was standing in the doorway, bearing his little lost boy expression, holding a bouquet of pink roses.

He looked terrible. His hair was messy, and his face looked like it hadn't been shaved in weeks. His eyes were glazed and bloodshot, like daggers piercing through every inch of her soul.

Shocked by the sight of him, she couldn't move. Her legs were locked in place.

"What are you doing here?" she angrily questioned.

Handing the bouquet to her, he crossed the threshold.

"Aren't you going to ask me in?" he asked, staggering past her.

Making sure to stay within a safe distance, Catherine left the door open. "I don't think that's a good idea," she replied. "You've been drinking."

His speech slurred. "I've been drinking, but I'm not drunk. I just want to talk."

Catherine's face turned flush. "There isn't anything for us to talk about. Even if there were, I wouldn't do it while you're in this state."

Closing in on her, he backed her into the door frame. "What state?" he grunted.

Catherine tried to get away from him, but he boxed her in, forcing her back into the foyer wall.

The stench of liquor rolled off his breath as he pushed his chest into hers. "All I want to do is talk. Can we please talk about what happened?"

Looking at him with a blank stare, Catherine didn't answer.

He inched closer and grabbed her chin, holding it steady with his hand. He tried to push his lips against hers, but she resisted by turning her face to the side. His nose pressed into her neck. "What's wrong? You used to like for me to kiss you," he said, inhaling the scent of her perfume.

Using all of her strength, she pushed him away. "I don't want to," she insisted. "And I don't want you here!"

Moving toward the door, her emotions exploded and she burst into tears. "Haven't you caused me enough pain?" she cried.

Regretting his actions, William lifted his hands in the air, and backed away. "I'm sorry that I hurt you," he said in a loving voice. "Please give me a chance to explain."

Catherine sat down on the foyer steps and cradled her head with her hands. Her fight had ended. She was ready to listen to his explanation. The truth was, she did want to know what had caused him to be unfaithful.

William squatted beside her. "The woman you saw me with. I dated her in high school. I ran into her on the way to our suite."

Crossing her arms over her chest, Catherine's expression didn't change while he continued.

"I know it's no excuse, but I was pretty drunk that night," he said, then hurried to add. "But I promise, she didn't mean anything to me. It happened that one time and I haven't seen her since."

He moved in front of her, gently placing his arms around her shoulders. "It's you that I want. Only you," he whispered.

The words struck her hard and she choked back her tears.

Looking up with an expressionless stare, she lifted his hands from her shoulders, and pushed them back into his chest. "It's over...I'm sorry...but it's over," she muttered.

At that moment, William realized how much pain he'd caused. How much damage he'd done. Overcome with sadness, he simply stood, and walked out the door.

Justin arrived a few minutes later. As he walked up to the entryway, he saw the door had been left open.

He rushed inside.

Just as he made his way over the threshold, he halted at the sight of Catherine sitting quietly, with her head in her lap, on the foyer steps. He could tell that something had happened, but didn't know what it was. That is, until he saw the bouquet of roses lying beside her on the floor.

He realized that William had been there.

"Are you all right?" he asked in a distressed tone.

Hearing the sweet sound of his voice, Catherine burst into tears and ran into his arms. "Oh, Justin. I'm so glad you're here."

He held her tightly. "It's all right," he uttered in a tender voice, consoling her.

Catherine backed away to tell him what had happened. "William was here," she whispered, wiping the tears away from her eyes. "There was a knock on the door. I thought it was you."

His face reddened. "Did he hurt you?"

"No. He didn't hurt me. He just wanted to talk."

Not wanting to upset him any further with the details, she smiled. "I'm all right," she said, reassuring him. "I asked him to leave and he did."

Pulling her to him, Justin sighed hard. Although he wanted to know the details of what had happened, he didn't ask.

He was just happy that she was all right.

That night, for the second time, Catherine and Justin spent the night together snuggled in each other's arms. Justin was so wonderful, so understanding. Early on, he had told her that he wouldn't pressure her into having intercourse, and like a perfect gentleman, he had kept his word.

Over the next week, Catherine and Justin spent most of their evenings together, watching old movies or listening to music. One of the things Catherine loved so much about him, was that they didn't have to go out. They were perfectly content just being together.

During that time, Justin mentioned that he wanted to have a dinner party and he asked if she would help to plan the event.

Excited, she willingly agreed.

In her spare time, Catherine worked with a party planner who, under her close supervision, made all of the arrangements for the event. The party would be held at his home the weekend before Antoinette's family gathering, and the guest list was to include their closest friends, and some of the contractors that Justin often worked with, including a builder, an electrician, and a roofer, along with their wives.

Catherine arrived at Justin's home early the afternoon of the dinner party. Before getting out of her car, she looked up at the stately mansion and took a deep breath. It was the first time she'd been at his home since their Christmas dinner when she'd left so abruptly and she was feeling a bit nervous.

Walking to the back of the car, she opened the trunk, retrieving a garment bag, her makeup kit, and the overnight bag she'd packed just in case the party ended late.

As she snapped the trunk shut, she heard the front door open, and Justin came into view. He smiled brightly, and all the signs of her uneasiness disappeared.

"Hi," he said with a huge grin, rushing toward her. "Here let me take those," he said excitedly, reaching for the bags.

Smiling, she thanked him, then walked with him to the front door.

"Come on in," he said, opening the door widely.

Taking another deep breath, she stepped inside.

"The caterers just arrived," he informed her, moving toward the staircase. He gestured up the stairs. "I'm going to run upstairs to put these in the guest bedroom. How about if I meet you in the kitchen?" he asked. She nodded in agreement.

Upon entering the kitchen, Catherine was greeted by the party planner. "Hello, Miss Sheldon. I'm glad you're here. I'd like to go over a few things with you."

"Sure," Catherine agreed with a bright smile.

Throwing her handbag to the side, Catherine rolled up the sleeves of her shirt, and got to work. While the catering staff began the food preparation in the background, the two ladies huddled over the island in the center of the kitchen to make last minute plans.

When they finished, Catherine gave the party planner a tour of the lower level of the house, explaining how she wanted everything set up.

A little while later, Justin found Catherine in the dining room. He watched proudly as she showed the party planner where everything could be found, from place settings to utensils. He'd shown her only once, and she'd remembered where everything was.

While speaking, Catherine looked up and saw him standing in the doorway. She smiled in his direction. "Is there anything you'd like to add?" she asked.

The party planner turned to him. "No. It looks like you have everything under control," he said with a smile, and he walked out of the room.

Her focus turned back to Catherine.

With an air of cool confidence, Catherine continued. "Great," she said. "I think that's everything. Just let me know if you need anything," she instructed and walked away.

When Catherine left the dining room, she went to find Justin. Just as she made her way around the corner leading to the den, he came into view, standing near the glass doors looking out over the gardens of his backyard. She walked up behind him, encircling his waist with her arms. "Hi," she whispered against the back of his ear, snuggling her chest against his back.

Her arms still around him, he slowly turned to face her. "Hello," he whispered.

Lifting his hands to her face, he stroked the skin of her soft cheeks and guided her mouth to his. They kissed, softly, gently. His hands wandered through her thick, velvety hair. Her legs weakened and she had an orgasmic reaction. It was the first time she'd ever experienced anything like that. At that moment, she wanted him more than ever.

With their lips inches apart, they heard someone clearing their throat to get their attention. "Excuse me," the voice cracked.

Smiling at one another, Catherine and Justin turned to see who was speaking.

"I'm sorry for interrupting," the party planner said, "but the caterers can't find any extra baking pans."

Planting a soft kiss on Catherine's lips, Justin smiled. "I'll be right back," he said, and he led the party planner to the kitchen. "They're on the top shelf of the pantry," Catherine heard him tell her.

Catherine sat on the sofa to wait for him. A few minutes later, he walked back in the room. With a huge grin, he sat beside her. "Now, where were we?" he asked, hoping to start again where they'd left off.

Catherine smiled. "It's probably best that we were interrupted. Right now isn't the best time," she pointed out.

She looked down at her watch. "In fact, we better go upstairs to get ready. We only have an hour and a half before our guests arrive."

"You're right," Justin agreed, glancing down at his watch.

Standing up, he helped Catherine rise to her feet.

"I think I'll begin with a cold shower." He laughed.

Giggling, Catherine took hold of his hand and they went upstairs.

After showering, Catherine dried her hair and pinned it in a glamorous style. She applied her makeup, rubbed perfume on her neck and wrists, and then put on her hose. She walked over to the closet where her garment bag was hanging and pulled out her dress.

Just as she had the first time she'd met Justin, she dressed in a simple black dress, cut right above her knees, and finished the outfit with a pair of black chunky heeled silk pumps.

On the bed, nestled inside her luggage, was the jewelry she planned to wear for the evening. Opening the bag, she pulled out the strand of pearls that Justin had given her for Christmas and put them on, along with a pearl bracelet and earrings.

When Catherine finished dressing, she headed downstairs to the dining room to check the table. She didn't realize it, but Justin was watching her from across the room as she inspected every place setting and arranged the place cards.

Feeling Justin's presence, she slowly turned to look at him. Their eyes met, and it was pure magic.

He smiled softly and she returned the smile, then he casually strolled toward her. "You look beautiful," he commented, gently kissing her cheek.

"And you look very handsome," she replied, seeing him dressed in a sport coat and a nice pair of slacks.

He wanted to comment on the strand of pearls, but the doorbell chimed. He reached for her hand, "Well, are you ready?" he asked excitedly.

"Yes. Let's go," she replied as they walked hand in hand to answer the door.

When Justin opened the door, Catherine smiled seeing Hugh and Antoinette on the other side. Feeling slightly nervous, she was immediately calmed by their presence.

While Justin shook Hugh's hand, Catherine gave Antoinette a warm hug. "I'm so happy you're here," she whispered in Antoinette's ear. Then Catherine turned to Hugh and gave him a kiss on the cheek.

After closing the door, the doorbell chimed again. "I'll talk to you in a minute," Catherine told Antoinette, excusing herself while Justin opened the door again.

Catherine smiled warmly when she saw that Justin's friends, Gary and Bridgett Moseley had arrived, along with the electrical contractor and his wife.

As they walked in, Justin graciously introduced Catherine to everyone. She warmly welcomed them and together, she and Justin led their guests into the large formal living room for cocktails.

While Justin helped the bartender take drink orders, the caterers passed out hors d'oeuvres.

When everyone had been served, Justin joined the men, who were now huddled near the fireplace, and Catherine sat down with the ladies in a cozy seating area on the other side of the room.

From where she was sitting, Catherine could hear a little bit of the men's conversation as they spoke about golf and fishing.

On the other side of the room, the ladies talked about their husbands and children. Although Catherine couldn't give any input in those two areas, she listened carefully, trying to retain any information that might help her later when she did have a husband and a family.

Within thirty minutes, the remainder of the guests arrived and soon after, they sat down for dinner.

Across the length of the table, Justin watched as Catherine fiddled nervously with the strand of pearls around her neck while the other ladies carried on a conversation amongst themselves.

Seeing that Catherine felt left out, Bridgett Moseley tried to break the ice. She mentioned that she had been using Catherine's skin care line for quite some time and she said that she was very pleased with it.

That started things off.

Others then chimed in on the conversation, asking for advice about fashion, makeup and skin care. One of the ladies even asked if Catherine would sit down with her, and possibly the others, at a later time to advise them on which colors worked best for them, and demonstrate to them, step-by-step, the proper way to apply their makeup.

Excited, Catherine agreed.

Changing the subject, the builder and his wife told funny stories about the trips they'd taken. One that stuck out in particular was about the time they'd taken their twelve year old daughter on a cruise with them. They said when their daughter found out there was no charge for room service, she didn't want to leave the cabin. She spent the entire cruise watching movies and ordering anything that she wanted. She was in heaven. And so were they.

The conversation changed again, when they found out that Hugh was the famous movie producer, Hugh Davenport. Everyone wanted to hear stories about their favorite movie stars, and of course, Hugh obliged.

Although most of the guests weren't wealthy, Catherine found them to be rich in other ways. With them, the atmosphere was laid back, real. There wasn't one stuck up person in the group.

Soon dinner had ended and the group moved to the den.

Glancing at one another from across the room, Justin and Catherine smiled. Around the room, the lines of social standing had been broken, and everyone was talking and laughing with one another. Tonight, they were all equal.

While the men helped clear the furniture, providing a dance floor, Justin walked over to the sound system and turned the CD player on. Soon after, songs from the seventies began to play, and everyone danced.

Catherine hadn't had that much fun in ages.

Around midnight, Catherine and Justin waved good-bye to the last of their guests. The party had been a success. And Catherine couldn't wait to get together with them again.

Snapping the front door shut, Justin smiled at Catherine and reached for her hand. Leading her into the den, she sat down while he walked over to the bar. "How about a glass of brandy?" he asked, pulling out two glasses.

Catherine nodded. "That would be great," she replied.

Crossing to her, Justin handed a glass to her. She thought he would sit beside her, but he excused himself and walked into the kitchen.

A minute later, he walked back in the room. "I hope you don't mind," he said, "but I let the caterers go home before they finished cleaning."

Taking a sip of brandy, Catherine smiled. "I don't mind at all," she replied, happy that they were alone.

She watched as Justin took off his jacket and walked over to the stereo. After sliding a CD into the player, he walked toward her. The smooth sounds of jazz began to play.

Grinning, he moved closer and held out his hand. "Would you like to dance?" he asked.

Accepting the invitation, Catherine took hold of his hand and stood up. Together, they swayed around the room.

Although it had been a while since they'd danced together, they moved in perfect sync with one another.

Cupping her hand behind his neck, she pulled him close, and shut her eyes. Her cheek brushed lightly against his. It was smooth. Inhaling the scent of his cologne, she remembered the first time they danced at Antoinette's party…How close they'd danced that night, how relaxed he'd made her feel.

If only she'd followed her instincts back then.

Not wanting to think about the past any longer, Catherine pulled away from him slightly and looked into his striking blue eyes. At that moment, she was exactly where she wanted to be.

Reaching forward, she glided her hands over his cheeks, guiding his mouth to hers. Closing her eyes, hers lips melted into his. A tingle ran through her spine.

Instinctively, Justin knew what she was doing. "Are you sure?" he whispered against her lips.

Without speaking, she licked her lips and nodded.

Reaching down for his hand, she led him upstairs, to his bedroom. As they entered, she led him to the bed.

While he watched, she pulled the covers back.

Justin shifted closer. His hands migrated to her back. They were hot. Gliding them across her smooth skin, he unzipped her dress. The feeling of his hands against her skin caused her upper thighs to pulsate. Catherine shut her eyes as Justin slid her dress off her shoulders. The dress fell to her ankles. Turning to face him, she stepped out of it, and he picked it up, laying it neatly on the chair beside the bed. Moving close to him, she watched as Justin unbuttoned his shirt, then she used her fingers to push it over his muscular shoulders.

Slowly, they undressed each other. Soon they stood before each other naked, with nothing to hide.

Reaching for his hand, Catherine guided him into bed.

Drawing a deep breath, she laid back while he kissed every inch of her body, exploring every part. His lips gravitated to hers, and their passion ignited.

Moving as one, they climaxed together, sending pulsating tingles through her body. It was electric. The moment one ended, another began. The pulsating didn't seem to stop. That was the first time that Catherine had ever reached multiple orgasms. It was the most amazing thing she'd ever experienced.

By the time they finished making love, they were both out of breath and exhausted. Moving beside Justin, Catherine slid her leg over his. "That was amazing," she said with a smile.

Agreeing, Justin grinned.

Catherine stroked Justin's chest and they began to talk about the party, how nice it'd turned out.

Laughing, Justin said that he'd noticed when the ladies bombarded her with questions for advice on skin care and makeup. He complimented her on how well she'd handled their questions.

After talking for a while, they fell asleep, and when they woke, they were still wrapped in the comfort of each other's arms.

CHAPTER 19

A soft ray of sunlight streamed through the window and Catherine opened her eyes. The day of Antoinette's party had finally arrived, and once again she and Justin were together.

Feeling wonderful, she rolled over, watching as Justin slept. Snuggling beside him, she traced the skin on his shoulder with her fingers. Still in a deep slumber, it didn't wake him.

Thoughts of the past few weeks churned through her head and she smiled. Although the time had passed quickly, the weeks she'd spent with him had been the happiest time in her life. And now it was clear, she was in love with him.

Trying not to wake him, she scooted to the edge of the bed and got up. Grabbing her robe from where it lay on the bottom of the bed, she put it on, then went downstairs to make a pot of coffee.

Waiting for the coffee to brew, Catherine leaned her elbows on the countertop and looked out the window. She watched a family of birds sitting on the birdbath, using the water to clean themselves. It was the first time she'd ever seen them using it, and it made her smile.

The coffee pot started gurgling as it finished brewing, and she looked down at it. When it finished, she made two cups and went back upstairs to see if Justin was still asleep.

As she entered the bedroom, she noticed that the bed was empty. Glancing around the room, she focused on him standing beside the window talking on his cell phone.

"Good Morning," he whispered with a smile.

He pointed to the phone. "One of my clients," he mouthed, and she understood. Setting his cup of coffee down on the end table, she sat in the chair beside him. While she waited for him to finish, she sipped her coffee.

Realizing that he was about to hang up, she put her coffee cup down on the table beside his, and stood up.

Flipping the cover to his cell phone closed, he looked at her. "I can't believe this," he said. "They want me to meet with them this evening."

"What time?" Catherine asked, knowing that Antoinette's party was going to begin at seven.

"Four," he grunted.

"Can't you meet with them next week?"

He thought for a moment. "No," he said. "I can't do that to them. They're a young couple, making plans to build their first home and they're really excited about starting tonight."

Seeing the disappointment in her eyes, he moved close and hugged her. "It'll be all right," he said. "But I think it'll be best if we meet at Antoinette's, just in case the meeting runs over."

Agreeing, they finished their coffee, then Justin started to dress. Catherine could tell he was getting ready to leave.

"Do you have to leave so soon?"

"Yes. I want to get home to write some notes for their house plans. I have a good idea of what they want, so I'd like to get a head start."

Agreeing with him, Catherine watched while he went to the bathroom to brush his teeth and splash water on his face and head. Then she went downstairs with him to see him off.

When he left, Catherine spent her day lazily around the house. She felt lost without him.

Later, she started to get ready for the party.

She took her time, dressing in an elegant, silver embroidered dress. After she finished, she opened the music box that Justin had given her and pulled out the beautiful strand of pearls that were inside. Looking into the mirror, she smiled putting them around her neck. They were perfect…

When she finished, she opened the drawer to pull out some tissue to carry in her purse. Inside the drawer, she saw the box containing the diamond ring that William had given her. Up until then, she had forgotten all about it.

She stood motionless for a moment, then reached down and picked up the box. The memories of her times with William began to come back. One at a time, they raged through her mind. But she didn't cry nor did she open the lid to look at the ring. Instead, she pulled the box out and walked over to her jewelry box. Calmly, she pulled out the diamond necklace that William had given her in San Francisco and gripped it tightly in her hand.

Carrying both pieces she went downstairs to her study. She knew exactly what she wanted to do…What she had to do.

Opening her telephone directory, she thumbed through, finding the telephone number for a delivery service that she often used. Without hesitation, she dialed the number, and the owner answered.

After saying hello, Catherine asked if his company could make a delivery that evening, and he agreed.

As soon as she hung up, she pulled a shipping box and a roll of packaging tape out from her credenza, and then she wrapped the package. When she finished, she addressed it to William.

An hour later, the delivery driver arrived to pick up the package, promising to deliver it immediately.

Without any second thought, Catherine handed the package to the driver.

As he walked toward his truck, she picked up her purse and walked out the door.

In the driveway, her limousine driver, Jackson, was waiting beside the car to take her to Antoinette's party.

Standing tall, she walked to the car, watching as the delivery truck pulled out of her driveway.

When Catherine arrived at the Drew Estate, she was greeted at the front entrance by Antoinette and Hugh. Antoinette looked simply beautiful and her face was glowing like that of a much younger woman. Catherine was thrilled to see how happy she was.

Of all the people in the world, Antoinette deserved to be happy. She'd been through a lot of tough times in her life, and now it was her moment to shine in the spotlight.

After speaking with the two of them for a while, Catherine decided to mingle in the crowded ballroom. Unlike other parties that Antoinette had held at her estate, the room was filled with only family and close friends and like another member of the family, Catherine knew everyone.

Although Catherine was having a great time, she truly missed Justin. She'd been there for some time and he still hadn't arrived. She didn't feel like mingling anymore, so she decided to take her glass of wine and go for a stroll down to the swimming pool.

Stepping onto the patio, she looked up at the sky. The night was clear; the sky was filled with stars and a full moon was beaming down on the gardens.

When she arrived at the pool, she looked around. Unlike the last party she'd attended at the estate, when she'd met William, there were a few people sitting around the pool enjoying the evening weather.

Catherine pulled a chair out from one of the tables and sat down. Feeling relaxed, she took a sip of wine, and closed her eyes. "Do you want to go for a dip?" she heard a familiar voice ask from behind. She immediately recognized the voice. It was William.

Startled, her eyes snapped open.

She didn't want to turn around, but she had to.

Turning her head slowly, she interrogated him. "How did you get in?" she asked harshly. "You weren't on the guest list."

He stooped down in front of her. "I received the package that you sent." Although she'd just done it earlier, she'd already forgotten that she'd sent it to him.

He gripped her hands, and gently stroked them. She looked away.

Slowly he moved his hands upwards to her chin, gently guiding her head to face him. "I just had to see you again," he said as his eyes filled with tears. "I've been lost without you. I'm here to ask for a second chance."

Catherine looked out over the glistening pool water and she slowly stood up, forcing him to stand also.

Seeing how desperate he looked, she moved closer, using the back of her hand to stroke his cheek, near his jawbone.

Sharing a hug with him, she kissed him on the lips.

"I'm sorry but I can't. I just can't do this again," she whispered softly against his lips, and then she backed away.

"I've had a lot of time to think about everything that's happened. I know you realize that you made a mistake. And you probably wish it never would have happened. But it did." She smiled, then continued. "And in my head, I've even forgiven you. But in my heart…in my heart…I don't think I can ever trust you again."

Tears rolled down her cheeks and she went on. "We were together for months and we never once talked about what was going on in my life. You know, just everyday stuff. As I think back now, I realize that every time we were together we always ended up in bed…sharing our bodies but nothing more. I know now, that I want a man I can trust, a man who will be true to me, someone to have children with, someone to have a future with." She stopped for a moment, and sighed deeply. "And you're not that man," she said sternly, without showing any emotion.

"And Justin Scott…is he that man?" he questioned angrily.

She stared blindly while he continued. "Yes. I know that you had been seeing him, that you spent time with him all of those months that we were together. And you never once said a word."

"Justin and I were just friends," she tried to explain.

"Just friends, right—," he snickered.

Catherine raised her voice. "Listen, don't try to make me look like the bad guy here. I never once slept with Justin. Not once while we were together. I was in love with you and you screwed things up by sleeping with that woman. You did this to yourself…"

Angry, she turned and began to walk away.

"But it was my mother," he called out.

Catherine stopped to listen. What did his mother have to do with his indiscretion?

As Catherine turned around, William ran up to her. "Yes. My mother," he repeated. "She orchestrated the whole thing. She told Tammy where I was going to be for New Years Eve. She's been wanting me to go out with Tammy for years now. She knew how I felt about you, and she wanted to break us up."

"I've never even met your mother," Catherine said. "Why would she want to do that to me?"

"It's not you," he said. "It's anyone that I date. She has it in her mind that I should marry Tammy."

Catherine looked at him suspiciously.

"I know it sounds crazy, but it's true…"

Catherine interrupted. "No," she said. "What's crazy is that you expect me to believe that your mother is to blame for what happened." She stopped to take a deep breath, then posed the question. "Did your mother sleep with that woman?"

Stunned, William stood silently and watched as she turned and walked away.

Although he pleaded with her to stay, she kept on walking…She had finally found the strength to walk out of his life once and for all.

As Catherine made her way up the steps to the balcony, she was overcome with a feeling of relief. She had taken her life back. She was free…

Once inside, she searched the crowd for Justin, but he still hadn't arrived. She quickly paced around the other rooms, looking for him, but he was nowhere in site.

She looked across the ballroom and saw Antoinette waving at her. She walked across the room toward her. "Antoinette, have you seen Justin?" she asked with a pained expression.

"Why yes. I saw him earlier. We talked for a while, then I told him you'd gone for a walk. He said he was going to find you."

Antoinette looked at Catherine with a strange expression. "That's odd," she said, thinking back. "Then, a little while ago, I saw him walking toward the foyer. I tried to get his attention, but he walked right past me. I figured that the two of you had an argument or something."

Catherine's face darkened. "No. We didn't have an argument. In fact, I had no idea he was here."

Worried, Antoinette repeated, "No idea he was here. You mean you didn't even see him?"

"Something else happened," Catherine remarked hastily, "but I'll have to tell you about it later. Right now…I have to go," she said, moving quickly toward the foyer.

Antoinette followed close behind. "Have to go, what do you mean?" Antoinette interrogated.

"I can't explain now. I'll call you later," Catherine called out, running down the front steps to her limousine.

Catherine was sure that Justin had seen her with William and he had probably misinterpreted what had happened. She had to explain.

She tried to call from her car, but there was no answer at his home. She tried to page him, then tried to call on his cell phone, but there was still no response. She had her driver go to his house, but all the lights were out, and his truck wasn't in the driveway where he usually parked.

She tried to think about where he would have gone. Then it struck her...He must have gone to the one place that gave him comfort...the cabin. It was worth a try. In her heart, she knew he had to be there.

Catherine knew it would take a few hours to get to the cabin. With that in mind, she had her driver bring her home so she could change her clothes and pack an overnight bag.

As soon as she arrived home, she asked Jackson to get her car out of the garage, then she ran inside.

A few minutes later, she ran back outside. The car engine was already running and Jackson was standing beside the car with the door open.

Throwing her bags on the passenger seat, she started to get in the car, but Jackson stopped her. "How about if I drive?" he asked in a soft, gentle tone. Although Jackson didn't know where she was going he was worried about her.

"No. This is something I have to do alone," she replied. "But thanks so much for offering," she said, and hurried to get inside.

The long drive to the cabin gave Catherine the opportunity to think about everything that had happened. She also had the chance to think about what she really wanted. The thought of losing Justin was much more than she could handle.

Holding the steering wheel firmly, Catherine drove carefully, making sure not to speed. Although she wanted to get there quickly, she knew it was best if she got there safely instead.

Halfway there, Catherine began to feel tired. She turned the radio up and set the air conditioner on high to blow cold air in her face, keeping her awake.

With only a few miles to go, she started to think about what she would say when she got there, practicing over and over again, hoping that she wouldn't screw up.

Looking out the window, Catherine glanced up at the sky. She could tell the sun would be rising soon.

Driving up to the cabin, she immediately spotted Justin's truck.

Parking beside him, she turned the ignition off. Taking a deep breath, she looked around the wooded area. She couldn't see any movement. She figured that Justin was asleep.

Leaving her bags in the car, she stepped out and walked across the gravel path. Her legs began to feel weak. She wasn't sure if it was from driving for so long, or because she was so nervous.

As she walked toward the porch, she looked up in the trees, listening as the birds chirped loudly around her. The steps of the porch creaked as she walked up. She hoped he wouldn't hear it and think she was an intruder.

Opening the screen door, she knocked, but there was no answer. She turned around to walk down the porch steps, and caught a glimpse of him fishing at the end of the pier.

Hesitating slightly, she paced down the path leading to the dock. Her heart started pumping through her chest, her hands trembling. Every step of the way, she tried to remember what she'd planned on saying, and how she would say it.

When she got to the middle of the pier, he turned around.

She stopped dead in her tracks. It was as if she'd hit a brick wall.

Once again, her heart began to pound, and her hands began to tremble.

Justin watched as she inched closer.

With a couple of feet between them, she stopped again.

She stood silently for a moment staring deeply into his eyes. But his eyes weren't the same. It was if they'd lost their brightness, overtaken by a sadness she'd never seen before. At that moment, she knew what he was thinking. He thought it was all over for them. He thought that she and William had reconciled, and were getting back together. But he was wrong, dead wrong.

The time they'd spent together began to flash though her mind. And it was then, right then that she knew exactly what she wanted.

She knew exactly who she wanted to spend her life with. It was him, only him. He was the only man that she'd ever truly loved. He was the only man who ever truly loved her.

Slowly, she raised her trembling hands. Tears rushed from her swollen eyelids as she got ready to explain.

Misty eyed, he turned, looking out over the water.

Pressuring him, she urged, "Justin. Please look at me. I have some things to say and I want you to look into my eyes as I say them."

Slowly, he turned to look at her.

"I know that you saw me with William last night. And I have a pretty good idea what it probably looked like from a distance. But if you would have heard our conversation, you would have known the truth."

"And what is the truth?" His voice cracked.

Walking closer she continued. "A few months ago, you said that you thought I'd been blinded by passion where William was concerned. You were right. I was blind…but I'm not blind anymore. For the first time, I'm seeing things very clearly. You have been the one constant man in my life. You stuck it out through thick and thin and continued to be my friend. I don't know why I didn't see that before now."

Tapping her hands against her heart, she continued, "I've always had a knack at looking beyond the mask that people seem to wear these days. But where William was concerned, I just didn't see it. I guess I didn't want to see it."

She reached up to stroke his cheek. Tears rolled down her face as she spoke. "The truth is…I'm in love with you. I've always been in love with you. I just hope that I'm not too late. I hope that you haven't lost faith in me…in us. Please tell me that you haven't lost faith?"

Without answering, Justin turned to face the water again.

Feeling unwanted, Catherine humbly lowered her head and slowly began to back away. It was clear he didn't want her.

Exhaling a shaky breath, she started to walk toward her car.

Suddenly, she felt his strong hands, gently gripping her arms. Pulling her close, he prevented her from leaving. "Now I have something to say," he said softly, pulling her even closer.

"You're right. I did see you with William. And when I saw you kiss him, my heart stopped beating. I was terrified that I'd lost you forever. I've never believed in falling in love at first sight. But with you, I did. It was then, back at Antoinette's party on the night we met that I knew you were the woman I wanted to share the rest of my life with. The woman I wanted to have children with."

His eyes welled with tears and he grinned. "I've never loved anyone as much as I love you."

"Oh, Justin. I love you too," she vowed.

As the sun rose in the distance, they embraced for a warm kiss, signifying not only the beginning of a new day, but the beginning of a new life…together.

Epilogue

❀

Three years had passed since Catherine had seen William. She'd heard through different sources that he'd moved out of the country, but no one knew where. One person said they'd seen him in Monte-Carlo playing in a high stakes poker game. Another said they'd run across him while traveling in Spain. Wherever he was, Catherine hoped he had found happiness in his life as she had.

Months after her breakup with William, she and Justin had married in a small ceremony overlooking the hills of Tuscany. But even after that, from time to time, she'd still catch herself searching through crowds for his face. Often wondering if she'd ever get the chance to see him again.

And now, even as Catherine pushes a stroller carrying her twelve month old daughter down Rodeo Drive, she still finds herself glancing around the city streets, hoping to catch a glimpse of him.

As she rounds the corner where Rodeo meets Brighton Way, she suddenly gets that chance.

Down the street, she spots him getting out of his car. Her heart begins to pound.

Taking a deep breath to collect her thoughts, she nervously steps in front of the stroller, pretending to check on her daughter.

With her back to him, she looks over her shoulder to take a quick peek. Having lost sight of him, she frantically searches the crowded sidewalk for his face, spotting him as he now stands directly across from her. Their eyes lock and they smile politely at one another. Time seems to stop as he crosses the street, moving in her direction.

As he nears, she studies his face and physique. Although his body still looks the same, his hair is longer and he's dressed more casually than he ever had while they were together.

He steps forward, looking down at baby Elizabeth first. He smiles, then looks up at Catherine. Saying hello, he moves closer and hugs her.

Pulling away, he looks down at Elizabeth again. "She's beautiful," he says. "She looks just like you."

Thanking him, she glances around nervously, then looks back at him. She looks into his eyes as he speaks, they're different now, more weathered than before.

He says he'd heard that she had married Justin and he congratulates her. Making small talk, he says that she looks wonderful and she says the same about him. As she stands before him, she wonders what would have happened if he hadn't been unfaithful. Maybe he would have changed. Maybe she would have married him.

In a way, she feels sorry for him. If what he'd said about his mother meddling in their relationship had been true, his only hope was to break free of her tight hold. She wondered if he'd had the power to do that. She'd probably never know if he had.

Time had passed and Catherine had forgiven him. For she knew that it wasn't his fault. All his life he'd been taught how to receive but not to give. He'd never been taught how to love.

Her life now is a good one. Justin is a wonderful father, a loving husband, just what she'd expected.

William looks down at his watch. He seems nervous.

"Well, I better get going," he says. "I'm supposed to meet someone in a few minutes," he explains, gesturing down the block. "It was great to see you again."

Nodding, she tells him to take care and he says the same. She watches as he walks away.

Catherine stoops down in front of the stroller. "That was an old friend of mine," she explains to her small child.

Baby Elizabeth smiles and coos at her mother.

Now three months pregnant with her second child, Catherine strokes her stomach lovingly as she rises up. Her thoughts turn to Justin.

Pushing the stroller, she continues her journey.

She can't wait to get home…

978-0-595-39208-7
0-595-39208-3

Printed in the United States
51232LVS00002B